DOROTHY E\

MISS PLUM AN

DOROTHY Evelyn Smith (*née* Jones) was born in 1893 in the Peak District of Derbyshire.

Her father was a minister in the United Free Methodist Church, the family eventually moving to London. However, Dorothy set many of her novels in Yorkshire, which she knew well.

By 1911 Dorothy was a part-time student at an art school, and in 1914, she married James Smith, the son of another nonconformist minister.

During World War I, Dorothy began to write poetry and short stories, some of which were published. The Smiths had moved to Essex by 1920 where a daughter and later a son were born. The couple remained in the county, and after James's death, Dorothy moved to a bungalow at Leigh-on-Sea to be near her son and his family.

In the early years of the Second World War, Dorothy Evelyn Smith began writing her first novel, *O, the Brave Music* (1943), the first of eleven novels ultimately published, the last in 1966.

Dorothy Evelyn Smith died at the age of 76, in 1969.

NOVELS BY DOROTHY EVELYN SMITH

O the Brave Music (1943)

Huffley Fair (1944)

Proud Citadel (1947)

My Lamp Is Bright (1948)

The Lovely Day (1949)

Lost Hill (1952)

He Went for a Walk (1954)

Beyond the Gates (1956)

Miss Plum and Miss Penny (1959)

The Blue Dress (1962)

Brief Flower (1966)

DOROTHY EVELYN SMITH

MISS PLUM AND MISS PENNY

With an introduction by
Elizabeth Crawford

DEAN STREET PRESS

A Furrowed Middlebrow Book
FM50

Published by Dean Street Press 2020

First published in 1959 by Robert Hale

Cover by DSP

ISBN 978 1 913527 35 8

www.deanstreetpress.co.uk

For

ANDREW DAKERS,

Friend of Many Years

INTRODUCTION

'WHAT Mary Webb did for Shropshire, Dorothy Evelyn Smith is now doing for Yorkshire', commented one US reviewer in 1955. However, although *Miss Plum and Miss Penny*, first published by Robert Hale in 1959, is set in a Yorkshire village and features the arrival of a mysterious stranger, the novel eschews wild romance for gently subversive humour. Instead of an orphan or gypsy character, central to other Dorothy Evelyn Smith novels, disruption is caused in Greeth by the equally rootless, but outwardly demure, Miss Victoria Plum. The novel begins on Miss Penny's 40th birthday, the latter content with her spinsterhood, and, after she performs a noble deed, we watch with fascination as she and the other inhabitants of Greeth struggle to escape 'the tenderest trap of all'—the trap of compassion, sprung by Miss Plum.

Dorothy Evelyn Smith positions the village of Greeth close to Huffley, the town that features in some of her other novels and which, in a 1944 review, the *Yorkshire Post* suggested carried with it 'a hint of Keighley'. Certainly, as a child, Dorothy did live for a short time in that town, but was born, very much the youngest of the three children of Francis Jones (1852-1940) and his wife, Hannah Stringer Jones (1859-1943), on 7 February 1893 in Derbyshire and christened at Hope, a village in the Peak District.

As a minister in the United Free Methodist Church, Francis Jones was obliged to move quite frequently and, after time spent in Keighley and Sheffield, the family lived in Leicester before, in the early years of the 20th century, settling in London, where he became chairman of the Hackney district of the United Methodist Church. Thus, Dorothy spent much of her childhood and youth not, as some of her heroines, running wild on the Yorkshire moors, but in Hackney, at 69 Ickburgh Road, Clapton. However, as both her parents came from Leeds, it is likely that family holidays may well have been spent in Yorkshire. Certainly, her novels speak of her love and knowledge of that county, its countryside, its people, and dialect. Set in autumn and winter, *Miss Plum and Miss Penny* allows the author to conjure up evocative scenes of Greeth transformed by snow, where 'every window framed a frozen picture of the most perfect artistry', of a Christmas Eve carol-singing expedition, and of the whole village forsaking their daily tasks to ice-skate on the frozen Tarn.

Nothing in detail is known of Dorothy's education other than that by 1911 she was a part-time student at an art school. Three years later, in June 1914, she married another Clapton resident, James Norman Smith (1886-1952). His father, too, was a nonconformist minister, a 'priest' in the somewhat esoteric Catholic Apostolic Church which at the turn of the 20th century drew a large congregation to its church in Mare Street, Hackney. Knowing this of her background, it is to be noted that Dorothy is not averse to creating in her novels unsympathetic tub-thumping preachers. In *Miss Plum and Miss Penny*, however, the vicar, Hubert Sturgess, is resolutely Church of England, a good soul, if hardly an advertisement for muscular Christianity.

James Smith worked all his life as an insurance clerk, with a break for service during the First World War. It was now that Dorothy, employed in the War Office, began to write poetry and short stories some of which, so far untraced, were published in magazines. The Smiths had moved to Essex by 1920 where first a daughter and then, in 1927, a son, were born. During these years they lived in Southend-on-Sea but in the early 1950s moved 20 miles north, to the remote village of Bradwell-on-Sea, where they bought a 17th-century thatched and weather-boarded cottage, every romantic novelist's dream. The name it still bears, 'Cobbetts', is likely to have been given it by the Smiths in homage to the house in Dorothy's first, very successful novel, *O, the Brave Music* (1943), the profits from which may well have enabled the cottage's purchase. Alas, the Smiths had only a short time together in which to enjoy 'Cobbetts'. Devastated by James' relatively early death and unable to drive, life at Bradwell became very difficult for Dorothy and she eventually moved to a bungalow at Leigh-on-Sea to be near her son and his family.

In the early years of the Second World War, because the shortage of print had affected the market for short stories, Dorothy Evelyn Smith had begun writing a full-length novel and was delighted when *O, the Brave Music* was accepted by Andrew Dakers, the first publisher she approached. She published her next four novels with him, clearly a happy experience because, although she moved to Robert Hale in 1952, it was to 'Andrew Dakers, Friend of Many Years' that she dedicated *Miss Plum and Miss Penny*, her ninth novel.

Her family remember Dorothy Evelyn Smith as an observer and natural storyteller, who held that the 'story wrote itself'. Certainly, *Miss Plum and Miss Penny* is driven by the characters, the resolution not necessarily what might be expected of a regular 'romance'. Sitting in her Leigh-on-Sea bungalow, the author must have relished setting her Yorkshire scenes, not only the snowy Greeth exteriors but also the interior cosiness of Miss Penny's 'The Laurels' and of 'the small, perfect house on the heights of Greeth', home of Stanley Hartley, described as a 'bachelor by choice'. It is unlikely that Dorothy ever enjoyed the services of a live-in housekeeper but, even in 1959, felt able to supply the Greeth households with a medley of characters such as Miss Penny's devoted Ada, Stanley's 'self-effacing' Mrs. Platt, and Hubert's well-meaning but slovenly Mrs. Hart, who between them 'mash the tea', 'mek a cheese omelet', and 'think on'. It was this homely framework that made novels such as *Miss Plum and Miss Penny* so appealing, particularly to readers in the USA.

Dorothy Evelyn Smith does not seem ever to have been interviewed by the press and, 50 years after her death, family memories are fading. But recollections that survive are of a woman who, besides listening to and making music, loved reading poetry, in particular Dylan Thomas' 1954 publication, *Under Milk Wood*. Knowing this, we can derive added pleasure as we encounter Alison Penny reading it at intervals throughout the novel, 'faintly worried' by some of the 'confusing passages'. 'It was rather more *outspoken* than she had bargained for . . . So very *Welsh*.' Sly Miss Plum confesses to have been reading the book in bed, the implication being that no passages would have confused her.

Dorothy Evelyn Smith, who was 50 years old when she published her first novel, had a remarkably long career and after *Miss Plum and Miss Penny*, despite the societal changes of the 1960s, produced two further novels before her death, at the age of 76, in 1969.

Elizabeth Crawford

CHAPTER ONE

1.

ON HER fortieth birthday Alison Penny woke, after a night of torrential wind and rain, to a world of stillness washed in pale sunshine.

Because of the violence without she had slept badly, waking unrefreshed; reluctant to leave her warm bed and dress, to go through the motions of living another day.

Her glance wandered languidly about the familiar room. Sunlight lay on the thick grey carpet in lemon-yellow pools and gilded the wings of the tiny statue of Eros that stood on the highboy. Pink-flowered curtains, glowing in morning light, hung motionless before closed windows: almost fanatical about fresh air, she had been obliged to get up in the night and shut them. The room, in consequence, smelled stuffy and she wrinkled her nose in distaste. I really should get up and open a window, she thought. But she lay still, too languid to obey this healthy impulse. Ada would open the window. Ada would soon be coming in with the Birthday Breakfast on a tray.

Ada's eyes, sharp as a hawk's behind the steel-rimmed spectacles, would watch the undoing of the meticulously tied parcel and judge the genuineness of pleasure in her gift. Ada would swoop on the discarded paper and string, folding and tying with an almost savage precision while making her caustic comments on the cards and letters piled beside the plate. And almost certainly she would turn at the door and say in her flat, north-country voice: "Nice to be some folks, laying abed for their meals!"

She said this every birthday. And Alison, who detested having breakfast in bed, submitting on this day of the year only because she knew what pleasure it gave, would summon up her special little-girl giggle and say: "You spoil me, Ada!"

And then the gratified sniff, the clump of feet down the stairs, the slam of the kitchen door and, presently, the rise and fall of Ada's singing, happily dulled by distance, of the more dismal items from *Hymns Ancient and Modern*. That meant that Ada was happy.

This Birthday Breakfast was Ada's triumph; her last stand in the long battle for supremacy which she had been losing slowly but surely ever since Alison was fifteen.

How strangely quiet everything was. No clatter of crockery downstairs, no automobile horn or bicycle bell from the distant roadway, no tradesman's whistle or dog's bark. No wind. . . . She glanced at her travelling clock but it had stopped during the night. It was always stopping. She shook it violently without effect and resolved to take it into Casson's this very day and have it fixed.

Perhaps, she thought, it is very early yet.

She curled away from the window and tried to sleep again, but the silence defeated her.

This silence. It was almost, thought Alison, symbolical. After the turmoil and frets of youth—all passion spent—she now entered the calm harbour of middle age. Henceforward serenity would be the keynote of her life: a serenity broken only once each year by the birthday letter from George.

This tranquil program, far from dismaying, filled her with a nostalgic content. Although she would have died rather than admit it even to herself, this was all Miss Penny now hoped from life: that this annual letter from George should keep alive the remembrance of how, in her early twenties, her heart had been broken by the three people she loved best in the world. Mummy, Daddy and George—in that order.

Wriggling onto her other side she began to plan how she would spend the day.

First, after ceremony of the Birthday Breakfast and, perhaps, an extra handful of bath salts in her bath, she would inspect her garden and assess the damage done by the gale. There was bound to be a good deal of restaking. Any snapped or fallen blooms must be rescued and placed in vases. Earth must be stamped down around the roots of roses and leaves brushed from paths.

This done, she would go into Huffley, walking all the way over the moor path, take the clock into Casson's and lunch at the café in Winegate. After lunch she would go to see *Good-by Geraldine*, the motion picture which had been well reviewed in all the Sunday papers. After a cup of tea she would take the bus home and eat the special dinner Ada would certainly have provided, and spend the evening watching television. Perhaps, as she sometimes did, she might invite Ada to join her, though such occasions were rarely successful. Ada had the irritating habit of making a running commentary throughout the program, mostly consisting of such remarks as: "There—I knew that's what she were up to, silly young fool!" "Why can't he open his mouth when he speaks? I can't hear a blessed word." Or: "Jumping about all over t'place like yon, kicking their legs up. It's not human, let alone decent. Yer pa would turn in his grave!" Upon which Alison, guiltily conscious that this was in the nature of an understatement, would feel impelled to turn the switch and banish the beautiful bodies, the flowing limbs to outer darkness.

No, she would not invite Ada tonight.

It might be pleasant, she mused, to invite either Stanley Hartley or Hubert Sturgess to watch with her and drink, perhaps, a glass of the elderberry wine before parting. Or even, as this was an occasion, a little of Daddy's port, five bottles of which still reclined in cobwebbed isolation on the cellar shelf. Really there was no possible reason why she should not ask one or even both of these good friends to her house. Even though Stanley was a bachelor and Hubert a widower, at her age it was quite ridiculous for anyone to imagine she was running after either of them because she offered this simple hospitality. If Winnie Maynard or Iris Cummings liked to raise their eyebrows at each other they were welcome to do so.

She pictured to herself Stanley, impeccably dressed as always, and looking more like a retired bank manager than any retired bank manager had ever looked, sitting in Daddy's wing chair, his well-kept hands folded upon his stomach, his handsome grey head politely inclined toward the television screen, calmly and dispassionately evaluating the worth of the performers. She saw him offering a cigarette, lighting it for her, placing an ash tray tidily at her elbow. Stanley himself did not smoke.

Now she remembered that Stanley did not drink, either, so Ada would have to make coffee, which she would do with a very ill grace. For some reason Ada disliked Stanley and had invented a variety of shockingly vulgar names for him which Alison had to pretend not to hear.

Hubert, of course, would be more companionable though far less restful. Hubert smoked one cigarette after the other, dropped ash all over himself and the floor and never sat still for a moment. He was, in fact, just as likely to end up by flinging himself down on the hearthrug, which Alison considered a ridiculous and undignified way for a parson to behave. Hubert would laugh immoderately in all the funny parts and clear his throat a good deal in all the pathetic ones. Also, he had an irritating habit of fiddling with the controls of the set, constantly leaping up to twiddle knobs, producing startling effects of sound and vision. "Too much contrast," he would exclaim. "This knob at the back here, this is the one to turn. And then this side one—so. It's quite simple when you get the hang of it. There, *that's* a bit better I think!" Then, almost immediately shouting: "Why is the blessed thing flipping round like that! What the blazes?"

From experience Alison knew that if you just sat still and let the thing alone, quite often it came right of its own accord. In any case she had a profound respect for the mysteries of television and if her set went wrong she sent for a man to fix it: and by *man* she meant Mr. Whittingham from the radio shop and not the vicar of St. Cuthbert's, however much he might fancy himself at the job.

On the whole, it might be more peaceful to sit alone in her living room tonight; alone with her television and her memories. She would read George's letter once again before putting it away with its predecessors in the cedarwood box, and perhaps shed a few not unpleasant tears for the twenty-two-year-old Alison who had sent George off to Canada alone because Mummy and Daddy had said so, and they knew best.

2.

The garden gate clicked and feet came crunching up the gravel path. Someone whistled *Bless This House* rather agreeably.

The postman? No, for the feet crunched around to the side entrance and she heard the thud of full milk bottles and the tinkling crash of empty ones.

Perhaps the postman had already been; in which case Ada would soon be coming in with the breakfast tray and the present, and George's letter and everything. She reached for the pink knitted bed jacket that lay on the chair beside her bed. She *must* be wearing it when Ada arrived.

She wondered what colour it would be this year. Pink, yellow, blue, white, lavender—she had had them all, in all their various shades. Every year Ada knitted a bed jacket for her birthday. Every year Alison had to register astonishment and gratification. Ada decreed that the bed jacket must be worn as a sleeping garment because of an innate conviction that Alison was delicate.

In theory Alison wore out one bed jacket each year. In actual fact she seldom wore the article after its presentation, though she religiously washed it at regular intervals and kept it lying on her bedside chair. How she hated the sight of a bed jacket! They were so ugly and hot. They rucked up into agonizing, cast-iron ridges during the night. They made her feel old.

Nonetheless Ada's feelings must not be hurt.

She dragged the pink abomination around her shoulders and slid down again in the bed. Her nose, tiptilted over the folded sheet, the thick brown plaits on either side of her round, pink face, the innocent eyes the colour of wet slate, made her look more like fourteen than forty.

Ah—now that really was the postman!

Thump thump. Thump thump thump. Thump. . . .

Excitement mounted from the pit of her stomach into a tight ball in her throat. A birthday was a birthday, even if you *were* forty. Her toes wriggled in anticipation.

And now came the slow clump of climbing feet, the wheezing sigh, the pause while Ada balanced the tray upon her knee to fumble with the doorknob.

Alison shut her eyes tightly.

"Happy birthday," Ada intoned, dumping the tray beside the bed.

Alison opened her eyes and blinked up into the harsh, lined face above her. She smiled affectionately.

"Thank you, Ada. Will you open the window, please. The wind was so strong in the night, I simply had to shut it." Sitting up in bed she reached for the tray. "What's this? . . . Oh, Ada—you really shouldn't, you know!" She began to fumble with the string.

It was a white one with a border of blue ducks with yellow beaks.

"How sweet! Oh, but how *beautifully* knitted, Ada!" She laid a cheek against the blue-and-white softness, fingered the blue silk ribbons.

"I made it a size larger. You've put on weight this last twelve-month."

Alison blinked and swallowed. She said brightly: "I must do something about that," and laid the bed jacket on the eider down. "And what a lot of cards!"

"Aye," Ada said flatly. She pounced on the discarded paper and string and went over to open the window. She stood staring out into the bright morning, her broad back dark against the brightness, smoothing the crackling paper over her stomach.

Alison waited for her to go. She poured out a cup of tea, tapped at the brown egg in the swan eggcup she had used since she was seven, and glanced at the top birthday card, which pictured a fatuous-looking Persian kitten talking into a telephone. Only Winnie Maynard could possibly have chosen such a monstrosity. Still, it was very kind of her. . . .

"I think I have everything I want, thank you, Ada," she hinted gently.

Ada turned and came back to the bed. She looked down at Alison, her hands still fidgeting with the paper, her lips pushing in and out, in and out, as they did when she was upset. She said abruptly: "Stop in bed all day if you've a mind. It'd do you no harm." Then, without another word, without a backward glance, she went from the room, shutting the door very quietly, as if illness were in the house.

Now what, thought Alison, startled, could possibly be the matter with Ada? If Ada were in one of her moods it was going to spoil the whole day. Stop in bed, indeed!

She drank some tea, took a spoonful of egg and removed the telephoning kitten from the top of the pile, revealing three tulips in glorious technicolor and the legend: "All the best from both of us," unsigned. The postmark was Amersham, so it must be from Cousin Hilda and her husband. She laid the tulips on top of the kitten, drank some more tea and ate a thin slice of bread and butter very slowly and deliberately. It was a point of honour with her to read her birthday cards and letters in the exact order in which they were piled on the tray. It made the excitement of George's letter all the more exciting, because Ada always put it right at the bottom.

The next card was, she considered, in rather poor taste. It was a plain postcard, completely filled by Grace Fletcher's enormous violet scrawl. "Have a drink and forget it!" it advised.

Really—What the postman thought defied speculation.

It was pleasant to turn to the severe picture of the Royal Exchange from Stanley. It was even pleasanter to discover that, in addition to wild ducks flying across a violent sunset, Hubert had sent her *Under Milk Wood*. This was a poem she had been meaning to read one of these days. Now she could— indeed, *must*—read it, and that soon, for Hubert would certainly wish to discuss the poem in detail on their next meeting. How kind of him, she thought. For a moment she wondered if it might not be something warmer than kindness on Hubert's part, but instantly she suppressed the thought. This was George's day; a day for the dear, dead past rather than the problematical future.

Such a lot of cards! Violets from Iris Cummings. Pink roses from her godchild, Peter. Welsh mountains with sheep. Sealyham terriers playing with a ball. Golden bells tied with a true-lovers' knot. A Pekingese peeping from a hamper. Two

Cairns peeping from a hamper. . . . And then the letters. One from an old school friend and one from Peter's mother, all about Peter. A business letter about the Women's Institute. Two receipts. The electricity bill. . . .

And that was the lot.

After sitting quite still for a few minutes Alison finished her egg, the bread and butter, the marmalade; drank three cups of tea.

She thought I knew it had to happen some time. He could not go on writing forever and ever. And she thought: it is astonishing how well I am taking this. I am quite calm about it. . . .

Indeed, the hands that lifted the tray really shook very little. It was just this sudden dryness of the throat, this queer little throb at the base of her skull.

She got up and took her bath, brushed her hair one hundred strokes, plaited it and wound the plaits around her head. She put on the new tweed suit and a silk shirt blouse, patted a little powder over her face and took a clean handkerchief from the box on the dressing table. Glancing anxiously into the mirror she decided that Ada was mistaken about her weight: still, a brisk walk never did any harm.

No sound of singing came from the kitchen.

She is sorry for me, Alison thought. I am going to have to put up with Ada being sorry for me. . . .

She went downstairs and put the tray on the kitchen table, saying briskly: "Now I must see what damage the gale did to my flowers. Did you ever know such a wind, Ada? It kept me awake half the night. And yet look what a beautiful morning it is now! Almost unbelievable for November."

Ada stared intently into a saucepan. She said: "There's another post at midday."

"So there is," Alison agreed brightly. "I shall be out for lunch. I'm going to walk into Huffley. I shall come back on the 5:40 bus. If there's anything you need, let me have a list, will you?"

She went out into the garden and busied herself with stakes and raffia. Ada's compassion followed her, enveloped her like an unwanted garment. Like a bed jacket. . . .

But the warm sun was delicious, the work familiar and soothing. There was less damage than she had feared and soon she was back in the kitchen, hands filled with late roses and early chrysanthemums which she arranged in vases with all her customary cleverness.

Ada watched furtively, pushing at the steel-rimmed spectacles; pushing her lips in and out, in and out; sniffing heavily from time to time.

"There—aren't they lovely?" Alison said, admiring the finished vases. "I shall put this one on the bookcase"—walking out of the kitchen, across the square, black-and-white-tiled hall and into the long, narrow living room filled with elegant, faded furniture—"and this, I think, will look just right *here*." She put the vase down by an early photograph of Mummy, all frills, sitting in a basket chair, hands folded on her lap, and Daddy standing behind her, possessive and aggressively male; very handsome in wing collar and tightish trousers; surprisingly youthful.

She stared at the blank, touched-up faces as one stares at the faces of people in trains. She did not know them. They were strangers, this man and this woman, joined together in holy matrimony, united in forbidding her to marry George and go away with him into a strange, new, exciting life of her own.

They had known best.

George, Daddy had explained with a comforting arm around her shoulders, was a rolling stone. A ne'er-do-well. An adventurer. Not nearly good enough for his little girl . . . George, Mummy had murmured, was not the *faithful* sort. She would be making a rod for her own back and they would never know a moment's peace. . . .

They were right, of course, and time had proved it. George was a rolling stone. He had rolled all over the place, into many countries; sometimes making quite a lot of money, sometimes cheerfully admitting to being broke. His letters which, for the first year or two were frequent, rarely bore the same postmark twice. And certainly he had not been faithful. That, too, he had admitted; adding candid details which had made her grateful that Mummy and Daddy had not insisted on reading them. And the letters had come less and less frequently until the Birthday Letter had become the only one she expected or received each year.

And now, not even that. . . .

Well, she could take it.

It was just this choking dryness, this little hammering at the back of her neck. . . .

"Have you made out your list?" she asked, holding herself very upright as she walked back into the kitchen.

"There's nowt needed," Ada said, her voice muffled by a cupboard door.

"No? Well then, I believe I'll be off so as not to miss one moment of this sunshine. Now where did I put my bag?"

Ada crashed out of the cupboard and faced her. She had been crying. Her eyes were all red and swollen behind the old-fashioned spectacles. She said harshly: "You'd 'a done a sight better to stop in bed an' get it over with. Walking all them miles, all on yer own. An' nowt to come back to—not even a letter. . . ." Her face became quite violently contorted.

Alison took a grip on herself. She put her arms around Ada's neck, kissed the hard, wet cheek with real affection.

"I have you to come back to, Ada."

"Me. . . . Nobbut an owd servant. Is that all you wanted out of life?"

"And," Alison continued, wiping the tears from Ada's cheeks with her own clean handkerchief, "I have my dear, comfortable home, the Glee Club, the Women's Institute, my Cubs, and several good friends. That is a great deal to have."

"What friends?"

"Well. . . Mr. Hartley, for instance."

"Yon flabby-belly!"

"Ada!"

"Well, he is. He wears corsets, like a blessed woman."

"Ada!"

"Well, so he does, an' everybody in Greeth knows it. Mean with his brass, an' all, an' finicky in his ways. . . . Even the Reverend Sturgess is better than yon Hartley. Not as I think a deal of him, neether. A regular jack-in-the-box, fit to drive a body crazy with his fidgets. Don't try an' mek out *them's* any substitute for a husband an' childer of yer own."

Alison drew herself up. She said with dignity: "You are overwrought, Ada. Make yourself a cup of coffee. Try to control yourself." She swallowed dryly. "I know," she added in a softer tone, "that you were always fond of George."

"He were a *man*," Ada blubbered. "Whatever he did or didn't do, George were a man, an' you ought to 'ave gone with 'im. Same as what I ought to 'a gone with Albert Fletcher."

Albert Fletcher. . . .

Yes, of course. Alison had almost forgotten about Albert Fletcher. He had worked at Grimling's, the ironmonger's in Huffley, and he had courted Ada. Unsuccessfully; because Mummy and Daddy had said Albert wasn't good enough for Ada, and they knew best. . . . With sudden clarity she recalled a violent scene in this very kitchen: Albert shouting and Daddy shouting, and Mummy and Ada weeping together; with herself shivering in the doorway, fascinated, terrified, when she should have been in bed. . . . She saw the popping, incandescent gas-light; Albert's cloth cap lying on the table; Albert's thickset figure, one hand deep in a pocket, the other pointing at Ada. "Choose," Albert had cried dramatically. "You can choose between them and me—an' I shanna give you a second chance, Ada Fawcett, mind that!"

Six months later he had married the only daughter of a prosperous baker and had done very well for himself, inheriting the business and becoming a Town Councillor. His wife had three fat little boys and a grand fur coat before you could say knife. . . .

"Oh," Alison said weakly. "Oh, Ada dear. . . ."

They threw their arms around each other, stood, in a close embrace. Something boiled over on the stove but neither heeded the ominous splutterings. They were away in the past; in the exciting, romantic, magical past. . . .

A thumping on the kitchen door jolted them back to reality. Ada opened the door, disclosing a towheaded youth clutching a bunch of bronze chrysanthemums.

"Mr. Hartley's compliments," the youth mumbled.

"All right," Ada said. She shut the door, dumped the chrysanthemums on the table and turned away to deal with the boiling pot.

Alison delicately touched a strong, curling petal.

"They are very fine blooms," she managed.

"Aye."

"You'll put them in water, won't you, Ada?"

"Aye."

"Well, I think I'll be off now."

"See an' get yersen a proper lunch. I've got a chicken for tonight, an' one of them cream jellies you're so set on."

Alison made a supreme effort.

"You spoil me, Ada!"

She even managed the ghost of a little-girl giggle as she picked up her handbag and left the kitchen.

3.

It was so warm walking that she almost regretted the yellow woolly scarf she had picked up at the last minute. However, she would probably be glad of it when she came out of the theatre. Better be safe than sorry.

She walked briskly along the moor path, breathing deeply of the clean air as Daddy had taught her, and in no time at all she began to feel better.

She had indeed so much to be thankful for. Good health, a comfortable income, a home of her own, a faithful, affectionate servant, a delightful garden, good friends and neighbours. . . .

But really, Ada had gone a little *too* far about Stanley. *What* was it she had called him?

The little-girl giggle suddenly bubbled up of its own accord. She wondered if he *did* wear corsets, and what he looked like in them. How did Ada *know*, anyway? How did anyone know?

Stanley was hardly likely to beg his elderly housekeeper's assistance in lacing them up.

A sudden vision of Mrs. Platt, with the corset strings in both
hands and one foot planted in the small of Stanley's back, turned
the giggle into a peal of laughter that rang out very pleasantly on
the morning air and made her feel even better.

I can still laugh, she thought triumphantly. I may be forty
and George may have forgotten me, but I can still laugh!

Three gulls flew inland with incomparable grace. The light
breeze caressed her cheeks. The smell of the moor rose all
around her, familiar, comforting.

Yes, they had known best; and God was in His heaven, all
was right with the world. . . .

After leaving the clock, which Mr. Casson kindly promised
to have ready by closing time, Alison drank an excellent cup
of coffee at Shuttleworth's, did a little window-shopping and
bought herself a pair of nylons.

It was still rather early for lunch so she wandered into the
almost deserted Recreation Ground and fed the ducks with bread
she had saved for that purpose. They were such comical little
things, turning upside down and beating the grey water with
yellow feet. One was so tame that it waddled up the grassy slope
to eat from her hand. She sat down on a bench to watch them.

The bench was already occupied by another woman who
sat slumped sideways, her face turned from Miss Penny and
the comical ducks. Someone, Alison wondered, who was wiling
away the time before an appointment?

Twice she glanced at the woman; willing to talk about the
little ducks, the wind last night, the wonderful change in the
weather. But the woman kept her back turned; and presently
Alison became aware that the woman was crying.

Her first reaction was a sharp feeling of revulsion. Crying in
public—showing any kind of strong emotion in public—was a
violation of Alison's standards of good behaviour. But immediately she reproached herself for inconsistency. This poor
creature had obviously come to the deserted Recreation Ground

for privacy. It had become public solely on account of Alison's own arrival. Clearly then, the right thing to do was to intrude no longer, but leave the mourner to her desired solitude.

She stood up, brushed the crumbs from her skirt and walked quietly away toward the iron entrance gates; vaguely sorry for the unknown woman but glad to be relieved of an uncomfortable encounter.

At the gates she gave a quick glance over her shoulder.

In after years Alison often asked herself what her life would have been—how much its pattern would have changed—had she not looked back at just that moment, but had walked straight ahead to her hot lunch and a comfortable seat in the theatre.

But she did look back.

And then she gave a shout that was half a scream and felt herself running, running faster than she had run for years, back to the duck pond into which the woman was slowly and deliberately walking. Already the water was about her ankles . . . Above her ankles. . . . Up to her knees. . . .

"Stop!"

The woman stopped and half turned, disclosing a face of such blank, unmitigated misery that Alison's heart quite turned over.

"Come here at once," she cried, in the voice she kept for Cubs who were getting out of hand, and which sometimes worked.

It worked now. The woman obediently retraced her steps, sloshing through the shallow water and climbing the grassy slope that ringed the duck pond, onto the gravel path.

"How *could* you!" Alison cried, trembling. "Oh, how *could* you—Oh, dear, we must get you home at once. Walking will be the best thing, you are less likely to take a chill. Do come along, please. I will come with you if you wish. I am afraid you are not well and the sooner you are home the better."

The woman stood before her, her face expressionless, her body quiescent, as if she had no volition of her own. Water dripped from the hem of her skirt and ran down the shapeless shoes.

"I have no home," she said in a flat voice.

Alison blinked anxiously.

"But you must have some place . . . a friend's house, or rooms . . . or a hostel, perhaps, where you can change into dry things?"

"No."

"But . . . well, where did you sleep last night?"

"On that bench," said the woman, staring over Alison's head with eyes from which tears seemed to have drained all colour.

Alison thought with a shock of last night's storm; of herself being obliged to leave the warm comfort of her bed to close the window against the violence of wind and rain. She felt speechless and, temporarily, helpless. Then she gathered her wits together, took the woman by the arm and began to urge her along the path toward the gates. She said more calmly: "We will go to the Y.W.C.A. I know Miss Sandys—a very nice woman—and there will be a fire to dry your clothes and a hot meal, at least. You must be very cold and hungry. We will say," she added gently, "that you slipped and fell into the pond."

"I've no money," said the woman, hanging back. Her wet shoes squelched horribly. The ducks, who had fled in alarm at the intrusion, began to line up again, hoping for more food.

"We will discuss that later," Alison said briskly. "The thing is to get those wet clothes off and some hot food inside you. It's only about half a mile. We could take a taxi, but it would be wiser to walk."

"I don't want to go," muttered the woman. "I don't want to live. I've nothing to live *for*. Why couldn't you mind your own business? Why didn't you let me alone? It would have been all over by now."

"That, too, we will discuss presently," Alison said firmly. "Now walk as quickly as you can. It will improve the circulation, and make you less noticeable, too."

The woman gave a harsh hoot of laughter, quite shocking in its suddenness.

"That's good!" she shrilled. "All my life nobody has ever noticed me except as a joke. Nobody's ever really known I was *there*. . . . And just because I get my feet wet. . . . Oh, that's rich!" Her voice choked on the laughter and tears poured down the pale, thin cheeks. "Rich—that's what that is!"

Alison waved wildly and a passing taxi slowed in to the curb. She bundled the hysterical woman into the cab and said: "The Y.W.C.A. please, as quickly as you can."

Staring out of the window, not to embarrass the poor thing, who was making every effort to control herself, Alison realized that this was a serious business and she was in it, up to the hilt.

If you saved a life, that life became your own responsibility. She had heard that somewhere and its truth seemed irrefutable.

She had commanded this poor creature to come out of the duck pond, and she had come out.

And that, thought Miss Penny—reluctant, sharply resentful, but logical as always—was quite definitely *that*.

CHAPTER TWO

1.

AT HALF past four Alison, having missed her lunch and being extremely hungry, consumed two large portions of jam sandwich and three cups of tea in the Winegate Café. On the floor beside her stood a brand-new suitcase in which reposed one pair of walking shoes, size six (narrow) and stockings to match, one grey tweed skirt, twenty-five waist, one rayon nightgown and various toilet necessities. Just enough, she told herself firmly, for one night's stay. Or, at the most, a week end.

Alison had missed not only lunch but *Good-by Geraldine* also, which was a great pity, for this was her last chance of seeing it. However, it was no use crying over spilled milk. She was more inclined to cry about what awaited her in Miss Sandys' sitting room at the Y.W.C.A.

Miss Sandys, nice woman that she was, had asked few questions. She had been willing to feed Miss Penny's friend, to dry her clothes, to let her have a good sleep. Further than that she could not go. The Y.W.C.A. was already filled to bursting point and really she could not see her way. . . . Of course, there *were* institutions. . . .

Alison had understood perfectly. Miss Sandys was tactfully intimating that people who "fell into duck ponds" should be put under proper control. Which, of course, they should. But under *whose* control?

She lingered over her last cup of tea. She drew patterns on the tablecloth with the handle of a spoon. She frowned into the future.

Now she needed help—but who could help her? Now she craved advice—but what advice could she accept that would appease her own conscience?

The thought of Hubert dropped into her mind like a pebble into still water. Ripples of hope and comfort spread and widened. Hubert would surely know what was best to be done. And there was Stanley, too: the practical, hard-headed businessman. My spiritual and financial advisers, she thought gratefully. Between the three of us we can surely find a home for this pitiful creature, congenial employment, a new outlook on life. . . .

Almost cheerful already, Alison paid for her meal, picked up the suitcase and walked out into Winegate.

It was not yet dark, but the shops were lighting up and looking almost festive, as if the spirit of Christmas, still more than a month away, already showed a tentative smile. She lingered before gay windows, admiring the glow and shine of a fruiterer's, smiling at cuddly toys, choosing the fur coat she neither needed nor could afford, sniffing appreciatively the smell of roasting coffee. She collected her clock and had a word with Mr. Casson about his invalid wife. She looked regretfully at the pictures of *Good-by Geraldine* adorning the theatre entrance.

I'm just marking time, she thought irritably. I'm putting it off. And she marched down Winegate, along Postgate Street until she reached the Y.W.C.A., on the door of which she knocked with unnecessary violence.

Miss Sandys was welcoming—even arch. "We are awake!" she whispered; and she clicked a switch and shut Alison into her private sitting room.

On a sofa, and covered by a warm blanket, the woman lay blinking in the sudden brightness. She stared at Alison and Alison stared at her; both embarrassed, neither knowing what to say.

"I don't know what to say," the woman whispered.

She sat up, swinging bare legs to the floor. Her underclothes were cheap and inadequate but they looked reasonably clean. Her arms and legs were very thin and her collarbone stuck out distressingly. She sneezed twice, fumbling for a non-existent handkerchief. Alison handed over her own: it was quite clean except for Ada's tears.

"Please don't try to say anything," Alison said awkwardly. She held out the bag. "I've taken the liberty of getting you a few things in case your own are not dry. I hope the sizes will be right—it was just guesswork, of course. Perhaps you would like to dress now. Our bus goes in twenty minutes so there is no time to waste."

"Our bus?" the woman repeated, staring.

Alison swallowed dryly.

"I have decided . . . I hope that you will accept my hospitality for tonight."

"I can't do that—you know I can't." The woman's voice was gruff: but already, Alison saw, she was pulling on the new stockings, the shoes, the warm tweed skirt.

"I think you can, and must—just for tonight. I have friends who may be able to help you. That is for tomorrow, however. Are the shoes comfortable?"

"Quite."

The woman fastened the skirt band and came to stand by the fire. She was much younger, Alison saw, than at first she had supposed. Not more than twenty-five—possibly less. Also, she was not bad-looking. Dark hair grew in a widow's peak over a broad forehead. Dark eyes, feverishly bright, watched her hungrily. Her mouth was thin and too small and the chin sloped sharply backward, but there was a dimple in it. . . .

"I can't make you out," she was saying huskily. "Either you're an angel from heaven, or you're just plain crazy."

"Neither, I hope." Alison forced a laugh. "Is this your skirt? And your shoes and stockings? . . . We must go at once if we are to catch that bus. By the way, I don't know your name . . ."

"Plum," the woman said sullenly. "Miss Plum."

"Miss Plum."

"That's right."

"And mine is Alison Penny."

"Miss?"

"Yes," Alison said brightly. "Now, shall we go?"

2.

All the way home Alison worried about how Ada was going to take it. On the telephone she had sounded far from enthusiastic.

"Fell into t'duck pond?" Ada had shouted. "What, is she clean daft, then?"

Alison did wish she could persuade Ada not to shout into the receiver. It was so unnerving.

But however aggressive Ada might be, Alison knew she could count on the spare room being ready, the bed aired and the gas heater burning at full blast. And there was always plenty to eat.

Glancing apprehensively from time to time at her companion Alison decided that bed-and-gruel was the order of the day. Violent shivers convulsed the thin body and on the cheekbones spots of colour burned with unnatural brightness. Oh dear, thought Alison, who had done a little mild volunteer work and had never quite got over it.

She thought with dismay of Miss Plum sitting on the bench in the Recreation Ground throughout the long, violent night; all alone, all friendless in the rain and the blowing blackness; completely cut off from human kindness and only a few feet away from the lapping water of the pond.

If I had been going to drown myself, she thought, *that* is when I should have done it. . . .

The bus swerved and the woman slumped heavily against her shoulder. "Pardon!" she rasped, righting herself with difficulty.

How lucky, Alison thought, that they had not far to walk. The Laurels stood only fifty yards from the bus stop and the suitcase was nearly empty.

"We are almost there," she announced. "Try and pull yourself together. There is only a very short walk and you will soon be in bed, all warm and comfortable." She signalled to the conductor, who put his thumb on the bell.

Nonetheless it was the longest fifty yards Alison had ever walked and by far the most uncomfortable, with Miss Plum on one arm and the bag on the other, and both heavier and more awkward than she could have believed possible. How thankful she was to be standing in her own hall at last with the thick, soft rugs beneath her feet and firelight flickering through the open door of the living-room, and the good smell of roasting chicken filling all the air.

"Here we are at last," she said briskly, ignoring Ada's stony expression. "Miss Plum has caught a chill, Ada, and is going straight to bed."

"Bed," Miss Plum whispered. She gave a staccato laugh that might have been a sob, took one step forward and slid into a heap upon the hall floor.

3.

When Ada had shut the door behind the doctor she cleared the table, mended the fire, gave a twitch to the long curtains of ruby velvet and came to stand on the hearthrug. She folded her hands over her stomach and looked down at Alison with grim determination.

"Well," she said harshly, "this is a nice to-do, it is an' all."

Knowing that no answer was required Alison said nothing. She lit a cigarette with what she hoped was not jaunty defiance and stretched her feet toward the fire.

"An' who's going to sit up all night with her?" Ada persisted.

"I am, of course."

"You!—you look about done up as it is. A hospital's where she ought to be. I reckon you never thought o' that."

Alison said: "You can't poke people into hospitals just anyhow. You have to get a doctor's authority." Her cigarette went out and she relit it, puffing inexpertly. "Anyway, I didn't feel it was a hospital she needed. It was a home. . . . She is not only ill but unhappy."

Ada sniffed.

"You could 'a done summat about that when she come out of the hospital, where she ought to be this minute." She shifted the steel-rimmed spectacles farther up her nose. "An' what if she's got summat catching? For all you know she's sickening for t'small pock, or black plague or summat. That'd be a fine thing, wouldn't it!"

Alison shut her eyes.

"Ada. . . . Please sit down and stop shouting at me. I've had about as much as I can stand for one day. My birthday, too. . . . If Miss Plum were seriously ill Doctor McKenzie would have had her removed to the hospital at once. She needs warmth and quiet and rest; a certain amount of nursing, which I am prepared to do, and good food which I know I can rely on you to provide. I don't know Miss Plum's story. I only know that she is a woman like ourselves; that she is ill and very unhappy and friendless. . . ." She opened her eyes, surprising Ada in the act of wiping her own. "Dear Ada, it's no use trying to pretend you're a hard-hearted old Gorgon because I know better. Between us we are going to make Miss Plum well again; give her new interests, a fresh outlook on life . . . I'm counting on you, Ada."

Ada sat down abruptly. She began to clean her glasses on a corner of her apron.

"She never *fell* into yon duck pond, did she?"

"No, Ada."

"That's what I reckoned. . . . Mark my words, there's a man at the bottom of this."

They sat silent awhile. Alison thought about George. Ada thought about Albert Fletcher and that stuck-up wife of his in her fine fur coat.

In no circumstances would either of them have walked into a duck pond. Yet each now remembered with a kind of furtive excitement that once, long ago, they might have had some reason for doing so.

"Well," Ada said at last, "I'll be off now. I'll set the clock for half-past two, an' then you can get to yer bed an' I'll tek over."

Alison protested weakly: "That only gives you five hours' sleep!"

"Napoleon never slept above four hours," Ada said authoritatively, "an' look what tricks *he* got up to!"

4.

Nursing Miss Plum was hardly an onerous task. She ate very little, slept a great deal and did exactly as she was told. She made no demands, rang no bells, took her medicine with meekness and was pathetically, almost embarrassingly grateful for the smallest attention. She spoke when she was spoken to.

Very soon it became unnecessary to sit up with her at night and, as Miss Grigg, the district nurse, popped in each day to give her a blanket bath, the nursing routine rapidly resolved itself into little more than carrying trays upstairs, keeping fresh flowers in her room and sitting beside her occasionally for cheerful little chats.

"She's no trouble at all," Alison marvelled. "You'd hardly know she was in the house."

"Them little scraps of things often has the best constitutions," Ada commented. "If you or me had been out on yon bench all night we'd 'a been in us boxes by now, an' safely under t'sod."

Doctor McKenzie's visits ceased and so did Miss Grigg's. The thermometer was put away in the bathroom cabinet. Ada's trays became solider, more savoury, and Alison no longer whispered and went about the house on tiptoe.

But still Miss Plum lay in bed, obedient and undemanding, speaking only when she was spoken to. Her dark hair straggled lifelessly on the pillow, her dark eyes watched Alison warily over the folded sheet, followed her about the room as the eyes of a dog watches a new master.

She needed encouraging, Alison decided.

"Miss Plum, you must be longing for a proper bath. I'm sure it wouldn't hurt you now to run along to the bathroom. I've put fresh towels for you—the white ones—and the water is lovely and hot. Here is a dressing gown, and please use my bath salts if you care to."

Miss Plum immediately got out of bed, pulled on the dressing gown and disappeared down the corridor. Alison took the opportunity of remaking the bed with fresh linen. She pulled an easy chair close to the fire and brought cushions and a travelling rug. From here one could look out over the garden, which would make a change for her.

Miss Plum reappeared, took off the dressing gown and got straight back into bed.

"Oh . . . I thought you might like to sit in this chair for a while, Miss Plum. You can see the garden from here. The chrysanthemums are really rather fine this year."

Miss Plum looked frightened—almost desperate.

"Is that what you want me to do?" she whispered.

"Well, I just thought it would make a change and help you to get back your sea legs. Would you rather stay in bed?"

"Yes."

"Very well. I'll get you another hot-water bottle." She went down to the kitchen and filled the kettle.

Ada eyed the hot-water bottle sharply.

"I thowt she were for gettin' up?"

"She doesn't seem to want to. I suppose she still feels very weak."

"She'll go on feeling weak while she lays abed. Very weakening, laying abed is. She'll have to mek an effort."

"I'm sure she will, perhaps tomorrow."

"Happen she will," Ada agreed. "An' happen not," she added under her breath as the door closed behind Alison.

Alison tucked the hot-water bottle under the bedclothes and smiled at Miss Plum. She said brightly; "You are looking much better today. We shall have you up and about in no time, I'm sure."

Miss Plum turned her face away and burst into tears.

Alison was aghast.

"Oh dear, please do stop crying, you'll make yourself ill again . . . Miss Plum, you really *mustn't*! Do try to pull yourself together!" She put her hand on the shaking shoulder. At once it was seized and held, moistly kissed. She pulled it away sharply, embarrassed, rather revolted.

"You are still weak," she said, feeling weak herself. "But now you will be getting stronger each day. Doctor McKenzie has sent you a tonic. It's on the table here—don't forget to take it every four hours. One tablespoonful. I should have a nap now and then you will be ready for your lunch."

Miss Plum continued to cry.

Alison tried her Cubs voice again.

"Please pull yourself together, Miss Plum."

And once again it worked. Miss Plum ceased to heave and sniff. She blew her nose loudly, mopped at her eyes and turned her strange, triangular face back to its normal position. She whispered: "I said you were either an angel or just plain crazy. Now I think you're both. Maybe all angels are crazy. I wouldn't know. I never met one before."

Three days passed and still Miss Plum was in bed. Obedient, undemanding, grateful—but in bed.

It was time, Alison decided, to seek advice.

5.

Stanley Hartley surveyed his tea table with a complacent eye. Everything upon it was good, plain and attractive, from the beautifully laundered linen cloth and napkins to the sponge sandwich he had made himself and which had risen to just the right proportions. Mrs. Platt was a good creature, an admirable housekeeper, but she could not make a sponge sandwich. Stanley could and did—whether Mrs. P. liked him messing about in her kitchen or not. This one was a beauty and no mistake. . . .

Orphaned at an early age and a bachelor by choice, Stanley had many years ago learned the desirability of doing things himself if he wanted them done properly.

A disastrous series of boarding-houses had impelled him to seek an apartment. Having found an apartment, the ephemeral nature of daily help and the high cost of eating in restaurants had brought home the necessity of learning how to cook simple meals, how to sew on buttons, darn socks, wash and iron underclothes and keep three rooms in reasonable order. To these tasks he brought the same dogged perseverance with which he tackled his daily work at the bank. When Stanley set his hand to the plough he never looked back. Never.

Such single-minded zeal and application not surprisingly brought its just rewards. And if at the same time it drove a blade-straight furrow deeply across the blossoming meadow of his youth—well, there were only twenty-four hours in a day and his multitudinous duties kept him occupied for sixteen of them. He had no time to be young. How long did youth last, anyway?

And so, as Stanley steadily climbed the tortuous road toward the manager's chair, he also perfected himself in the arts of grilling steaks, slightly underdone, of achieving mashed potatoes, snow-white and without a single lump, of astonishing guests with soufflés insubstantial as a dream, savoury soups that had never known a can and excellent coffee. His rooms were swept and clean, his suits impeccably pressed, his linen glossy and his hands well-kept.

His friends—he had not many—groaned in perplexity. "I don't know how you do it, old boy. It's a miracle." Their wives, sipping the admirable coffee as they gazed at crisp chintzes, well-dusted Chelsea china, polished windows and paint quite free from fingerprints would murmur assent, with guilty—but somehow comfortable—memories of dishes stacked in sinks for tomorrow, foul old pipes on mantelpieces, sticky marks on doors and downtrodden carpet slippers kicked off anywhere just before they came out. Somehow, wives were always a little more tolerant of husbands after a visit to Stanley's apartment.

By the time he could afford a really good housekeeper Stanley had lost all need or desire for one. It was not until his retirement, when a hitherto unsuspected passion for flowers had flung down its coloured challenge, that housekeeping became irksome.

Who, after all, would choose to darn socks rather than snip away the dead roses? Who would not prefer a greenhouse to the kitchen sink? Who would stuff indoors with mop and duster when they could be out in the bright and blowing sunshine, with a view right over the moor to far-off Huffley and the smell of the sea coming in on the wind? How Stanley blessed the day he had left his apartment for the small, perfect house on the heights of Greeth!

So he advertised for a housekeeper.

He endured the first one for a week. The next lasted three months before taking herself off in a genteel huff. The third, a too large, too lively-looking female in a puce hat, never stayed at all: having run a ribald eye over Stanley from his fine grey head to his elegant, polished shoes, she announced without further preamble that the place wouldn't suit her, and departed to drink a Guinness in the Fox and Hounds. "When I work for a man it's got to *be* a man," she commented to the barmaid. "And if I run a house, I run a house and not a bloody museum!"

Stanley tried daily help, and they chipped his precious china and boiled his eggs to bullets. He tried a lachrymose lady who offered to oblige; and her husband, most disobligingly, broke his leg immediately and could not be left. He attempted to train a shiny-faced child of fourteen, who kept the radio on all day at full blast and ate everything in sight.

Then, just when life was becoming an unendurable nightmare, somebody found Mrs. Platt for him.

An excellent creature, Mrs. Platt. A silent creature. A creature with a bird's appetite, a deferential voice, a self-effacing personality. She could not make a sponge sandwich but she could and did do practically everything else to perfection, apart from dusting the Chelsea figurines and making Stanley's bed— tasks he would allow no one but himself to perform.

And so, after the lonely ploughing, the reaping. The golden plenty. The winter's warmth and rest. At last Stanley had time to look upon the cosy little world he had created for himself. He looked, and found it good.

His discovery of flowers made him an enthusiastic gardener. He joined the Glee Club, mingling a mediocre baritone with all the other mediocre booms and squeaks and fluting trills, thoroughly enjoying the whole business. He learned to play a cautious game of bridge. On occasion he took the plate around in church and was punctilious in purchasing lavender bags at sales-of-work. He knew most of the village people to nod to and made a few friends.

Stanley was content—no, more than content—he was happy. He had achieved everything he wanted from life.

Occasionally—but only very occasionally—a doubt, no bigger than a man's hand, crossed these clear skies and he would, wonder if, perhaps, he had not missed something after all. He would surprise a soft, mysterious glance between husband and wife. . . . He would feel the cling of a child's hand long after the child had flung heedlessly away. Sunset, lingering over the moor, would arouse strange sensations in his aging breast. . . .

Occasionally, but very occasionally, he would wonder if it might not be a good idea to marry that nice little Miss Penny.

But only occasionally, and it never lasted for long. There were too many complications. Sharp words were as common as soft glances—nay, commoner! The thought of school fees, measles, careers, incessant uproar in the house, cancelled out the cling of tiny fingers. Sanity was restored. . . .

He felt particularly pleased with life today, surveying the. dainty arrangements for his tête-à-tête with Miss Penny: the really excellent sponge sandwich, the bronze chrysanthemums; in their crystal vase, the loganberry jam that had set so beautifully, the leaf-thin squares of bread and butter. . . .

Mrs. Platt entered apologetically with another cup and saucer. She whispered: "The Reverend Sturgess has come with Miss Penny. I'll mash the tea right away."

Stanley shot an aggrieved glance through the window and saw that Hubert was indeed accompanying Alison up the path. They were laughing together quite loudly. Hubert bent and pulled something from the earth. If that was a weed, Stanley thought pettishly, it was probably the only one in the garden; and trust Hubert to find it!

He advanced to greet his guests with all his considered charm and dignity.

Hubert pressed the chickweed into Stanley's palm. "My good deed for the day," he commented with his schoolboy grin. "We must all club together and buy you a hoe, old boy."

"Splendid," Stanley returned blandly. "And then you will be able to borrow it for the vicarage garden, and what an excellent thing that will be!"

Laughing, they all moved into the square, pleasant sitting room with its bright fire, gay rugs and cushions and dainty tea table. Beyond the deep windows lay the garden, still ablaze with bronze and yellow and red chrysanthemums, and beyond the garden the moor slept in her sober garments of winter, livened here and there by a glimmer of gorse.

"Ah, this view!" Alison exclaimed, enchanted. "The loveliest view in Greeth I always think. How lucky you were to get this house, Stanley!"

"I was indeed. Take this chair by the window, Alison, then you can feast your eyes as long as the light lasts. Hubert, where will you sit?"

"Not for me, old boy," protested the vicar. "I only dropped in about the Old Folks' Christmas treat, but there's no hurry, no hurry at all. I didn't know you were throwing a party."

"Oh, it isn't a party," Alison cried. "I invited myself to tea— didn't I, Stanley? And please do ask Hubert to stay. As a matter of fact I want your advice as well, Hubert, so really it's quite fortunate that you came."

"No, really," Hubert said weakly, hovering.

"Sit down, Hubert," Stanley said patiently. He placed a newly manicured hand on Hubert's shoulder and pressed him into a chair. "And now, I suppose I shall have to be mother?" The other two smiled and murmured, knowing full well that in no circumstances was anyone else allowed to pour the tea in Stanley's house. He lifted the fluted silver teapot and held it reverently, like a chalice.

Hubert fidgeted in his chair. They didn't want him, of course. If Alison had needed advice from both she would surely have invited the two of them to her own home. They were just being kind. He wished he had not come or, having come, that he had the courage to take himself off without making everybody feel awkward.

Behind a genial façade of backslapping and bonhomie Hubert hid an unconquerable distrust of himself; an unsureness of his welcome into other people's homes; a sort of angry mixture of pleasure and humility at the least sign of friendliness.

As a priest he was never free of this malaise. If the church services were ill-attended, as they usually were, he blamed the dullness of his sermons. On the rare occasions when a good congregation turned up, suspicion gnawed at him: had he made an ass of himself last week? And were they hoping for a good laugh? It had been the worm at the core of his marriage with Edna—so desperately sweet, so agonizingly brief!—and it spoiled the relationship between himself and Ronnie.

During term time he thought of his fourteen-year-old son with tenderness, counting the weeks until he should be home. But as soon as Ronnie jumped from the train he knew it was starting all over again: the over-anxiety to please, the cowardly evasion of authority, the all-boys-together attitude that Ronnie openly despised. Once Ronnie had brought a friend home for the holiday, but that had been even worse. Suspicious of their laughter, resentful of their silences, uneasy if they were out of his sight and irritable when they sprawled about the house grumbling that there was nothing to do, it had been a disastrous experiment, never repeated.

He thought: I am maladjusted to life; and took the slice of sponge sandwich Stanley was offering. "This looks delicious. Don't tell me who made it!"

"Why not?" Stanley paused with the cake knife suspended in mid-air.

There you were—he'd put his foot in it again. . . .

"Just my fun," he said hastily. "Everybody knows the excellence of your cooking. I envy it. *I* can't even fry an egg without breaking the yolk. As for baking a cake—" He bit into his slice, making gratified faces and overdoing it, as usual.

"And what is all this about the Old Folks' Christmas treat?" Stanley asked in a careful voice.

"Oh, nothing much. Just that they want you to dress up as Santa Claus and give out the presents. But we'll talk of it another day."

"Santa Claus for the Old Folks?" Stanley's eyebrows made a nonsense of the idea. "And why me?" He handed Alison her second cup with a hand that was not quite steady. For one frightful moment he had feared that Hubert, who was probably quite fifteen years his junior, was inviting him to the Old Folks' party as a *guest*—and in front of Miss Penny, too. . . . It was true that his age made him eligible. True, also, that most eligible inhabitants of Greeth attended the party irrespective of social standing. Nonetheless the idea was intolerable to Stanley.

In his relief he staggered up and down the room in sprightly imitation of an old man weighed down by a heavy sack.

Miss Penny clapped her hands.

"Oh, but why not, Stanley? I think it's a lovely idea. I believe they will appreciate it more than the children do: children are so blasé these days. And you will do it beautifully. You simply must say yes!"

"We must see. We must see." Stanley sat down again behind the teapot, pleasantly puffed up with his small success. He had no intention of saying anything but yes. It answered the whole vexed question for at least another year—probably for many years ahead. "And now," he continued, bending his handsome head toward Miss Penny with a nice mixture of deference and camaraderie, "what was it you wished to consult *us both* about, my dear Alison?"

"Oh, dear!" sighed Alison, who had forgotten her problem in enjoyment of the party. "It's about Miss Plum . . ."

CHAPTER THREE

1.

THE day Miss Plum came downstairs the weather changed for the worse. Icy winds battered at doors and windows, roared menacingly in chimneys and sent smoke swirling darkly about the roof tops. Sleet slanted across the windows in peevish gusts, depositing a dangerous slush upon the roads. It was so dark indoors that lights were burning the whole day long.

Winter had clamped down on Greeth.

Alison made up a tremendous fire and put rugs ready in the most comfortable chair. "Perhaps," she said doubtfully to Ada, "Miss Plum should wait for a better day."

"She'll tek no harm," Ada said dryly, "without she roasts to death! If you don't get her down them stairs today she'll stop in bed until spring—so you can mek up yer mind to it."

A faint bumping sound sent them scurrying out into the hall. They stared, aghast, at the descending figure of Miss Plum. Even Ada for once was speechless.

For Miss Plum was dressed in her outdoor clothes and was weakly manoeuvring the suitcase from step to step, weeping silently but bitterly the while.

Alison sprang up the stairs and wrested the case from Miss Plum, who immediately sank down and mopped at her streaming eyes.

"Miss Plum! What on earth are you doing?"

"Going away," Miss Plum sobbed hollowly. "That's what you want, isn't it? And I don't blame you, either. I've been a nuisance far too long. . . . You've been goodness itself, but I know when I've outstayed my welcome. No doubt I'm a dim type but at least I know *that* much."

"My dear Miss Plum," Alison said, more warmly than she actually felt, "of *course* you are not leaving today—your first day out of bed! What nonsense. You are not leaving this house until you are perfectly well and strong. Your chair is waiting for you by a lovely fire, and we are going to make ourselves comfortable and have a nice little chat. And Ada is going to bring us a cup of tea—aren't you, Ada?"

"You've nobbut just had yer dinners," Ada objected.

"Never mind that. A cup of tea is what we need, Ada, and the sooner the better, please. . . . Now come along, Miss Plum, and we'll soon have you comfortable. Lean on me and take it slowly."

Ada pushed at her spectacles and departed, slamming the kitchen door. Alison helped Miss Plum downstairs, divested her of her outdoor garments and tucked her up cosily in front of the fire.

Miss Plum continued to cry.

"I meant to go," she kept repeating. "You ought to have let me go. I'm a nuisance to you. I've been a nuisance to everybody, all my life."

After drinking two cups of strong tea and eating a buttered scone Miss Plum became calmer. She lay relaxed in the easy chair, gazing at Alison with dog-like devotion.

"You're too good to be true," she murmured dreamily. Touched, but embarrassed, Alison picked up some mending. Miss Plum almost snatched it from her. "At least let me do that for you. Oh, please don't deny me such a small thing!"

"It's only an old pair of stockings. I wear them for gardening. I doubt if they are worth anyone's trouble."

"*Trouble!* As if a little thing like this could be a trouble after all you've done for me!" Miss Plum began to weave the needle to and fro with rapidity and, Alison noticed, remarkable neatness.

2.

Deprived of occupation, Alison sat rather helplessly watching the agile fingers, the dark, down-bent head, the long, narrow feet crossed at stick-thin ankles. She thought about her talk with Stanley and Hubert and the advice they had given her—for once they had been in complete accord—to get rid of Miss Plum at the earliest possible moment.

That was all very well, Alison had replied, but where, in fact, could Miss Plum go? She appeared to have no money, no friends, no home, no resources of any kind.

At this Hubert had frowned and fidgeted, flinging cigarette ash onto Stanley's carpet, and had submitted that really, you know, he was sorry, but it did not sound a very likely story.

Stanley had been more forthright. Such a situation, he had declared, poised elegantly on the hearthrug in his smooth grey suit and matching suede shoes, might conceivably have been possible fifty years ago—though unlikely, even then—but in these days of Welfare states, National Insurance, compulsory education, the emancipation of women and what-have-you, it was well-nigh impossible. This Plum woman was either a consummate liar or she was crackers. In either case Alison had done all and more that could possibly be expected of her, and must now put the woman kindly but firmly outside the door. If necessary, he had added sternly, Alison might call upon him for assistance: though Hubert, of course, as the vicar of the parish, was the more obvious choice.

He had then taken a little brush and shovel from the hearth and swept up Hubert's cigarette ash with a good deal of ceremony. A two-minutes' silence had been observed while he did this.

Hubert, looking rather frightened, had murmured that of course if there was anything he could do. . . . Though it sounded to him more like Doctor McKenzie's pigeon. . . .

"What could Doctor McKenzie do that he has not already done?" Alison had demanded.

"Well, he's the medical health officer, you know." Alison had pulled her little-girl face. "But Hubert, Miss Plum isn't *catching*!"

"Well, then, there's always the Salvation Army."

"Oh, no." Alison had been decided about this. "I hardly think so, not for Miss Plum."

"Well, then. . . ."

It seemed they had come full circle.

Alison had felt bitterly disappointed. She had imagined that she only needed to mention Miss Plum to Hubert and Stanley for them immediately to remove the whole burden of responsibility from her shoulders with ease and dispatch. Whereas all they had actually done was to suggest impossibilities and ask a lot of silly questions to which she did not know the answers. . . .

3.

Watching the flying fingers it occurred to Alison that now, if ever, was her opportunity to ask Miss Plum a few questions. Oh dear. . . .

She racked her brain for the correct approach. Miss Plum cried so very easily and Alison found tears unnerving. Oh *dear!*

She swallowed with difficulty and got out: "And what are your plans, Miss Plum, when . . . when you are well enough to leave?"

The flying fingers ceased to fly. The down-bent head slowly raised. Spaniel eyes of desolate devotion rested on Alison.

"My plans?"

Alison cleared her throat, bent to adjust a blazing coal that threatened the hearth.

"You must surely have some idea of where you will go—what you will do . . ." she said awkwardly.

"I have a very good idea," Miss Plum replied in a chill whisper.

And once again Alison saw the thin, drab figure wading slowly into the duck pond; heard the horrible squelch of shoes; felt the fear, the overwhelming pity, the revulsion. . . .

"I want to help you, you know," she said earnestly. "I guess that you have had a hard life with a great deal of unhappiness, but it is only guesswork. Would you care to tell me something of your story? I don't wish to pry. But I don't see how I can help you if I know nothing about you. Why, I don't even know your Christian name!"

The darning dropped into Miss Plum's lap, the dark gaze slid away to the thickening twilight of the December afternoon. The small mouth pinched itself into nothingness.

"No—you don't even know my name."

"What is it?" Alison asked; and added encouragingly: "Mine is Alison."

"And mine," said Miss Plum, "is Victoria. . . . Now laugh!" she shouted so suddenly that Alison jumped in her chair. "Go on— have a good laugh. Fetch that woman out of the kitchen and let her laugh, too. Go on, I'm used to it. Victoria Plum . . . *Victoria Plum!*" Her own laughter shrilled from the tight mouth. She clasped her hands around her knees and bent her head upon them, and the narrow shoulders shook. Muffled but vehement her voice continued: "Can you imagine what it's been like all my life, as long as ever I can remember? The endless jokes, the sniggers, the embarrassed looks. . . . No, you can't even begin to understand what it's done to me. Nobody could . . ." She sat up, fell back against the cushions, pushed her fingers through her hair. "It was bad enough when I was a little girl. I was plump and pink, rather pretty, though you wouldn't think it now. All the grown-ups used to pinch me and make silly, greedy faces, asking me if I was ripe yet, and all that sort of stupid nonsense. I hated it. I got so I wouldn't come in the room when we had company. . . . When I went to school it was worse—much worse. Children can be fiends to each other. My parents were poor, they couldn't afford a good school—not that it would have made any difference. All children are the crudest creatures on God's earth. Somebody made up a silly song about plum jam. They used to dance round me in the playground, singing it. They used to call after me in the street. The teachers weren't much better: I was always good for a laugh . . . I suppose if I'd been tough I could have stuck it. But I wasn't tough. I never have been tough . . . I wasn't clever at school. I couldn't do sums or grammar or remember dates, and I hated most of the lessons. But I *was* good at needlework. I used to take a prize each year. It was the sheerest hell . . ." Miss Plum sat upright, her hands gripped together in a bony bunch. In a pompous, artificial voice she recited: "'First prize for needlework—*Victoria Plum*' . . . You can imagine the titter that ran round the hall. . . . One year I stumbled as I went up the steps. One of the people on the platform caught me in his arms. A great red-faced fool of a man. 'A very ripe plum indeed,' he

said. 'It fell right into my hand!' That got a wonderful laugh!"
She lay back again, flexing her fingers. "My parents died soon
after I left school and there wasn't any money. I was too genteel
to work in a factory and I wasn't trained for anything better. I
looked after an old aunt until she died. She left all her money
to a distant cousin. He gave me fifty pounds and advised me to
buy some clothes and try for another job as a companion." She
groped for her handkerchief and blew her nose violently.

"And you did that?" Alison asked timidly.

"That's what I did. That's what I've been doing ever since.
. . . Companion to one stuffy old woman after another. . . . Fat
old women with disgusting habits; thin old women with bad
tempers and revolting ailments; old women with religious
mania; old women who made me stand behind the curtains and
spy on the neighbours. Greedy old women; sly, mean, lying old
women; cruel, sadistic old women. And all of them, all the time,
being funny about my name. Old women," cried Miss Plum,
pulling at her dark hair, "I hate them! I hate them all! I never
want to become an old woman myself. I hope I die young." She
began to cry again.

Ada's head came around the door. It was surmounted by a
ceremonial beret: bottle-green, pierced by a quill rampant.

"I'm off," she announced baldly.

Alison slewed around in her chair.

"Off? . . . Oh, Ada, you're surely not going out in this weather!"

"It's my day."

"But Ada—you know perfectly well you can go out any day
you like. Why choose a day like this?"

"I'm going to Huffley to see me cousin Annie. It's her birthday," Ada replied stolidly. "I've left yer suppers ready. See an'
don't let yon stew burn when you hot it up, an' think on to fill
t'dish with water when you've done."

"Oh, Ada, do be careful, the ground is like glass."

"Chap'll be coming with the oil. I've put cans outside an'
t'money under 'em, so there's no need to open t'door. Yer afters
is in t'fridge. See an' shut door properly. It wants a good bang."

A good bang was what Ada gave the living-room door and the front door and, after a rather slithery descent down the path, the gate also. Alison watched her headlong passage, feeling rather frightened and forlorn. She did not know how to cope alone with Miss Plum; how to cheer or advise her about the future. There seemed, indeed, to be no future for one so spiritless.

Gazing out at the dreary twilight she found herself wishing quite desperately that she had never set eyes on Miss Plum. I ought to be ashamed of myself, she thought, trying to feel ashamed. When I remember how fortunate I am, how happy my own life has always been. . . .

It would be wiser, she decided, to invite no more confidences for the present but to leave well alone until Miss Plum was stronger.

With a resolute air she pulled the velvet curtains across the windows, switched on more lights and returned to her seat by the fire.

She said brightly: "I shall call you Victoria, if I may. It is one of my favourite names, and it suits you, too."

"Oh, do you really like it?" Miss Plum said eagerly. "And may I call you Alison? Oh, how sweet you are, how awfully kind and sweet. . . . And have you any more mending I can do? I've finished these stockings. No, really, I don't want to read or play cards. I just want to do something for *you*. Please!"

So, as the day deepened into night and sleet slashed at the windows and wind howled about the house, Miss Plum and Miss Penny sat cosily before the fire employing themselves with mending and fancywork; listening to a little talk about budgereegahs on the radio, watching an amusing little comedy on television; eating the savoury meal that Ada had prepared and washing up together afterward. They remembered to fill the stew pan with water and the door of the refrigerator was firmly banged. Victoria went early to bed hugging a hot-water bottle and looking almost happy. Alison settled down again to wait for Ada's return.

She felt tired and rather headachy and she sneezed several times. She thought gloomily: I'm going to have one of my colds, and went into the bathroom for ammoniated quinine. She ate a chocolate to take away the taste and respectfully opened *Under Milk Wood*, which she was determined not only to read but to understand, so that she could discuss it with Hubert when Victoria Plum had departed and her days were once more her own.

Spurred on by this comforting thought she pegged away at *Under Milk Wood*. It was rather more *outspoken* than she had bargained for, but it must be quite all right or Hubert would not have given it to her. She quite enjoyed parts of it. So very *Welsh*. . . . But of course there were other parts—well, really. . . .

At school she had enjoyed poetry lessons very much. *O, young Lochinvar is come out of the west,* and *I stood on the bridge at midnight, as the clock was striking the hour.* And crying over *When I am dead, My Dearest, sing no sad songs for me. . . .*

Poetry had been quite her *thing* when she was a girl. Of course, times changed. . . .

Ten o'clock. . . .

Ada was very late. Goodness, the last bus must have gone past by now, and Ada must have missed it!

Suddenly she felt rather frightened. In all her life she had never been alone in the house at night. Strictly speaking, of course, she was not alone now because of Miss Plum. But somehow Miss Plum only made the aloneness more alone.

Resolutely she turned again to *Under Milk Wood*.

> SECOND VOICE. Chasing the naughty couples down the grass-green gooseberried double bed of the wood, flogging the tosspots in the spit-and-sawdust, driving out the bare, bold girls from the sixpenny hops of his nightmares.

Goodness! . . .

Faintly worried, Alison shut the book and laid it on the table.

It was her fault, of course, for not keeping up with the modern trend in poetry. No doubt Hubert could explain the poem perfectly. Not, perhaps, in *too* much detail. . . . Enough, though, to enable her to enjoy it as a whole, while ignoring confusing passages.

Tomorrow, she decided firmly, she really would tackle the book. She was too tired tonight; too thick-headed with the cold she was certainly going to have, quinine or no quinine.

She drank a small glass of Daddy's port and felt a little better.

Perhaps Ada's cousin Annie's husband, who was a greengrocer, would bring her back in his truck. She would sit up a little longer, just in case, even though Ada had her own key. It was so depressing to come back to a darkened house with no fire, no hot drink, no welcoming voice.

She sat closer to the fire sipping Daddy's port, while the wind howled like a demon around the house.

She thought about Miss Plum. Victoria . . .

A lot of nonsense, she thought crossly. Whatever one might feel about parents who could conceive of such a name—surely it was not a *tragedy*?

Her own name had given rise to a good deal of schoolgirl wit. The bad Penny. Two-headed Penny. Penny plain. Penny bun. . . . Somebody was always thinking up a new one. Irritating at times, perhaps, but she had always laughed as loudly as any of them. Louder. . . . She had never let it get her down. Certainly it had never given her the urge to walk into a duck pond.

Even George had called her Tuppence.

George . . .

Alison realized, almost with a sense of guilt, that she had not once thought about George since her birthday.

She poured another little glass of Daddy's port and settled down to have a nice think—and perhaps a nice little cry—about George.

At half past ten, Ada's cousin Annie's husband telephoned to say that he couldn't get his truck to start, but that a neighbour who drove a taxi would bring her home within the hour. "God willing," added Cousin Annie's husband, who was a cautious man and a local preacher in the obscure religious sect to which he belonged. Furthermore, this voice went on, with no wish to alarm Miss Penny, it must be admitted that Ada had had a right nasty fall and her ankle was paining her; and if it wasn't putting Miss Penny to too much trouble, it would be a good idea to prepare a bed on the ground floor, on account of all them stairs being out of the question.

Something then went wrong with the line and Alison was left clutching a dead receiver. She gave a little groan of dismay and sneezed heavily.

"What is it?" said Miss Plum's voice from the top of the stairs. "Is anything wrong, Alison?"

"It's Ada. She's done something to her ankle and they're bringing her home in a taxi. I must make up a bed down here immediately. . . . Oh, dear, I knew something would happen if she went out in this weather!"

Miss Plum descended with a firm tread. She said crisply: "The sofa bed in the breakfast room. It won't take five minutes between us. You fetch blankets while I get hot-water bottles and make a good strong pot of tea."

Immediately the house became a hive of activity.

Long before Ada and her two supporters arrived, doing a sort of concerted war dance up the icy slope of the garden path, everything was ready: the gas heater popping away in the breakfast room, two hot-water bottles in the sofa bed and tea stewing in its pot on the kitchen stove.

Ada, loudly and bitterly lamenting, was urged and bullied into bed. The supporters were comforted with boiling tea and dispatched with gratitude. Doors were locked and bolted and lights extinguished. Bedsprings creaked wearily as the three women settled themselves at last for the night.

It was not until she was just on the verge of sleep that a sudden and rather frightening thought smote Alison.

Today was Miss Plum's first day downstairs. How, then, had she been aware of the sofa bed in the breakfast room? How had she been able to lay hands with such unerring precision on teapot and tea caddy, milk, sugar and biscuits? How had she known where the spare hot-water bottles were kept?

The all too obvious answers sent her shrinking farther under the bedclothes.

During her protracted convalescence there had been numerous opportunities for Miss Plum to snoop and, clearly, she had snooped. While Alison and Ada, believing Miss Plum asleep, were out upon their lawful occasions, she must have sneaked downstairs and made herself familiar with the whole house. Opening drawers and cupboards. Poking bony fingers behind cushions and curtains. Moving the books in the bookcase. Touching jewellery, photographs, ornaments, kitchen utensils and the best china in its rosewood cabinet. Turning keys, counting linen, reading letters. . . .

Oh, no—this was too much! I cannot bear this, Alison thought. Oh, why on earth did I stop her from leaving this afternoon! That was my chance. . . .

It was not theft she feared, for she did not think Miss Plum would steal from her. It was the deceit, the cunning, the unforgivable prying that made her shrink with distaste. She thought fiercely: she shall go tomorrow! Not another day shall she stay in this house. . . . As soon as breakfast is over she can pack her bag and go. Stanley and Hubert were right.

Stiffened by indignation, she felt capable of going into Miss Plum's room there and then and having it out with her. And indeed she might have done so had not a heavy bout of sneezing convinced her of the foolishness of leaving her warm bed.

Sleep is out of the question, she thought; and composed herself for a night-long vigil.

She never knew what woke her. Whether it was the sleet rattling against the windows to the shrieking accompaniment of an east wind, or the mouse-like chiming of the travelling clock that Mr. Casson had mended, or the postman's knock. Whatever it was, she was instantly aware in every aching inch of her body that there would be no getting up for her today. She felt awful. She felt half *dead*.

"Ada!" she called. The sound came weakly, cracked and hoarse; its hoarseness frightened her.

And then, of course, she remembered that Ada, like herself, was imprisoned in bed, the victim of circumstance. It was no use calling for Ada. It was no use Ada calling for *her*. Both Ada and herself, if they called at all, must call for Miss Plum. And with this thought Alison came suddenly and completely wide awake. She sat up in bed shivering violently and pulled the new bed jacket around her shoulders.

On the table beside the bed reposed a tray of tea. The teapot was a little brown one from the kitchen, but the cup and saucer were the Coalport ones out of the cabinet in the living room. (How had Miss Plum known that the key was kept in the little mug with roses on it, second from the left on the three-cornered shelf?)

Alison drank some tea. The cup chattered against her teeth and her fingers were icicles but her head felt hot and light. I must get up, she thought desperately. Ada cannot get up so I must. I will not allow Miss Plum to have charge of my house. Ada's cousin Annie must come and stay, as she did when Ada had quinsies. Or I must get a nurse or a home help or somebody . . . I will not be left at the mercy of Miss Plum.

She drank some more tea.

And where *is* Miss Plum? she thought suddenly, suspiciously. The house was so silent. No movement; no smallest sound of living. . . . She stretched a hand toward the bell cord, then drew it back uncertainly; half afraid to break the chill silence and bring the day and all its problems crashing around her bed.

But at that moment came the sound of a spade scraping along the front path. A discordant sound, setting the teeth on edge, yet reassuring, too. Somebody beside herself was alive, at least, and employed in clearing away the treacherous film of sleet. It could hardly be Miss Plum, who had only yesterday risen from her own sickbed—yet who else could it possibly be?

She tugged at the cord. The sound of the bell came faintly from the kitchen, but the scrape of the spade neither faltered nor ceased. She must be mad, Alison thought, quite panic-stricken. Out there in this frightful wind, scraping away all to no purpose, for it will be as bad as ever five minutes after she's finished. She will make herself ill again—and then where shall we be! A fine thing if the whole lot of us are stuck in bed!

There was nothing to do but wait. Cowering under the covers, shivering and aching, she waited; listening to the gusty rattle of sleet against the windows, the howl of the wind, the excruciating scrape-scrape of the spade on the garden path.

She told herself it must end soon.

And presently it did end. A door banged. There was the thump-thump of boots being discarded. She's been wearing my Wellingtons, she thought resentfully. And then came the sound of feet running upstairs and Miss Plum came bursting into the bedroom, hair beaded with sleet, cheeks aflame, eyes alight with the eager, dog-like devotion that Alison found so disturbing.

"Oh, you are awake," cried Miss Plum. "Have you drunk your tea? Was it cold? Shall I make you a fresh pot? How are you feeling? Oh, you poor thing, you look awful! I mean awfully ill. Shall I take your temperature?"

"Miss Plum," Alison whispered, "please send for Doctor McKenzie at once."

"Oh, but I *have*. He said he'd come as soon as possible. He said you were to stay in bed, both of you. And he said could I manage? So I told him I could manage perfectly, of course. Well, I should hope so, after all you've done for me! And *please* call me Victoria as you did yesterday."

"Victoria," Alison said faintly.

"Thank you, Alison. Now I'll get you another hot-water bottle and make you comfy. You just lie still and don't worry about anything; I shall manage, I promise you. I'm going to enjoy it. I mean, *poor you*, of course—but at least it gives me a chance to show my gratitude."

And Miss Plum seized the cold rubber bottle and bore it away, smiling victoriously; a smile which Alison felt was intended to be reassuring but which was, in fact, nothing of the sort.

CHAPTER FOUR

1.

THE news of Alison's influenza and Ada's sprained ankle soon spread through the village and everybody rallied around. Little pots of custard and jelly arrived in covered baskets. Bunches of grapes bloomed purple and green on fruit dishes. Flowers filled every vase in the house. Magazines were piled beside each bed. People called with kind inquiries and offers of help on their way to the shops, and when the doorbell was not ringing the telephone was—or so it seemed to Miss Plum in that first week of her self-imposed authority.

The gifts she accepted with gratitude and all offers of shopping were accepted; but any suggestions of help in the house were refused with such firmness that they soon ceased. After all, Alison's friends agreed, Christmas was almost upon them and they were all as busy as they could be. And what with the appalling weather and all its attendant ills, well. . . . And this Plum woman who had so mysteriously appeared in Alison's house seemed perfectly competent. Who Miss Plum was and why she was there Alison's friends would have given a good deal to know; but until dear Alison recovered there seemed little hope of finding out. The vicar, when pumped, was vague, and Mr. Hartley, who was nursing a cold of his own, unapproachable. As far as Greeth was concerned, the mystery of Miss Plum would have to be shelved for the time being.

Hubert told himself guiltily that he ought to visit Alison. Quite certainly it was his duty as her vicar. But influenza was infectious and he caught things so easily. . . . There were the Christmas services to think of. And there was Ronnie: what kind of a Christmas would the boy have if his only parent were in bed with influenza? He did so want Ronnie to have a happy Christmas this year. He had made such plans, dreamed such dreams. . . . He and Ronnie were really going to get together these holidays; really understand each other and become firm friends . . . Ronnie was growing up fast. Soon he would be fifteen. Soon he would be leaving the nest, fluttering on uncertain wings out into some unknown world of his own choosing, where hawk and owl and predatory cat awaited his defenceless passage. It was so desperately important to become Ronnie's friend as well as father before that happened.

If only Edna were alive, he sighed. If only there were someone to help him with Ronnie, to bridge the gap between them in some magical, feminine fashion. . . .

He had wondered sometimes if Alison would marry him. Alison was kind and sensible. She was excellent with children—look how she managed those Cubs. She had a little money, too, which would not be unwelcome, though Hubert was the least mercenary of men. And she was quite nice-looking in her own way. She could not, of course, compare with Edna—but then, who could?

Hubert's wife had, in fact, been a limp blonde; too tall, too pale and much given to asthma. But she had loved Hubert devotedly and had thought him wonderful, a king among men. She was enshrined, therefore, in his memory as a second Helen of Troy.

But, he thought bleakly, Edna was dead and Ronnie needed a woman's influence. Should he take the plunge and ask Alison to marry him? Would she mind leaving her cosy, well-appointed home for the doubtful amenities of an over-large and dreadfully draughty vicarage? And there was his housekeeper to be considered. He could hardly dismiss Mrs. Hart after ten years faithful service and put Ada in her place—even supposing Ada consented to be put. Equally, he could not expect Alison to part with Ada. And what reason had he to suppose that Alison would take him, even if he asked?

Oh, dear, how dreadfully complicated life was! In any case he would have to wait until Alison recovered from her influenza.

Until Christmas was over. Until Ronnie had returned to school. . . .

He bought a bunch of violets and took them to the door of The Laurels himself, where Miss Plum accepted them with the assurance that Alison was a great deal better and that Ada could now hobble about with the aid of two sticks, and that she herself was managing splendidly. Yes, it meant a great deal of work but there was *nothing* she would not do for dear Alison. Nothing in all the world. She then gave Hubert a smile of great patience and courage and laid the cold, wet faces of his violets briefly against her cheek.

Hubert departed feeling rather touched. He had not imagined Miss Plum to be anything like that.

Stanley made a sponge sandwich and sent it to Alison by Mrs. Platt.

In his neat handwriting he inscribed upon the card: "From Stanley, with love," feeling rather skittish as he wrote. He was undoubtedly a great deal better today—and it *was* nearly Christmas, anyway, at which time one was expected to love all one's fellow creatures.

"Carry it carefully," he cautioned. "A sponge sandwich broken is a sponge sandwich spoiled: somehow it never tastes quite the same."

Mrs. Platt delivered the cake, enquired after the invalids and asked if there were anything she could do to help.

Miss Plum thanked Mrs. Platt, but no, there was nothing; she was managing perfectly.

"It's a lot of work for one pair of hands. Special food to cook and everything, and up and down stairs all day long."

Miss Plum replied that she was prepared, if necessary, to work her fingers to the bone for Miss Penny. Mrs. Platt thought, though she was not sure, that there were tears in her eyes as she said it.

"She seems a very decent sort of young woman," she told Stanley on her return. "Very nice feeling she showed, I thought. She doesn't look strong enough to be tackling that lot alone, but she wouldn't let me do anything for her."

"And how are the invalids?"

"Getting on well. Miss Penny is sitting up in bed and Ada's about on two sticks. It seems they're through the worst of it. . . Did you say Miss Plum was a relative of Miss Penny's, sir?"

"I have no recollection of saying so, Mrs. Platt," Stanley returned evenly.

"Oh. I just thought. . . . Would you like your tea now, sir?"

"If you please, Mrs. Platt, if you please."

Eating buttery crumpets before a blazing fire, with a Chinese screen around the back of his chair to ward off the slightest draught, Stanley pondered this problem of Miss Plum which recent circumstances had caused, temporarily, to be shelved.

Clearly, Alison's illness had consolidated Miss Plum's position in no small degree and he doubted if Alison would have the strength of will to send the woman packing, at any rate until after Christmas. And by that time something else might easily have cropped up, and the longer she stayed the more difficult it would become to get rid of her, and so on and so forth.

He had promised Alison that if the situation got beyond her he would himself step in and take a hand. And so he would, he told himself, stretching his legs full length and applying a small green bottle to each nostril in turn with infinite caution.

It was not a job he cared about. It was the sort of job from which any person of sensibility would prefer to be excused—especially as the young woman in question appeared to be rather different from Alison's vague description of her. Hubert had seemed quite impressed. Mrs. Platt, too, had evidently felt sympathy and even admiration for Miss Plum. Doctor McKenzie, who had been keeping a professional eye upon Stanley's cold, had referred to her as "a good lassie" and had said that Alison was lucky to have her in the house.

As soon as my cold is quite gone, thought Stanley, I will go and see for myself what this Miss Plum is really like.

2.

Alison and Ada, immured in their separate prisons, were filled with conflicting emotions concerning Miss Plum.

True, she worked extremely hard, dashing up and down the stairs, in and out of the garden, to and from the village with the greatest energy and enthusiasm. She never complained. She never, even if she felt it, showed irritation. On the other hand, hot-water bottles were never really hot enough, mashed potatoes had lumps in them, doors banged with nerve-shattering frequency, blanket baths were nightmares of damp inefficiency and urgent bells were ignored as frequently as much-needed little naps were interrupted.

There was also the vexed question of Miss Plum's refusal of help in the house, about which she showed an adamantine resolution. "That Mrs. Platt," she cried scornfully, "saying there was too much for one pair of hands! I told her. I said, if I worked my fingers to the *bone* for you it wouldn't be enough."

"But Miss Plum—Victoria—why *should* you work your fingers to the bone?" Alison returned with the feeble irritation of convalescence. "Naturally people wish to help at a time like this. I'm sure Ada's cousin Annie would have been very willing to come."

"So she informed me," said Miss Plum stonily. "Only yesterday she came pestering at the door, saying she knew your ways and your likes and dislikes. She said she knew the house and had often helped Ada out."

"So she has," Alison replied sternly, "and it was wrong of you, Victoria, to turn Ada's cousin away as you did, without even allowing her to visit Ada. Very wrong indeed."

"Ada was asleep."

"Ada could have been wakened. She must have been most disappointed to miss her cousin, who is the kindest creature, and *most* competent."

Miss Plum looked stricken.

"And I am not, I suppose you mean."

"I meant nothing of the sort."

"Oh yes, you did. I know you meant it, though you're too sweet to say it outright . . . I know the fish was a bit peculiar yesterday, and the pudding wasn't as light as it should have been. I know I don't make even a pot of tea as well as Ada or her cousin Annie could make it. But I do try. I do so *want* to do everything for you myself. It's my *chance*, don't you see, to show my gratitude. You've done your very best for me. Now let me do my best for you—even if it's a poor best. Dear Alison," cried Miss Plum, dropping on her knees beside the bed and laying a cheek against Alison's hand, "let me give you all I have to give, however poor it may be."

So what could Miss Penny do but smile at Miss Plum and praise her in the most tactful manner she could think of; assure her that she and Ada were eternally grateful, and what they would have done without her defied description?

Doctor McKenzie called on a morning when Miss Plum had taken the bus into Huffley on a shopping expedition.

"Well, you're all right now, lassie," he pronounced. "You can get up when you feel like it. Take it easy for a bit. Don't start spring-cleaning, or any woman's nonsense of that sort. And don't go out-of-doors for a day or two. The wind's still in the east."

"How is Ada, Doctor?"

"Och, Ada's fine. She doesn't really need those sticks."

"She hasn't been upstairs yet."

"She soon will be. Take it slow, the both of you. You've always got Miss Plum."

Oh, surely not for *always*, Alison thought desperately.

The thought gave her energy. She got out of bed and clothed herself warmly. Her face in the mirror was a ghost's face, hollow of eye, lank of hair, colourless as the December morning outside. But at least, she thought triumphantly, I've lost weight. I look quite thin, in fact. Ada's bed jacket is *miles* too big!

"Ada!" she cried joyfully, "I'm coming downstairs."

"You'll do nowt o' t'sort," Ada's voice replied. "I'm coming up."

"Oh, no, Ada! Please don't try to climb the stairs. You'll start your ankle off again. Doctor McKenzie *said* I could get up, and I want to do it now, while Miss Plum is out. I'm nearly dressed and I shan't be a minute."

It was surprising how weak she felt. I might have been ill for months, she thought. But she steeled herself to air the bed properly, to give a quick, dismayed glance into the bathroom and, rather guiltily, into Miss Plum's bedroom, and to negotiate the long flight of stairs: they were thick with dust and one stair rod was treacherously adrift; a truly shocking sight.

Ada, who was building up an enormous fire, got stiffly to her feet. "Nay!" she said, rather tearfully, and enfolded Alison in a comforting clasp.

"Oh, Ada, how lovely to see you again!" Alison was on the verge of tears herself.

Ada made a pot of really hot, strong tea. They sat drinking it, smiling and chattering, happy to be together again.

"It were a right bad sprain," Ada said importantly. "I reckon I were lucky not to have broken both me legs."

"My temperature went up to 102° one day," Alison returned. "I felt quite lightheaded. I thought I was a little girl again. I thought I heard Daddy's voice in the hall. Perhaps I did. . . . Oh, Ada, we must never again be ill *together*!"

"How did you mek out with *her*?" Ada's head jerked vaguely in the direction of Huffley.

"Oh. . . well, she was awfully *kind*, you know. But I did wish she would give me a really hot bottle. And of course the meals weren't quite . . . but she was awfully kind, didn't you think so?"

"She means well enough, but she hasn't got any knack. Hurry, scurry, clatter-bang, all the day long; and milk boiling over on my stove, and them stairs that thick with dust, I can't abear to think about 'em, let alone look; and food either half raw or frizzled up to nowt—you'd think a child of ten would know better. . . . Well, never heed, luv, it's over an' done with, and I'm tekkin' charge from now on. So she can tek hersen off as soon as she likes. Sooner," added Ada on a grim note.

Alison said uncertainly: "Where will she go?"

"How should I know? That's her business."

"It's ours, too, Ada. Mine, I mean. I made it my business when I stopped her . . . when I helped her that day in the Recreation Ground. I can't just turn her out of doors, you know. She has no home, no relatives and no money at all. I don't know how she even paid for fare into Huffley."

"I gave it her." Ada pushed at her glasses defensively. "I took it upon meself to give her ten shillin' a week, for expenses, like. I hope I done right?"

"Oh, Ada, that was thoughtful of you! I must come to an arrangement with her. I must pay her for all she has done for us. I'll do it right away, as soon as she returns."

"She'll get her unemployment benefit, I reckon."

Alison shook her head.

"She has never been employed in that sense of the word. She seems to have lived exclusively with old ladies who thought that giving her a home and a little pocket money was all that was necessary."

"You wouldn't believe it could happen, not in these days," Ada said incredulously.

"Apparently it can—given Miss Plum's rather unusual nature and circumstances." Alison gazed rather perplexedly into the glowing heart of the fire. Ada, her mouth pursed up, gazed gloomily at Alison.

"If you don't watch out," she warned, "you're going to get saddled with Miss Plum for the rest of yer life."

"No!" cried Alison sharply.

"Having a kind heart's one thing, luv, and having a soft head's another. . . . She's got to stand on her own two feet, and sooner you mek her realize that, better it'll be for all on us."

"But not just before Christmas, Ada. It wouldn't be *human*!"

"Longer you put it off, worse it'll be," Ada said implacably. She stood up, smoothing her apron over her stomach. "I'll be getting back to me kitchen. She's coming back on the 2:30 bus. She's bringing some fish. But if she thinks she's going to cook it, she's got another think coming. You an' me's going to eat some decent food again."

She stumped away, leaving Alison to her own thoughts, which were neither clear nor happy ones. The depression attendant upon convalescence wrapped her as in a heavy cloak. Despite the joy of reunion with Ada and the pleasure of being downstairs again, she felt weak and apprehensive; quite unequal to the task of coping with Miss Plum and the problem of her disposal. Every now and then she glanced uneasily at the clock, but time refused to stand still: every tick brought the return of Miss Plum nearer.

What would be her reaction when she found Ada in command of operations and herself established before the living-room fire? Would she make a scene? Would she try to wrest authority from Ada, or order Alison back to bed? Would she, worst of all, resort to tears?

She ate the perfectly poached egg on crisp toast and the creamy milk pudding that Ada provided, took a little nap and woke to indulge in a delicious pipe dream about Miss Plum being kidnapped out of the fish shop by a lot of men with spotted handkerchiefs tied over the lower parts of their faces, and strong American accents; of Miss Plum vanishing mysteriously and irrevocably and never being seen or heard of again.

But alas, even as she dreamed, Miss Plum's footsteps came at their usual headlong clatter up the pathway to the house.

Alison seized the nearest book and began feverishly to read.

Come now, drift up the dark, come up the drifting sea-dark street now in the dark night seesawing like the sea, to the bible-black airless attic over Jack Black the cobbler's shop where alone and savagely Jack Black sleeps in a nightshirt tied to his ankles. . . .

Oh, dear—*Under Milk Wood*. How nice. She would be able to finish it during her convalescence and then, when next she saw Hubert, they could have a cosy little chat about it.

And before you let the sun in, mind it wipes its shoes . . .

Steps were coming down the hall. The door was opening. The door was shutting. Somebody—and it could only be Miss Plum—was standing in an awful silence behind the chair, breathing rather heavily down her neck.

Unable to bear the silence Alison twisted around crying: "Surprise, surprise!" in an absurd squeak she found herself unable to control. Now for it! she thought.

But there was no outburst, no tears, no recriminations.

"And what a lovely surprise," Miss Plum exclaimed. She came to kneel on the hearthrug, unwinding herself from a long, striped scarf and holding thin, blue fingers to the flames. "You couldn't have given me a nicer one. And Ada, too, working away in the kitchen as if she'd never known an ache or a pain in her life. . . . How well this repays me," she said softly, "for the little I have been able to do!"

"Dear Miss Plum," Alison cried, more warmly than she actually intended, "whatever should we have done without you?"

"You would have had Ada's cousin, who knows your ways and is such a competent manager," Miss Plum reminded her. "Your food would have been properly cooked and your hot-water bottles boiling hot, and everything would have worked on oiled wheels. I'm afraid I was selfish to refuse her help, and you were right to scold me. But I so wanted to do everything for you myself. It was my chance, you see. My—my last chance, perhaps. . . ." For a moment Miss Plum covered her eyes with trembling fingers; but almost immediately she recovered and stood up with an air of brave determination. "And now I must clean those stairs," she added brightly. "They've been on my conscience for days, but I never managed to get around to them."

Alison wondered if she should protest. But really, somebody had to clean the stairs and neither herself nor Ada was fit to tackle them yet. So she sat in rather guilty comfort before the fire, clutching her book in tense fingers while Miss Plum thumped and scraped her way down the dusty staircase and presently was heard to attack the loose stair-rod fixture with a hammer and stifled little shrieks of pain.

3.

Ada brought in the tea. Almost immediately the doorbell shrilled and she returned to the living room accompanied by the Reverend Hubert Sturgess and Mr. Stanley Hartley, both looking nipped about the nose and openly thankful to see teapot and buttered scones waiting before an enormous fire.

The visitors registered astonishment and delight at finding Alison downstairs once again; and Alison was pleased enough to have their company—though she could have wished for time to do something about her hair and improve the pallor of her cheeks before receiving them. Also, she was so bundled up in bulky woolen garments that her new and cherished fragility was not easily apparent, which was quite maddening. With great presence of mind, however, she refused to have the room flooded with electric light and instructed Ada to put a match to the tall pink candles which stood in brass sconces on either side of the clock. They all agreed that candlelight and firelight were ideal accompaniments to conversation and wondered why people didn't do it more often, while Alison sat well back in Daddy's wing chair and looked as fragile as possible in the circumstances.

A movement in the far corner of the room caused all heads to turn. And there in the shadows sat Miss Plum, on the very edge of a hard chair, with hands clasped and eyes downcast and a general air of doing her utmost to obliterate herself entirely.

"Miss Plum!" Alison cried rather sharply. "I had no idea you were in the room. Why are you sitting there in the cold? Come and have your tea by the fire."

The two gentlemen leaped to their feet and a general reshuffling of chairs took place which resulted in Miss Plum, despite her protests, being awarded the most advantageous position, directly in front of the leaping flames.

"We have met before," Hubert reminded her, handing the buttered scones. "But Mr. Hartley has not yet had that pleasure, I think."

"I, too, have been ill," Stanley said impressively. "Today is the first time I have ventured out-of-doors for a full fortnight."

"And you came to see me," Alison cried. "How kind that was, Stanley! I do hope you haven't overtired yourself."

"If I have," Stanley replied gallantly, "could it have been in a more rewarding cause?"

Hubert briskly pricked this bubble.

"I picked him up a few yards from his gate," he grinned, "and I will deliver him safely back again. He'll take no harm."

"The excessive jolting from the springs of the ancient vehicle to which Hubert refers as a *car* have left me somewhat shaken," Stanley returned equably, "otherwise I am none the worse for venturing forth. Indeed, how could I not benefit from such warm comfort and such delightful company!" He looked at Alison as he spoke: but Miss Plum was, of course, one of this delightful company, which made the small compliment a little smaller in Alison's eyes.

"And have you finished *Under Milk Wood* yet?" Hubert was inquiring eagerly.

"Not yet, I'm afraid I have not felt well enough for much reading, but I am looking forward to finishing it now that I am up again."

"Are you familiar with the poem?" Hubert asked Miss Plum.

"Oh, yes," she replied fervently. "I have been reading it in bed each night. I think it is simply wonderful . . . I hope you don't mind, Alison?" she added anxiously.

"Why should I mind?" Alison's tone was so brusque that everybody glanced at her, and then glanced away again feeling sure they had been mistaken.

Hubert felt gratified. He had heard the poem read on the Third Program. For him it had been a memorable and moving experience which he had longed to share with some kindred soul. He had greatly hoped that Alison. . . . However. He turned his attention wholly upon Miss Plum, gesticulating vigorously with a slice of cake and showering crumbs all over the hearthrug.

In the face of such competition Alison found conversation with Stanley well-nigh impossible and was presently moved to suggest that, if everyone had quite finished, the tea table might be moved back.

This was done, and then Hubert offered cigarettes all around. Stanley, being a non-smoker, merely waved the suggestion away. Alison took one, though she had never felt less like smoking. Miss Plum accepted with eagerness. "I can't afford to buy them," she said simply, "but I do love to smoke." She turned apologetically to Alison, and for the second time in an hour asked: "You don't mind?"

"My dear Victoria," Alison said, wrestling with a strong desire to slap Miss Plum hard, "I see no earthly reason why you should not smoke if you wish to. It is certainly no concern of mine." She then turned to Hubert and resolutely engaged him in talk about the Old Folks' Christmas Party, the activities of the Women's Institute and the problem of coping with her Cubs until she should be strong enough to take over again. Iris Cummings, who had kindly filled the breach, had now herself gone down with flu, and there was difficulty in finding anybody both competent and willing to take her place.

"There's such a lot of this beastly flu about," Hubert complained. "Really, quite an epidemic!" Lowering his voice he added: "I suppose Miss Plum could not be persuaded to take the job on until you are fit again?"

Alison threw away the cigarette which she was not at all enjoying and flicked ash from her skirt.

"The best way to find that out," she said stiffly, "is to ask her."

It was not possible to ask Miss Plum anything at the moment, for she was listening to the story of Stanley's life, which appeared to be almost, if not quite as entrancing to her as it was to him. Indeed, so avidly did she listen to every word, her dark eyes glowing and her long, thin fingers twined convulsively together, that Stanley was quite touched.

"But that's enough of me," he said, skilfully combining a laugh with a sigh as he passed a manicured hand across his handsome silver hair. "Ancient history. Ancient history. Especially"—he added with a courteous inclination of the head—"to one so young and, if I may say so, charming. I must not bore you another instant."

"You are not boring me at all," Miss Plum declared with soft insistence. "I have been alone all my life, and so I can understand better than most folks just what you have suffered."

Stanley glanced at her, startled and a little displeased.

This was not at all the reaction he had expected. What he had intended as a success story suddenly presented itself in the light of a lament. Not the clarion note of *"Alone I did it,"* but the minor pianissimo of *"I had to do it all alone"*—which was a very different kettle of fish.

And yet, wasn't it true, after all? Had his solitary way of life been dictated wholly by choice? Had there not been times when the thought of a gracious womanly presence in his home had seemed desirable? Had he not sometimes pictured a son who should follow in his footsteps? Or a daughter whose gentle companionship would reward his declining years? Why had he never done anything about it?

There had been women who had shown themselves attracted by him. That girl in the green frock whom he had escorted home from night school several times when he was a struggling junior clerk. The waitress at the café where he had occasionally taken a cup of tea after a Saturday afternoon's shopping: a real beauty she had been, though he was cautious about redheads. And there was the bright-eyed little widow who played the accompaniments for the Glee Club and who had been left very comfortably off—mink coat, Jaguar, three weeks on the Continent every summer, and what-have-you. . . .

He had thought sometimes that Alison would not be averse to marrying him. It was unfair to judge her by today, for she was not yet recovered and was obviously a little on edge—though she seemed to have plenty to say to Hubert!

Lapped in the warm comfort of this candlelit room Stanley thought rather gloomily of his own home upon the edge of the moor. Mrs. Platt had taken herself off to the "Pictures," so the fire would be low, the room cold, the curtains undrawn: the dark, wild night would stare in upon him, battering at the panes with chill malice. He would have to heat up his own supper, make up his fire, remember to switch on his electric blanket . . . !

He felt old and neglected and suddenly rather frightened.

"Miss Plum—" he said uncertainly, turning to look at her.

And Miss Plum was looking at *him.* . . .

But suddenly Ada was in the room, switching on the electric lights without being told to, nipping out the candles, clattering fire irons, glancing significantly at the clock.

"Yes, indeed, we ought to be off," Hubert was saying. "We must not tire you out, your first day up—or is it *down*?" His laugh brayed out and cigarette ash showered down his waistcoat. Silly ass, Stanley thought peevishly, wondering why Alison encouraged him by laughing too.

Miss Plum escorted the visitors out. Alison and Ada stood by the fire, rather self-consciously avoiding each other's eyes.

"Yer bed's ready, any time you've a mind to go," Ada said. "*She* made it. But *I* put bottles in—two of 'em, and blazing hot."

"Ada, you shouldn't attempt those stairs yet," Alison protested weakly.

"And I'm bringing yer supper up, an' all. I don't want me ankle getting set. There's some of the soup left, an' I'll mek you a cheese omelet."

Sounds of laughter came from the hall and the peculiarly feeble brand of badinage which seems inseparable from leave-takings. Then the door banged and shortly afterward Hubert's car could be heard spluttering its refusal to start. But presently, with a series of small explosions and an inadvertent shriek of the horn, the car moved off and there was no sound but the bluster of wind about the house and the quiet shift and crackle of blazing coal.

Ada's hands moved rhythmically over the starched curve of her apron. She said harshly: "Well, have you settled when she's going?"

Before Alison could reply Miss Plum came back into the room. She stood before Alison and Ada, smiling with a sort of eager apology at each of them in turn.

"Oh," she cried, "isn't it kind of Mr. Sturgess! He has asked me to help him with the Cubs."

CHAPTER FIVE

1.

THE Old Folks Christmas Party, held annually in the Village Hall, was considered to be quite an important local event.

There were a great many elderly people living in Greeth, not only among the villagers themselves but among those who had come from Huffley and other large towns nearby to enjoy their retirement in its quietness and clean moorland air. These residents lived mostly in small but comfortable homes filled with every gadget and modern convenience the mind of man had so far invented. They nearly all possessed small cars, radio and television sets. They gardened optimistically, played bridge and canasta; they donned black ties and went off to mysterious Reunions, or had their hair curled and were escorted to Ladies' Nights in black net with sequins and a good deal of costume jewelry. Some played golf. A few followed hounds rather precariously on borrowed bicycles or even on foot. Not one of them admitted to being old, except facetiously in reference to lumbago or blood pressure or the rapid thinning of hair.

But, almost without exception, they attended the Old Folks' Party. It had become the Thing To Do.

It was no good pretending you were not yet sixty-five, when everybody knew perfectly well that you were all that and more, so you might as well swallow the pill with a good grace. You could always pretend that the party was fun. Actually, it was quite fun when the thing got going, though there were always a few sticky moments at first.

Any person of sixty-five who dared to give up a seat to any other person of sixty-five, or who sprang up kittenishly to help hand around the tea, was heavily snubbed by the rest of the gathering. Nobody, naturally, relished a shrimp-paste sandwich offered by some old duffer at least two years his senior; and all were prepared to stand until their legs collapsed beneath them rather than accept a chair from a contemporary: there is a limit, after all, to human tolerance.

It was the understood thing that if you were a Guest you were a *Guest*: you sat, and you ate, and you were entertained—and you lumped it.

Young things of fifty-odd might press food and drink upon you, find you a chair, even inquire after your ailments. *Their turn would come*, you reminded yourself darkly. But woe betide the Guest who pretended, even for an instant, to be a Host. . . .

Things improved when tea was over and the games began.

However sourly you may have been regarding your neighbour, it is well-nigh impossible to do so when he is throwing a parcel at you which you must catch and pass on without delay to your neighbour on the other side, with the piano thumping out *The Blue Danube*, and everybody shrieking at the top of his voice. However upstage you may have felt a moment ago, you simply cannot keep it up during the rough-and-tumble of musical chairs. And of course there was the conjurer or the ventriloquist or the fellow who did imitations of radio and television stars, which you were quite certain you could do better, frequently demonstrating this upon the spot. Toward the end of the party came the community singing. Carols, vaudeville songs, old-time favourites—they all went with a swing. You took down your back hair and let yourself go, so that, by the time you emerged into the nipping cold of another winter's night you couldn't have cared less if old So-and-so had had the infernal nerve to offer you his chair, or that little woman with the dyed hair had raised her voice in speaking to you—almost as if she expected you to be deaf!

Stanley, as a more or less recent addition to the society of Greeth, made his preparations for being Santa Claus with some complacency, completely unaware of the enormity of his intentions.

Having inspected—and rejected—the scruffy, red-flannel garment and dingy cotton-wool wig that were offered, he hired from a London firm, at no little expense to himself, a truly magnificent outfit; silvery beard, ringlets, black top boots, ermine hood and all. If he were going to do the thing, he might as well do it properly.

He rather fancied himself in this get-up and spent a good deal of time rehearsing his performance before the long mirror in his bedroom; practicing a jocose wagging of head and finger, a superb swing of sack to floor, and going to a great deal of trouble to discover any small details about the lives of Greeth residents which might be turned into telling little jokes that would bring the house down and make his performance a memorable one. "Ah," people would be saying in years to come, "but you should have been here when Mr. Hartley was Santa Claus—that really was something!"

The party was usually held about two weeks after Christmas, which gave Stanley the best part of a month in which to achieve perfection.

He was glad of something to occupy his time, for there was little to do in the garden at this time of year, and such preparations as he made for Christmas were already completed. Having discussed the menu with Mrs. Platt, he left the actual preparation and cooking of the feast, with one exception, in her hands. This exception was sauces. No woman, in Stanley's opinion, was capable of cooking the perfect sauce, and no sauce was worth serving unless it *was* perfect. And, as any sauce must be cooked and served at the very last moment, this always led to a certain amount of confusion, the kitchen being small and both Stanley and Mrs. Platt large. Mrs. Platt, meek creature as she was, decided, each Christmas Day, that this was her Last, and usually spent the afternoon packing her box and crying into it. However, it always blew over by the day after Boxing Day.

Being of a frugal nature, Stanley made a practice of buying his Christmas presents in the July sales. He wrapped, directed and stamped them immediately and laid them ready in a drawer. His Christmas cards never varied: just a plain white card, in impeccable taste, bearing the message, "With The Season's Greetings from Stanley H. Hartley," engraved in gold. Several years ago he had bought up about one thousand of these cards at a very reduced price, so there was no fear of any last-minute rush, and he would be able to Post Early for Christmas without the slightest inconvenience for many festive seasons to come. It was a great weight off his mind. He had a superior smile for those folks who went roaring into Huffley at the eleventh hour in a frenzied search for Something for Aunt Agnes, or to scramble for expensive and tasteless reproductions of Alpine peaks or coaches tallyhoing through villages alight with tinsel, or sentimental puppies peeping out of stockings. No, Christmas was never permitted to spring a surprise on Stanley.

2.

Hubert, of course, always had to make a last-minute rush. Hubert's cards were invariably mailed too late to reach their destinations by Christmas Day: he had, in fact, been asked more than once by their recipients which Christmas Day they were intended for. He gave few presents. A pound for his housekeeper, ten bob for his gardener and a book for Ronnie—that just about took care of the gift problem for the Reverend Hubert Sturgess. The small anonymous postal orders that found their way into the poorer homes in the village were nobody's business but his own.

It had been different when Edna was alive.

Shared with Edna, Christmas had been truly a season of happiness and good will toward all men. When her health allowed Edna had been a good manager and so, although she almost invariably had her asthma around this time, it had not seriously disrupted the pattern of their lives. Presents and cards had been dispatched in good time, puddings and cakes were ready, mince pies baked and a little tree for the baby Ronnie already decorated with candles and coloured balls. Hubert had been able to enjoy his Christmas—even to conduct the well-loved services without feeling miserable if the congregation were too small or suspicious if it were too large.

His housekeeper, Mrs. Hart, was a well-meaning woman, but she had a home of her own in the village, and one could hardly blame her if she considered her husband and children first at this time of the year. She did her best. There was always a cold chicken in the vicarage larder, a pudding which needed only to be heated up, mince pies with fluted edges and a concoction which Mrs. Hart referred to as a trifle, consisting of sponge cakes partially moistened with custard, encrusted with shredded coconut and crowned with crystallized cherries: a commodity which exercised a peculiarly laxative effect upon the vicarage household—its sole merit in Hubert's eyes.

Hubert and Ronnie just helped themselves; and it might have been worse—Oh, much worse!

It was bitterly cold and Hubert shivered as he stood on the Huffley platform waiting for Ronnie's train, which was unaccountably late.

It was going to be a success this time. It *must* be. He and Ronnie were really going to get together. It only needed a little patience, a little understanding on his part—and perhaps, he thought humbly, on Ronnie's part, too. Ronnie was all he had left of Edna.

He beat his woollen-gloved hands together, peering along the shining curve of the track for the first sight of the train.

Sam Ellis came whistling from the warm fog of the porters' room. He nodded with seasonable affability to the vicar and mentioned that the weather wasn't too bad for the time of the year.

Hubert inquired after Sam's four children and was reassured regarding their well-being. "Hearty little bastards, the lot on 'em," Sam stated with pride, cocking a challenging eye at the vicar. "Reckon you'll be glad to get your lad back, an' all."

"Yes, indeed," Hubert said eagerly. "It seems so long since I saw him. He spent the whole of the summer holiday in Italy, you know, with some school friends. I haven't set eyes on him since Easter. I expect he'll have grown quite a bit."

"Aye, he'll be—what?—fourteen, now, I reckon."

"Nearer fifteen. Dear me, that makes me feel quite old!" Hubert exclaimed with his nervous laugh.

"Aye we don't get no younger, none of us," the porter agreed, beating his arms across his chest. The signal fell with a metallic thud. "Here she comes, then. Happy Christmas to you, sir." He lounged slowly down the platform wondering why he had said *sir*, when it was against all his principles. But you couldn't help liking the poor little sod, he thought. Pity he couldn't afford to get himself a new overcoat. Sam didn't go much on parsons, but he supposed they did a job of work like anybody else, and why not pay 'em for it?

Hubert watched the red eye of the train coming around the bend. He felt quite buoyed up by the little encounter with Sam, who was often surly and unapproachable. He wondered if he ought to have rebuked him for swearing, but knew that he was not brave enough. They don't mean anything by it, he thought excusing both himself and Sam.

The train hissed to a standstill, doors opened and people began to spill out onto the platform. He felt quite sick with excitement. He began to hurry along the length of the train, looking for Ronnie.

When he reached the end he turned and ran all the way back again. He must have missed him somewhere in the crowd. Pushing and apologizing, he began to battle his way back against the tide of outgoing passengers.

The boy *must* be on this train. If he had missed it he would have telephoned. If he were ill they would surely have wired from the school. . . . But suppose he had been taken ill during the journey? Suppose . . . one heard of such awful things. . . . He began to leap up and down, peering into one compartment after another. He heard himself stammering: "Have you seen a boy . . . ?" Faces stared at him dispassionately or with veiled amusement and he knew he was acting foolishly. But he had to find Ronnie. . . . His excitement turned sour in him as he dodged and ran and jumped in and out of compartments, explaining and apologizing.

The train was getting up steam. Porters were slamming doors, trundling hand trucks piled high with luggage. "Mind your backs!" they cheerfully cried.

The crowd thinned, a whistle blew and a flag flapped briefly. The train gave a grunt and began to shunt along the edge of the platform.

Ronnie, Ronnie. Where was Ronnie! . . .

"Hello, Pop," a voice drawled behind him.

Hubert swiveled around and came up against a coat button. He raised his head higher, past a school tie and a chin fuzzy with down and a mouth that was so like Edna's that the heart faltered. . . .

"Where were you?" he heard himself shouting thinly. "Where have you been? I looked everywhere."

Ronnie grinned down at him.

"I saw you. Jumping up and down like a dog on a string. I've been leaning against this pillar all the time, watching you. God, you looked funny!"

Hubert stared up at his son; stared into the grinning, unfamiliar face so unexpectedly high above his own; at the fuzzy chin, the dark line across the upper lip, the stream of cigarette smoke issuing from the mouth that was so like Edna's. . . .

He gave a sob. He felt sick with a violent upsurge of anger. He hated this grinning, smoking, moustached stranger who dared to jeer at him with Edna's mouth. Suddenly his hand swung up and he struck at the mouth with a crack that seemed to shatter the silence of the now empty platform like a pistol shot.

Then he went slowly out to his crazy little car, leaving his son to follow or not—as he chose.

3.

Ada took Christmas as calmly as she took most things in life.

There was a lot of extra work, but work was a thing she had never been afraid of. Before the holiday she always gave the house a good clean from top to bottom, rubbed away at the silver until it fairly knocked your eye, polished floors to danger point and spent her evenings madly knitting or poring over cookbooks for novel ideas about sauces, homemade sweets and trimmings for the turkey. She was perfectly aware that the whole dinner would be cooked and served in precisely the same manner as it always had been cooked and served at The Laurels ever since she had come there, more years ago than she cared to remember.

When Alison's mother and father were alive Christmas had been a time of lavish entertaining; of noise and bustle; of people coming and staying and going, with fires blazing in every bed-room; of carol singers wanting wine and hot mince pies; of tradesmen giving presents and accepting tips; of Alison hanging up a long woollen stocking on the end of her bed and waking Ada up at some frightful hour of dawn to show her what she had found in it.

Happy days, happy days. . . .

Rocking away before her kitchen fire, Ada's mind often roved backward over those good old times when life held nothing more complicated than an aching back or an overbaked pie crust.

Sometimes, less happily, it dwelt upon the present. Sometimes, shrinkingly, it reached out delicate antennae toward the future. She tried not to let this happen very often, for there was no point in crossing your bridges before you came to them—and with every day that passed it seemed to Ada that the future loomed more black and threatening, and she herself felt less competent to deal with it.

Stoning raisins before the kitchen fire, she wondered what her life would have been had she married Albert Fletcher. Would she, too, have been the mother of three sons, the possessor of a fur coat and a Morris Ten? Much more likely Albert would still be selling tin tacks and she making do on his wages in some poky little back-street house. Albert would never have got where he was today without his wife's money. Still, she thought, I might have had the little lads. . . . And the knife remained suspended in mid-air as her mind timidly explored this avenue down which her feet would never now adventure.

To Albert the man she seldom gave a thought, for she felt she was too old for such foolishness—though she had been right set up with him in those long-ago days when he had come courting her at the kitchen door. Black curls Albert had, and a thick, strong body and a high colour. And he could do tricks, she remembered suddenly with a sense of surprise. Tricks with cards and handkerchiefs and that. . . . He used to bring her presents from the ironmonger's shop. Some pattypans shaped like shells and a little gadget for mincing ham and cheese, and a newfangled can opener. She still had the can opener. She pulled out the table drawer, and sure enough there it lay: she had used it for years and years without giving a thought to its donor, and it was still good, it was still the best can opener she had ever used. "Nay!" she muttered, shutting the drawer sharply and getting on with her raisins.

A shocking temper Albert had. She recalled with a pleasurable sense of the dramatic that last scene in this very kitchen when she and Albert had called it off for good. "Choose between them and me," Albert had demanded, red in the face. And: "I shanna give you a second chance. . . ." He had thumped the table and shouted, and the Master had thumped the table and shouted. The Mistress and Ada had wept copiously and Alison— just a chit of a girl she had been then—had come downstairs in her nightgown and stood listening in the doorway with her eyes sticking out like chapel hat pegs. Nay . . .

Aye, well, the past was past. It was today that mattered now and what today would turn into when it became tomorrow.

It had all started, of course, with Alison's birthday, and no letter from George.

Ada was not deceived about Alison's attitude to George. Her heart was no more broken than was Ada's own heart. Time, and their own good sense and mutual affection had seen to that. They had lived together in great content for many years now. Alison had her yearly letter from George; Ada had her can opener. All the sad sweets of romance without any of their disadvantages, as you might say.

The non-arrival of the birthday letter had upset the balance of their lives. And right on top of the upset—while they were still, as it were, wobbling—Miss Plum had to turn up, gumming the works up properly.

If we don't get shut of Miss Plum soon, Ada thought, slashing at the raisins with deep animosity, Alison will go an' do summat daft, like getting hersen wed to yon flabby-belly Hartley, or happen the vicar—and then where shall we be!

It was a thousand pities, in Ada's opinion, that Miss Plum had not been allowed to walk slap into her duck pond, and have done with it. . . .

4.

Alone in the living room Alison was getting her Christmas cards ready for mailing.

She wore the new dressing jacket around her shoulders; not because she was in the least chilly, but because she had snapped at Ada several times today for no good reason, and she was feeling repentant.

She chose a card picturing a village so deep in snow that only the roofs of the houses were visible, and wrote: "To Ada, with much love, from Alison." That was the sort of card Ada admired. She would be sure to remark: "That's where I like to see snow—on a Christmas card!"

Silly, perhaps, to send a card to someone living in the same house. But it had always been their custom, and a very pleasant one, too.

By the same token, she supposed she would have to send one to Miss Plum.

This was not so simple a matter as it might have seemed, for there were not many cards left to choose from and most of them were singularly inappropriate to the occasion. There was one exactly like Ada's—but that would never do: Ada would be mortally offended. There was one depicting a frozen pond with worried-looking ducks standing about on it. That, naturally, was out of the question! One with guests arriving at the open, lighted doorway of an inn, stagecoach in background, seemed a possibility until one read the words inside: "The more we are together, the happier we'll be!"

"No!" said Alison quite violently. And so was left with the choice between a plain card with the word: "Greetings" in a depressing shade of puce (what on earth had moved her to buy

it!) and a hunting scene so crudely coloured that it was difficult to believe she had actually paid fourpence for it. But there
it was, marked on the back with so vehement a pencil that even
after using an art-gum eraser with great force the price could
plainly be seen.

Well, it couldn't be helped. Alison chewed the end of her pen
for some minutes, finally inscribing the card with the words: "To
Victoria, with all good wishes, from Alison Penny."

That seemed to be that. Anxiously consulting her list she
decided that nobody had been forgotten. She tidied away her
writing materials, pulled the dressing jacket closer around her
shoulders and went to visit Ada in the kitchen.

Ada was stoning raisins. She received Alison with dignity, as
befit one who had been snapped at for no good reason but bore
the injustice with Christian fortitude.

"Queer kind of puddens we'll get this year," she remarked
dourly. "First time I've made 'em this late."

"I'm sure they'll taste lovely, as they always do," Alison
soothed, pulling a chair up to the fire and perching on the edge
of it. "Let me help."

"Nay, I'm nearly done. Your ma always reckoned to have
the puddens boiled by the end of November at latest, but everything's bin agen me this year. I've done best I could, an' nobody
can do more." She sighed heavily, glanced at the clock and said:
"It's time she were back."

Alison also glanced at the clock. She said hesitantly: "I expect
the Cubs were a bit high-spirited tonight. I don't suppose she's
had any experience of managing a crowd of little boys. It was
kind of her to try—"

Ada stood up and wiped her hands on a damp cloth.

"Pity you never went yersen. If you'd wrapped up and had
Braithwaite's taxi, I don't reckon you'd have tekken any harm."

"I didn't really feel up to it," Alison murmured.

"Don't talk so daft. You've bin out of yer bed nearly a week,
you've walked as far as the shops an' you're eating hearty. You
could 'a done it if you'd had a mind."

"Mr. Sturgess had already asked her to help, Ada, and she seemed so pleased."

"And so she gets her foot in t'vicarage, as well as in this house. . . . Nay, have some sense, lass! If you don't watch out she'll be running the W.I. before you can say knife, an' singing in t'Glee Club, an' tekkin *Parish* magazine around. Nay, I wouldn't put it past her to marry t'vicar—an' if that didn't give 'im summat to jump about for, I don't know what would!"

Alison stood up. She said coldly: "Really, Ada, you forget yourself"—exactly as Mummy would have said it twenty years ago—and left the kitchen, registering extreme displeasure.

But no sooner was she alone than her face quivered and blurred into tears. Kneeling on the hearthrug with her head in Daddy's wing chair she cried as if her heart would break as, indeed, it felt like doing at that moment.

How could anything so essentially simple, she mourned, be at the same time so involved? Having rescued her from suicide, must she therefore carry Miss Plum upon her shoulders for the rest of her life? A female Sinbad, eternally burdened? . . . Yet how could she drive her forth knowing, as she did, that Miss Plum was penniless, friendless, and lamentably lacking in courage: knowing, as she did, that such a person would lose no time in finding another duck pond and making a thorough job of it this time? She couldn't allow that to happen; she could *not*, however much she might dislike Miss Plum. Especially at Christmas. If only she could *think* of something. . . .

Ada stumped into the room, shut the door with a bang, and gathered Alison up into hard, loving arms. She rocked her to and fro like a baby.

"There, there, my lamb, don't tek on. I never meant to upset you. You an' me's got to stick together whatever happens. We're not going to let yon Plum woman come between us—not after all the years we've bin together. Give over crying now, or happen you'll start me off, an' all."

"Oh, Ada, if only I'd never gone into the Recreation Ground that day. I know it's wicked even to think it, but I can't help it however hard I try."

Ada deposited Alison in a chair, pushed at her spectacles and seized the poker.

"You know what I think?" she said, attacking the fire with unnecessary vigour. "If you'd never run back shouting at her, she'd have come out of yon duck pond of her own accord—an' pretty quick, too! She's no fool, our Miss Plum! She knows a sucker when she sees one."

"I wish I could believe that."

"You can. What's more, if you was to turn her out this very night she'd have found herself another sucker before twenty-four hours was up. There's one born every minute. . . . Committing suicide teks *guts*, luv—and guts is what Miss Plum was born without."

"I couldn't turn her out at Christmas time, Ada."

"Happen not. What I say is, as soon as Christmas is over go into t'Labour Exchange an' tell 'em all about it. Let them sort it out—what do we pay rates for?"

Alison looked a little happier.

"I do believe you're right, Ada. How clever of you! Oh, dear, I feel much more hopeful already. I think we will both have a glass of Daddy's port, by way of celebration. I'm sure we deserve it."

The port soothed their frayed nerves, set the seal on their reconciliation—even made them a little merry. They were giggling cosily together when Miss Plum returned from helping with the Cubs.

Alison gave Miss Plum a glass of Daddy's port, too. Now that she had some hope of getting rid of Miss Plum, she felt almost affectionate toward her, begging for news of the Cubs and their behaviour, and praising her for her efforts. "They are dear little boys, but very high-spirited; sometimes they get rather badly out-of-hand and it's quite a job to control them. I think you did splendidly—and all alone, too!"

"Not alone," Miss Plum corrected. "Mr. Sturgess was there to help me. Young Mr. Sturgess I mean. Ronnie. . . . He asked me to call him Ronnie."

Alison sat up straight. She could hardly believe her ears.

"*Ronnie?* . . . Ronnie Sturgess *helped* you with the Cubs? . . ." It was not so long ago that Ronnie was a Cub himself—and a very unlicked one at that! To the best of her knowledge Ronnie had never in all his life lifted a finger to help anybody.

"He's such a nice boy," Miss Plum murmured. "So very tall and handsome. His father told me he was only fourteen but you'd never believe it. He saw me right home to the gate. I told him it wasn't necessary but he insisted . . . I don't think he's very happy at home, you know. I don't believe his father really understands him. Such a nice man! But I always think a growing boy needs a woman's hand, don't you?"

Alison did not reply. She stared at Miss Plum, startled, fascinated, as if she were a being from Outer Space. She was still staring when Miss Plum dabbed genteelly at her lips and went up to tidy herself for supper.

Ada also went from the room. She pushed at her spectacles with grim triumph, but she refrained from saying: "*I told you so*"—though sorely tempted.

CHAPTER SIX

1.

ON CHRISTMAS Eve the weather which, for so long, had been execrable, suddenly decided to reform, and early risers, peering apprehensively from bedroom windows, were rewarded by scenes of sheerest beauty and delight.

The cruel east wind had died in the night and trees stood motionless, their outstretched arms sleeved in glittering white. Snow lay untouched, immaculate, on roofs and roadways, lawns and flower beds and curving garden paths; transformed crazy old tool sheds into enchanted palaces and the black bones of rosebushes into dancing fairy rings. Television masts became things of beauty, like glistening banners held aloft, and every window framed a frozen picture of the most perfect artistry. The sun, climbing from the east, lighted the whole scene with a golden radiance as the sky slowly unfolded wings of cloudless blue in benison.

There were those who muttered sourly: "Wait while it thaws!" But they were few in number and disregarded: the general feeling in Greeth was one of thankfulness and deep delight in this overnight miracle.

Standing on the doorstep of the vicarage, Hubert lifted eyes of humility and gratitude to his God. After the long weeks of darkness Christ was about to be born again; and the still, shining world made ready for His coming.

"Help me to be worthy of this miracle, Lord," he silently prayed. And then: "Help me to be worthy of Edna's love, and of the gift of the son she bore me. . . ."

He was bitterly ashamed of his treatment of Ronnie; even more ashamed because, so far, he had done nothing to atone.

Through long, wakeful hours, lying cold and comfortless in his lonely bed, he had agonized over the affair. To strike his son like that—in public—for what was, after all, no more than a childish prank! What had made him do such a thing? What had come over him? His own son. Edna's son. The little baby that had lain in the crook of her arm, the living presence of their love. . . .

Was he, perhaps, a little mad? he had wondered fearfully. Did madness lie at the core of this terrible unsureness that beset him; his excessive doubts, jealousies, suspicions? Oh, God, not that. Not that. . . .

A childish prank. . . . No, it had been more than that, surely. Such behaviour could not be dismissed so lightly. There had been an adult cruelty in Ronnie's face, a shocking callousness in his laugh. *God, you looked funny!* No, he could not forgive; there was no forgiveness in him.

For hours he had knelt beside his bed, chilled to the bone, chilled to the heart; bony knees sore from contact with the cheap, harsh carpet. He had padded about the dark, silent house making cups of tea, swallowing aspirins in hope of sleep; reading at his desk huddled in an overcoat; standing irresolute outside the door of Ronnie's bedroom, listening, waiting, hoping for he knew not what. Then back to the cold bed to snatch what rest he could before the night was entirely gone.

They had not spoken to each other.

After that scene on the station platform he had shut himself into his study, shaking with anger and humiliation.

Ronnie had been there all the time, watching his agitation, his flurried, clumsy, desperate searching. He had leaned against a pillar and *watched*. With a cigarette sticking out of his mouth—Edna's mouth—and that grin on his face, so suddenly high above his own. *God, you looked funny!* Ronnie had actually said that. . . .

He had heard the taxi arrive; the bump of suitcases in the hall; feet going up and down the stairs, in and out of the kitchen. Stealthily opening the study door he had heard Ronnie talking to Mrs. Hart. She had given him a cup of tea. They had laughed together about something (about *him*?) and presently doors had banged and there had been silence. Mrs. Hart had gone home. Ronnie had gone—where?

Let him go, Hubert had thought violently. Let him go right away and stay away. We have nothing in common. We are nothing to each other.

For two days and nights they had lived in the same house without speaking, without contact. Once Ronnie had started to climb the stairs as Hubert had been coming down, and the boy had simply turned away and disappeared through a doorway.

Hubert had eaten all his meals off a tray in his study. Whether Ronnie ate at home or abroad he had no idea. He told himself he did not care. His heart felt squeezed and hard, his head ached perpetually, he could not get warm: nothing could make him warm.

The long vigils on his knees were useless. Prayer did not help because he would not be helped. His heart was closed to love, squeezed dry of love, hard and painful with lack of it.

Nothing so terrible had ever happened to him. Not even when Edna died: not even then. . . .

Now that the snow had fallen and the wind gone, the air felt almost warm. Hubert lifted his hands, and in each palm the sun dropped a warm, golden gift. It seeped through his clothing and dispelled the awful chill. It flooded his heart with radiance softening the hard core of his resentment and dispelling the darkness of his soul.

Tears pricked behind his eyelids as he gazed upon the immaculate, shining world, and he was filled with humility and gratitude.

"Help me to be worthy of this miracle. . . . Help me to be worthy of Edna's love, and of the son she bore me even as Thou were't born of Mary. . . ."

He turned and went into the house; blundered up the stairs to Ronnie's room.

Ronnie was asleep.

One hand lay outside the covers, the fingers clenched. His dark hair curled against the pillow, his lashes lay darkly on rounded, childish cheeks. He looked, indeed, no more than a child, despite the dark line above his upper lip and the down covering those cheeks. His mouth was slightly open showing a glimpse of strong white teeth. His bared throat looked tender, vulnerable.

Standing by the bed, Hubert gazed down upon his son and saw with astonishment, and for the first time, that the boy resembled himself more than Edna. The mouth was Edna's; but the tall brow, the short, pugnacious nose, the vacillating chin were his own legacy. Had he also bequeathed his nature to Ronnie? The doubts and suspicions, the cowardly evasions, the weaknesses that all his life had beset him? Was that the whole trouble between himself and his son—that Ronnie was made in his image, lacking serenity, courage—faith, perhaps?

As if he felt his father's gaze upon him the boy stirred, opened and shut his eyes again.

Hubert put out a hesitant hand.

"Ronnie. . . . Can't we be friends? We have nobody but each other. And it is Christmas Eve, the birth time of our Lord will soon be here."

"I don't want a chewing out," Ronnie muttered. And cravenly Hubert forced a laugh.

"Of course not. But let us put an end to this stupid . . . misunderstanding, shall we?" he said eagerly. "I was wrong to strike you and I am dreadfully sorry for it. But you hurt me, you know. You hurt me deeply."

"I only said you looked funny. And so you did. You should have seen yourself!"

"Yes, I expect I did. You are too young to understand. When you have a son of your own, perhaps . . . But come, don't let us waste any more of this glorious day. It really is glorious, Ronnie. Get up and look. Snow and sunshine, and no beastly wind— doesn't it look grand?"

Ronnie heaved himself off the bed, towering over his father as he yawned and scratched.

"I wonder if there'll be any skating?"

"Not yet. In a day or two if this weather holds. We might walk up to the Tarn together this morning"—he was trying his hardest not to sound too eager—"and inspect it. Take some bread and cheese in our pockets, eh?"

"I hate walking. Anyway, I'm going into Huffley. Miss Plum asked me to help her with some shopping."

"Miss *Plum*?"

"You know—that dame up at The Laurels. I gave her a hand with the Cubs. She's been ill, you know, and there'll be rather a lot to carry, so I offered to go along. As a matter of fact I rather like her. Her name—believe it or not—is Victoria! I didn't know how to keep my face straight. Victoria Plum . . . God, what a name to give a kid!"

"Ronnie, please don't use such expletives," Hubert said nervously.

"Come again?"

"Don't say *God*, like that. Loosely."

"Oh, God, you sound like a television panel. All right, then: dear me, you sound like a television panel." He glanced at his watch. "I've got to hurry if I want any breakfast. I may not be back by lunch, so don't wait." He fished a package of Players from a pocket of his jacket and opened it.

Gulping painfully, Hubert said: "Ronnie, I'd rather you didn't smoke yet. You're far too young."

To his enormous surprise Ronnie threw the package onto the table. He said: "O.K. I don't like it much, only a lot of the chaps do. It's just showing off really." He gave his father a sudden smile; a child's smile, sweet and brilliant, that brought a lump to Hubert's throat and made his heart beat quicker.

"Is the bath water hot?"

Hubert's face fell.

"No, as a matter of fact I'm afraid it isn't. I really must get something done about that boiler. I'll see about it as soon as Christmas is over. But you can have your bath tonight, Ronnie— it gets simply boiling by tea-time."

A few minutes later Mrs. Hart, frying bacon in the kitchen, heard them descend the stairs together and stand at the front door to admire the as yet untrodden snow. She heard the vicar's eager comments and young Ronnie's yawning replies.

And about time too! she thought austerely. Mrs. Hart was sick of the whole set-up. The study door locked and *Do Not Disturb* hanging on the handle. Young Ron sulking about the place or else being that fresh she'd a mind to smack his face for him. Meals served separate or not eaten at all. . . . It wasn't good.

Once the study door had been unlocked. Greatly daring, she had entered and had surprised the vicar on his knees in the act of prayer. Tears had been running down his cheeks. He had opened his eyes and stared at her, still kneeling; both of them too shocked for speech. Blundering from the room she had run downstairs and shut herself in the kitchen. She had felt acutely embarrassed, almost with a sense of outrage. In all her life she had never seen anyone praying like that—except, of course, in church, which was the proper place for such things. . . .

About time they made it up!

Mrs. Hart knew all about it. The whole village by this time knew all about it. Mrs. Hart's husband, who worked in Huffley, had heard the story from Sam Ellis, who had seen the whole thing. Smacking the lad's face like that in public, and calling himself a Christian! Not but what young Ron could be a limb of Satan when he liked. But what sort of example was that to set to folks! Calling himself a Christian. . . .

She slapped another couple of rashers into the pan and sniffed loudly. Nice goings on, indeed!

It just goes to *show*, thought Mrs. Hart ambiguously.

2.

Every year on Christmas Eve the church choir, augmented by the Glee Club, went from house to house singing carols.

Nobody enjoyed this outing more than Stanley Hartley; providing, of course, that the weather was not inclement, and he was free of those heart flutterings (which he was convinced were only wind) and the touch of sciatica with which he was often afflicted at this season.

None of these phenomena having reared its ugly head this year, Stanley set out in good time for the church, insulated against the cold by so many cardigans, pullovers and scarves that it was a marvel he could put one foot before the other.

A large and enthusiastic party was gathered in the vestry. This was proper carol-singing weather; the sort usually found on Christmas cards and nowhere else. This was the real thing!

Everybody seemed in the highest spirits. Some of the choir-boys indeed were already getting a little boisterous, but that would work itself off after an hour or so of trudging from house to house with refreshments, suitable and unsuitable, every half-mile or so. If not, a few well-directed clouts on the head would bring them to order, as Stanley knew from experience. Hubert, he noticed with some surprise, was being exception-ally boyish! Bubbling over with bonhomie. He appeared to be on the best of terms with Ronnie—if that great gawk of a lad really could *be* Ronnie. According to Mrs. Platt, who had had it straight from Mrs. Hart, they were not on speaking terms. There had been some sort of scene at Huffley station. . . . It just proved how futile it was to listen to gossip, Stanley thought severely and, it must be admitted, a little flatly.

Alison was there, looking perfectly restored to health. Her cheeks glowed pinkly above a collar of grey fur and her hands were tucked into a snug little grey fur muff. She looked, Stanley thought, quite charming.

He maneuvered a position by her side and kept it for the whole of the evening.

Hubert also thought Alison looked charming, and quite ridiculously girlish for her age which, as she had frankly admitted to him, was forty.

Five years younger than himself. And at least twenty years younger than Stanley, who was so selfishly monopolizing her. Was there anything between them? Surely not. Surely she'd have more sense than to throw herself away on a fat, pampered, self-centred. . . .

He caught himself up sharply. These were nice thoughts for Christmas time, the season of good will! And they were, moreover, sour grapes; for if he found it hard to imagine Alison marrying Stanley, he found it still harder to imagine her marrying himself. Stanley might be an ass, but at least he was a good-looking ass. He was a well-off ass. He had a comfortable home and no encumbrances. He wasn't a dithering, neurotic, cowardly half-wit. . . .

They moved off into the snow. Lighted lanterns swinging from tall poles were borne by two of the choirmen. Somebody carried a fiddle, somebody else a piano accordion. Two choirboys cuffed each other in high spirits and were separated with tolerance. Laughter ran to and fro as they made their way along the straggling High Street toward the War Memorial, which was their first stop. The firm snow squeaked under their shoes and was rosily lit by the lanterns. Mr. Clegg, the choirmaster, fussed importantly from group to group, heavy with last-minute warnings and reminders.

At the War Memorial they formed a circle around the lanterns. The fiddle tuned up, the accordion murmured, there were a few coughs and anxious clearing of throats and then they were off to a good start with *O, Come All Ye Faithful*, and this was followed by *While Shepherds Watched*. A small crowd quickly collected and money chinked cheerfully into the collecting bag which Stanley had been deputed to hand around. Then they were off again; this time for Wyck Farm, whose hospitality was known to be so lavish that the choirboys set off at a run.

Stanley jingled his bag with satisfaction. "If we do as well as this at each stop, I shall require help in carrying it," he declared.

Ronnie slipped around to Alison's other side. He said rather pettishly: "Isn't Victoria coming?"

"Victoria?" Alison repeated in mild astonishment.

"She said she might come, this morning. She's not ill again or something, is she?"

Summoning up her Cubs' voice Alison replied: "Miss Plum is very well. She was a little tired, I think. She went into Huffley this afternoon and it was very crowded."

"I know. I was with her."

"You were *with* her?"

"And why not?" Ronnie inquired in the tolerant tone often employed by the very young toward the old and feeble of intellect, who must be humoured.

Alison decided to ignore it. She said briskly: "Miss Plum does not belong to Greeth. She is here for a short time only, as my guest."

"I know all about it," Ronnie stated. "Everything. I think she's had a rotten deal, all her life."

"If Miss Plum has confided in you, Ronnie—and I must say I am surprised she has done so on so short an acquaintance—then you will know that Ada and I have done everything possible to help her."

"And in return she did everything possible for you and Ada."

"Yes, indeed," Alison returned honestly.

"And now you're going to throw her out on her ear!"

Alison counted ten, as Daddy had always advised her to do in moments of anger.

She wondered how much of this conversation Stanley had heard as he plodded along on her other side, galoshes squeaking in the snow and the collecting bag clutched to his bosom (in default of a strong room).

And then they were at the farm where, after *Good King Wenceslaus* and *Silent Night* they were regaled with coffee and mince pies, and where Stanley, to his ill-concealed distaste, was kissed under the mistletoe by the lively daughter of the house.

As soon as they were on the move again Ronnie reappeared at her side, continuing the conversation as if it had never been broken.

"She worships the ground you walk on."

Counting ten was no help. In any case Alison no longer felt angry; only desperate and rather frightened, though she hardly knew why.

"Miss Plum and I are very good friends, Ronnie. You are only a child and cannot be expected to understand the why's and wherefore's of the case. But I must thank you for helping her with the Cubs."

"I was passing the Village Hall and I heard a frightful racket going on, so I went inside and cracked a few heads against the wall. She was crying," he said moodily. "The little beasts."

Remembering the many occasions on which Ronnie had nearly reduced her to tears, in the not distant past, Alison made no comment and they walked in silence for a while. Then Stanley said abruptly and quite inaccurately: "I think your father wants you," and reluctantly the boy slouched away.

"Oh, dear," murmured Alison weakly. She had so looked forward to the carol singing, and now it was all being spoiled.

Making no foolish pretense of not having overheard, Stanley stated firmly: "What Miss Plum needs is a home of her own and a husband."

Goaded, Alison inquired tartly: "And do you propose to supply them?"

There was a silence so prolonged that she felt impelled to glance at him; surprising an expression on Stanley's face that could only be described as a smirk.

This sent her spirits lower, if possible, than before. She did not know what to say. There was nothing to be said. There was nothing to be done. Nothing, nothing, *nothing.* . . .

Miss Plum had sprung the tenderest trap of all—the trap of compassion—and they were all caught in it, helpless, bewildered. Herself, Stanley, Hubert, Ronnie: all together in the trap awaiting the pleasure of Miss Plum.

Only Ada was not in the trap. Only Ada retained the tough rectitude of common sense and the courage to declare it. *Guts is what Miss Plum was born without. . . . She knows a sucker when she sees one. . . . If you don't watch out you're going to get saddled with Miss Plum to the end of your life. . . .*

If the girl married Stanley, Alison thought, or even Hubert, I could wash my hands of her.

But even as the thought was born she knew it to be false. Stanley and Hubert were her best friends. United with Miss Plum neither could long sustain that role. Instead, Miss Plum would be her best friend; the door of The Laurels always open to her; the life of the village shared with her; the cosy intimacy with either spiritual or financial advisor shifted on to the narrow shoulders, the spaniel gaze, the bony, clinging fingers of Miss Plum forever and ever. . . .

"God rest ye merry, Gentlemen," piped Alison; and shuffled her feet in the snow and shivered, and ate a mince pie she did not want, and clutched her little muff of grey fur closer to her bosom.

Surely it had turned much colder since they set out?

"I think the weather is changing," she said to Stanley.

"I had not noticed it," he replied. But he wound one of his mufflers a little tighter, just in case.

Hubert materialized on Alison's other side.

"Isn't this marvellous!" he cried, beating his woollen-gloved hands together. "The very spirit of Christmas is abroad. It is a night straight out of Dickens!"

"Ronnie is looking for you," Stanley said crushingly.

"Then he will have no difficulty in finding me amongst only thirty people," Hubert returned, refusing to be crushed. "What an unusually good turn-out! Most gratifying." He cast the glowing end of a cigarette into the turn-up of a tenor's trousers in front, and there was a small skirmish while it was removed and the conflagration beaten out. "And where," he inquired, when order was restored, "is our Miss Plum tonight? I understood that she might join us."

Alison wondered what would happen if she suddenly screamed and beat Hubert over the head with her hymn-book.

Such excesses were, however, rendered unnecessary, for Hubert disappeared as abruptly as he had arrived. It had occurred to him that, if Ronnie really had been seeking him out, he could ill afford to ignore the gesture just at the moment when, however slight, contact had been made between them.

3.

The night wore on. Crunch of trodden snow, creak of gates, flood of sudden light from open doorways; clamour of welcome; hot mince pies, hot cocoa, hot coffee. *Good King Wenceslaus*, *Silent Night*, *While Shepherds Watched*, *Away In A Manger*. Hearty farewells, good wishes shouted and returned, girlish shrieks and male laughter.

Enthusiasm waned with the trodden miles. Footsteps began to lag and yawns were loud upon the quiet air. A choirboy, with every reason, was sick behind a bush. People straggled behind and two engaged couples disappeared altogether. A fiddle string broke with a snapping whine. Stanley's bag became burdensome.

Clearly it was time to pack up.

In the general relief at this decision spirits rose once more to seasonal heights. The collecting bag, most gratifyingly heavy, was given into the choirmaster's custody. Hubert thanked everybody with lavish praise and wished them a happy Christmas. They all roared: "And the same to you!" There was a good deal of hand-shaking, back-slapping, and shouted pleasantries as the members of choir and Glee Club fanned out and away into their various homeward directions.

A large saloon halted, offering a lift to five passengers—seven, if they didn't mind sitting on each other's knees.

Stanley accepted immediately, for he had developed a blister on his left heel, to say nothing of the stiffness in his right arm due to carrying the collecting bag. Hubert, after an embarrassing display of refusal, suddenly climbed in and sank back with his eyes closed. Fat Mrs. Jenkins from the post office was hoisted up with cheers and laughter and old Ted Gunter, the cowman from Cross Farm, was finally persuaded in. Three of the smallest choirboys were thrust and squeezed inside and the doors of the car, with some difficulty, slammed shut, when somebody remembered Miss Penny, who was a long way from home and who had, moreover, recently been ill.

Everybody asked each other where Miss Penny had got to but nobody knew. She had been there only a few moments ago but was now vanished. Voices shouted for her, but there was no answer.

"She must have gone ahead," Stanley said. And he reflected comfortably: Alison is young, it will not hurt her to walk.

Hubert did not even open his eyes. He had never felt so tired in all his life. But he felt sure he would sleep tonight now that he and Ronnie were friends again. Bed, thought Hubert blissfully. Bed!

Alison walked steadily, hands clasped inside the little fur muff and head erect. She heard the hullabaloo behind her but she paid no attention. It was infinite comfort to get away from them all.

She was not unduly weary for she was accustomed to taking long walks, nor was she in the least nervous of walking alone in the night. In any case, it was almost as bright as day with the flat shine of the snow and the brilliance of stars crowding the clear sky in breath-taking beauty.

It had been a very successful carol singing—the best for many years, she thought; and she tried to keep her mind on this and to rejoice.

She tried not to remember that infuriating smirk on Stanley's face; to forget that Ronnie and Miss Plum had gone into Huffley together and that Miss Plum had concealed the circumstance from her; to pretend that Hubert had not sounded disappointed at Miss Plum's absence. But she could not control her thoughts.

Men! Alison thought, quivering. And she remembered George with a sudden sharp poignancy. George, who had courted her so passionately, yet had managed so well without her; who, until this year, had so faithfully remembered her birthday but had now, it seemed, forgotten even that.

It does not matter at all, she told herself bleakly. I am forty. I am past my youth—all passion spent—and that is what men care about. Faithfulness does not matter to them, nor integrity, nor intelligence. Not even beauty matters so much to men as youth.

The stars gazed down upon her, coldly dispassionate. Trees, outlined in frosted purity, watched her passage. Glow of family windows shut her out. The church clock struck ten solemn reminders of time passing, time lost. . . .

As she neared The Laurels her pace quickened: sharp, eager impact of footsteps loud upon the hard-beaten floor of snow.

Bed, thought Alison gratefully. Bed and two hot-water bottles, and something hot and savoury on a tray and Ada tucking me in. Ada scolding me a little. Ada spoiling me. . . .

And tomorrow, she thought, it will be Christmas, and I will put all my worries and problems behind me. And then Christmas will be over and Miss Plum will go—Miss Plum will go!—and there will be no problem. Not any more. . . .

The gate swung to behind her, clicked shut with its usual competence. Lights shone from all the windows, giving welcome. The porch lantern guided her footsteps up the steep slope of the path.

While she fumbled for her key the door opened and light streamed out, blinding her.

She was inside, sitting on the monk's bench and bending over her overshoes before she noticed the feet confronting and a little below the level of her gaze.

Big feet. Male feet in rather peculiar-looking suede shoes coming out of trousers in an exceptionally hairy variety of Harris tweed. . . .

Her gaze went on and up. Over a well-filled pullover knitted in loud checks; past powerful shoulders and a flamboyant tie partially concealed by a luxuriant beard of brown flecked with grey, and so to a remembered grin, to the remembered blueness of eyes, to the sudden shock of baldness rising above a grizzled ring of curls. . . .

"George!" she whispered, white-lipped, clutching the monk's bench with frantic fingers.

"Well, well," said George's voice; harsher than she remembered—but yet remembered. "Happy Christmas, Alison, if it's not too early—or too late. . . ."

She felt herself pulled upward. She experienced the startling, unfamiliar prick of whiskers, the smell of whisky, horrid yet somehow exciting, the disturbing grip of muscular arms about her shoulders. She thought confusedly: I am being kissed under the mistletoe. By a man. By George . . .

"Long time no see!" boomed George.

She stared at him across the chasm of twenty years, seeking for words and finding none.

Where is Ada? was her panic thought. And then: where is Miss Plum?

Half-pulled, half-carried, she entered the warm, firelit living room; and George slammed the door on their reunion.

In the kitchen Ada sat like a stone as she listened to the voices, to the silence.

The supper tray was laid. A pan of milk, already once boiled, was hot upon the stove. What now? thought Ada, for once unable to cope with a situation. And she muttered: "Nay!" and continued to sit like a stone.

On the upstairs landing there was a whisper of skirts, and the door of Miss Plum's bedroom closed with a soft click.

CHAPTER SEVEN

1.

WHICHEVER way you look at it, twenty years is a long time.

In twenty years the world, still licking its wounds from a major war, can be plunged into yet another major war; can survive and emerge to lick its wounds all over again and to compound elaborate and devilish schemes for a third and still more effective abomination of abominations, forgetting all else.

In twenty years old folks have died off, the young have grown up and already a new generation is appearing to make its mark in the fields of art, politics, law, religion and life in general.

But even after twenty years there still remain a few who remember with tenacity the small happenings which, at the time, had seemed not so small. The kindness of a neighbour, the death of a dog, the unimportant tragedy of a love affair gone awry. . . .

There were inevitably those in Greeth who remembered the young fellow with the blue eyes and the mop of brown curls and the lean, rangy body, who had come courting Alison Penny twenty years ago: a gawky young fellow, as fresh as they came, but likable enough. He'd been a foreigner from Beck Mills, ten miles the other side of Huffley. Greeth had never held a high opinion of Beck Mills folks, many of whom had married with the gypsies and had inherited some of their less admirable qualities, adding insult to injury by invariably beating the Greeth team at darts.

Today, few of the Greeth folks could care less what had happened to Alison Penny's pitiful little love affair. But there were those who remembered.

Old Minnie Clegg at the End House remembered the lad giving her a fresh grin and a wink as he pedalled past her gate almost horizontal over his handle bars. Old Snaith, up at the Spinney Cottage, remembered a pretty little lass slipping through the larches to join the lad, who flung his machine on the grass and clasped her in his arms in the scented, violet dusk of June evenings. Old Snell from Wheelwrights, who now led a cat-and-dog existence with a widowed daughter-in-law down in the village, remembered an angry father stamping down the meadows and stamping up again, propelling before him a weeping girl; leaving behind a sullen youth to kick at the turf and mutter maledictions and finally to go off breakneck on his crazy bike with the wind flattening his brown curls and filling the back of his shirt like a balloon.

Some had declared that the girl's father was right to put a stop to it. Others, remembering their own youthful battles with parental authority, had championed the girl. "What, it's her life, isn't it?" they had demanded of each other as they gossiped on doorsteps in evening idleness or leaned on spades down on the allotments out of the way of the womenfolk. . . . Small happenings. And twenty years is a long time. But a few remembered.

Peering between kid-gloved fingers as she knelt in church on Christmas Day, old Mrs. Clegg recognized in the bulky figure in the Pennys' pew the gawky boy from Beck Mills of twenty years ago. Bearded he might be, running to fat and bald on top—she was not deceived: yon was the lad there'd been all the rumpus about. Her toothless gums champed up and down and her eyes glinted self-importance. She could hardly wait to get home and spread the news.

There he was, as large as life and twice as natural, sitting between Miss Penny and that woman who was living with her that nobody could find out about. This was a titbit indeed and was bound to liven up Christmas dinner and afford her respectful attention from all!

Old Thomas Snell, who had been sent out for a walk with his two youngest grandchildren, while his daughter-in-law dealt with a leg of pork and treated herself to a nip of gin in private, was the first person Mrs. Clegg met. Even while she cackled the news into Thomas's good ear the three of them passed on their way home to The Laurels: Alison walking quickly and looking very pink, George stepping out with a rolling gait and laughing loudly about something, and the young woman the village couldn't find out about slipping along just behind them in a subdued manner.

"That's him," Minnie Clegg declared. "I'd pick 'im out of a thousand!"

"Might be, an' might not," old Snell replied, aiming a clout at his youngest grandchild who was trundling a Christmas toy over his bad foot. "Can't see as it matters one way or t'other." But he bundled his charges back home as soon as he dared and nipped off to The Goat with a surprising turn of speed for his age.

The landlord of The Goat had resided in Greeth for no more than five years and knew nothing of Miss Penny's affairs. Twenty years ago he had been roaring at recruits on a barracks square and wished most passionately that he were still doing it. He suffered from insomnia, kidneys and a nagging wife and his cup was full without having to listen to old Snell spluttering ancient history. He admitted, under pressure, that he had a gent in the first floor front bedroom. A nice, open-handed sort of party, come from San Francisco. And if anybody wanted any further information they could always ask the party most concerned.

"There you are!" old Snell cried. "Why should anyone want to come here all t'way from San Francisco?"

"Ah, you got something there," agreed the landlord sourly.

"Unless it was to see somebody, I mean."

"Even so," said the landlord, running a cloth over the slopped surface of the bar and sucking his teeth spitefully.

By nightfall it was all over the village.

2.

Concocting his sauces under the patient but disapproving eyes of Mrs. Platt, Stanley pondered the circumstance.

Who *was* the gross-looking fellow who had shared Alison's hymnbook and who had whisked her out of church and away before any of her friends could so much as wish her the compliments of the season? Shuddering, he recalled the padded shoulders, the unspeakable tie that was the only possible excuse for the equally unspeakable beard.

Who was he? Cousin? He had never heard Alison speak of any male relatives. Business associate? Hardly, on Christmas Day. A refugee of some sort? He dismissed the notion instantly: the fellow was too prosperous-looking; too obviously English, despite the appalling get-up.

Remembering her rosy confusion over the sharing of the hymnbook (for he had kept a pretty sharp eye upon them), and her precipitate exit from the church, Stanley brooded sombrely on the possibility of Alison having a Past, and of this fellow being a part of it. He discovered to his surprise that he disliked the idea very much. Such a soft, pretty, confiding little creature! He was very fond of her indeed. The idea of marrying her had never appealed to him more than when he saw her sharing a hymn-book with that bearded brute with the tie and the pointed, lemon-coloured shoes. . . .

"Is the sauce burning, sir?" Mrs. Platt asked meekly.

"Certainly not," Stanley shrilled, snatching the pan from the flame and stirring madly.

"Oh, good. . . . Everything's ready when you are, sir."

Flicking brown specks from the over-cooked sauce Stanley thought indignantly: if she wished to marry, I was the obvious choice. Indeed, the only choice—unless one includes Hubert. And who could take Hubert seriously! And he thought: my Christmas dinner is ruined. I shall eat only a mouthful. Then I shall take a digestive tablet and go to sleep—if I am able to sleep.

"Who was the funny fellow with the beard?" inquired Ronnie, pushing Mrs. Hart's trifle about on his plate.

"I don't know," Hubert replied. "I have never seen him before."

"I never want to again. My God, what shoes! And did you spot the tie under all that fungus?"

"Ronnie, I have asked you not to blaspheme."

"Oh, sorry! It doesn't mean anything."

"Then why say it?"

Ronnie said peevishly: "This stuff is practically uneatable. Why don't we have the pudding?"

"It takes an hour to heat up. I thought we'd have it tomorrow. I shall be quite free tomorrow. I thought we might go for a good long walk in the morning. Take some bread and cheese—or we might get lunch at a pub. Then at night we'd have a good dinner and listen to the wireless. How does that sound?"

"It sounds madly gay," Ronnie said coldly. "And what about the rest of today?"

"Well, I'm afraid I shall have to rest this afternoon," Hubert said apologetically. "I was up very early, and I haven't been sleeping very well lately . . . I'm afraid it's a bore for you, but Mr. Hartley has invited us for supper tonight."

"Oh, God—that old pansy!"

"Ronnie!"

"Oh, for pity's sake, Pop! You don't mind if I say *Oh, goodness*—which actually means exactly the same thing. . . . Anyway, I don't expect anyone will mind if I decline Mr. Hartley's kind invitation with thanks."

"I shall mind," Hubert said a little sharply. He lit a cigarette and began to pile the plates together.

Ronnie walked about the room kicking idly at the furniture.

"As a matter of fact I thought of going up to The Laurels."

"Have you been invited?"

"Does that matter?"

"On Christmas Day—yes, I think so. Especially as Alison has a guest."

"I'm not going to see Alison. I'm going to see Victoria."

"Victoria . . . ?" Hubert gazed helplessly at his son. He didn't know what to say. He felt in a muddle and he was too tired to try to sort it out. In spite of everything he had not slept well last night, and all he wanted was to sleep. To sleep for hours and hours and hours. . . . Sometimes he longed most passionately to fall asleep and never to wake again. He always asked forgiveness for this because he knew it was terribly wrong. He had to think of Ronnie. He had to keep awake, alive, as long as Ronnie needed him. That was what fathers were *for.*

"Perhaps if you went up to The Laurels about tea-time, and came on to Stanley's later . . . ?" he suggested. He carried the dirty dishes into the kitchen and piled them up on the drainboard for Mrs. Hart's attention the following day.

Ronnie stood in the doorway watching the small, thin figure slowly climb the stairs towards the hope of oblivion. He thought of his mother. He did not remember her very clearly, but there had been a difference in the house when she was alive. A brightness; a sort of softness; a feeling of safety that he had never since experienced.

What a bore the holidays were! Six whole weeks stretched out before him, fairly rattling with boredom. Going for long, exhausting walks with Pop being hearty and all-boys-together. Being asked out to tea by one elderly parishioner after another. Helping with the Cubs and the Old Folks' Christmas Party, and the magic lantern for the kids. . . . There might be a movie worth seeing in Huffley, but more likely not. There might be some skating if only this weather would hold. . . . He raked out his old skates from the attic, but they were in a shocking condition and he couldn't find any oil.

His father had dropped cigarette ash all over the tablecloth and there was a sticky smear where custard had been spilled. With a sudden disgust he gathered up the cloth and thrust it into the laundry basket. Then he swept the hearth and carried in a bucket of coal. On a sudden impulse he washed up the dirty dishes and ran a duster along the ledges in the dining room. He began to feel virtuous, responsible and much less bored.

He went upstairs and changed into his best clothes and flattened his dark curls with sticky white cream out of a bottle. He peered with dissatisfaction into the mirror. He really would have to start shaving. And why was he so devilishly afflicted with pimples?

Quietly he opened his father's bedroom door.

Hubert lay on his back, fast asleep. His mouth had fallen open and he made small snuffling noises at the back of his throat. His hair looked thin and lifeless: one lock fell across his forehead in limp abandon, rising and falling to each stertorous breath.

An unaccountable lump rose in Ronnie's throat as he stood there looking down upon his sleeping father. He was an ass, of course, but he *was* his father. Mother must have loved him once. . . .

I love him, too, he thought with surprise, and felt an impulse to wake him and tell him so. But he turned away and went silently from the room.

Outside, the short daylight was nearly done and windows glowed behind coloured curtains snugly drawn. The cold and the white, deserted street and the sense of secrecy behind the curtained houses filled him with a rising excitement, and he thought of Victoria with a pleasure that was half guilt. Perhaps I shall kiss her under the mistletoe, he thought. . . . She was old, of course: in a few years she would be a hag. But she was a woman: warm; rather small and silly; dark-eyed, dark-haired and some-how mysterious. When she looked up at him in her timid way he felt like a man. He felt wonderful. . . . She opened, just a tiny crack, the gate leading to the unknown.

Fingering his downy chin Ronnie thought: I'll buy a razor first thing when I get back to school.

He went down a long slide with skilful ease; went back and did it again; gave a skip and began to run over the flattened snow whistling cheerfully.

3.

George lay in drowsy discomfort in his bedroom at The Goat. It was quite dark, but the luminous hands of his watch told him it was still only four o'clock. No need to move for a couple of hours yet.

The bed was soft enough: the discomfort arose from his having eaten and drunk a great deal too much in the middle of the day. After attending church with Alison and escorting her home to The Laurels to take a glass of sherry and then walking all the way back to the village, he felt exhausted. He hadn't taken that much exercise in a good many years. He never took any exercise at all if he could possibly avoid it. And he'd been mad

to eat a hot, three-course meal after four pints of very indifferent bitter and a couple of shorts. Quite mad. He'd been warned
often enough. Groaning, he turned on his other side.

He wondered why he had come to Greeth at all. Curiosity, he supposed. It was curiosity that killed the cat, wasn't it?
Feeling as he did at present, he wouldn't be at all surprised if it
killed *him*. . . . All that church-going. All that tramping about—it
was enough to kill anyone. . . . He belched resoundingly and felt
a little better.

But why *had* he come to Greeth?

In the last twenty years he had returned to England a number
of times and had never before felt the impulse to come back to
the scene of his youthful affair with Alison.

Not that he had forgotten her. Indeed, he had taken pride in
cherishing the one and only innocent romance of his whole life;
had deliberately kept its memory alive by sending her a letter for
her birthday each year.

It had sometimes occurred to him that she might no longer be
Miss Alison Penny of The Laurels, Greeth, Yorkshire, England,
but Mrs. Somebody of anywhere in the world, with a husband in
a bowler hat and striped trousers and a baby carriage parked in
the hall. He had never truly believed it. And anyway, his letters
would have been returned. . . .

During the crowded, amorous years, he had thought of her
continually—well, *fairly* continually—with an unquenchable
sentimentality. As he wearied of one affair, and before another
was begun, his thoughts had turned nostalgically to the strong,
heather-scented winds, the rolling hills, the bird-haunted dales'
the cleanness, the greenness of Yorkshire, England; to the slight
confiding figure of Alison unchanged, unchanging in her innocent love for him. Reason told him she might have married,
might have become soured and stringy or blowzily acquiescent,
but he had thrust reason behind him. My English rose, he had
thought fondly, even while appraising the chic and provocative
little rumps of Parisian girls waggling along boulevards greenly
burgeoning in spring, or the languorous glances of South American beauties from balconies set against white, blazing walls.

My tender English rose. . . .

And how little, in reality, she had changed. Pink, prim, pretty as a tightly furled bud guarded by thorns—just as she had always been. She looked a little older, had grown a little fatter, and she wore a small air of authority that was amusing. But the thorns were still there. Father and mother, who had convinced her that they knew best, were dead and gone. She was mistress of her own home, her own money, her own life. But the thorns remained, as always.

For twenty years George had dreamed that he needed only to snap his fingers and Alison would come flying to London, New York, Rio, Timbuktu—wherever he happened to be. But clearly this was not so. The roots of his little English rose went deep, and he would have a hard job to transplant her.

George had, in fact, been considerably taken aback by his reception at The Laurels.

First Ada goggling and gasping in the doorway like a hooked fish, then bursting into tears and rushing into the kitchen leaving him stamping snow from his shoes on the door mat. Then that queer little dark creature creeping up on him from the living room, staring like a mouse at a crouching cat and finally disappearing into the shadows of the upstairs regions without having uttered a sound.

Then Alison coming in from her carol singing. . . .

Leaning over the side of the bed George produced from his grip a bottle of white pills, two of which he dropped into a glass of water. He lay there watching them fizzing. Two now and two more in a couple of hours and he'd feel more like himself. . . .

After that first kiss under the mistletoe, the first incoherent tossing to and fro of questions, answers and explanations, Alison had pulled herself together in a remarkable manner. Ringing bells, offering glasses of Daddy's famous port, extending hospitality and accepting its refusal with equanimity. Keeping him at arms' length with astonishing dexterity. Accepting his presence with tolerance and dismissing him well before midnight with a dignified ease. . . . Yes, you had to hand it to her!

"You did not remember my birthday this year, George."

He had stammered like a schoolboy that he had planned to arrive here on her birthday, but had finally been unable to make it. "Just a little matter of business," he had explained; and had been disconcerted by her tinkle of laughter.

"A very attractive little bit, too, I imagine, to detain you for two whole months! Will you take another glass of port?"

Disconcerting. Rather shocking when you came to think of it.

Brought up as she had been, she should have known nothing about such things. Or if she had known, she should have concealed her knowledge, accepting his "bit of business" with feminine tact.

George was very conventional in his views about women, and easily shocked.

He lay still waiting for the pills to work, dozing a little from time to time.

He began to feel more comfortable. Life once more seemed tolerable, even exciting and rewarding in certain aspects.

He thought about money of which, at the moment, he possessed a great deal and had reasonable hopes of turning into a great deal more. He thought about the yacht he had had his eye on for some time and wondered if the point had now been reached when its present owner turned mulish and would go no lower. He thought about women and decided that he had done with all that. In the future women would mean nothing more to him than Alison. He would buy the yacht and sail away with Alison and himself aboard, together at last. They would sail into the sunset; into the sunset of their lives: he and his little English rose, with nobody to say them yea or nay. And their sun would go down in glory. . . .

He became emotional—even rather maudlin—about this, and wished he had bought her a Christmas present more worthy of her long years of devotion. Why had he picked on earrings, and flashy ones at that? The wrong sort, anyway, because he had forgotten her ears were not pierced. . . .

Suddenly he felt cheap, unworthy. He rolled off the bed and switched on the light. The lamp shade was dusty, the bulb

encrusted with fly droppings. He caught sight of himself standing under the light scratching and yawning. He looked awful.
Paunchy, yellow, soiled. Not unlike the light bulb, in fact.

He went into the bathroom and found to his surprise that,
though the tub was stained, leprous with rust, the water was
boiling hot and the towels clean and outsize. He shaved very
carefully and took a quick bath, towelling vigorously until his
skin glowed and smarted with an illusion of health and youth.
He put on clean undergarments and a dark suit that made him
look slimmer. He chose a sober tie and brushed brilliantine
into hair and beard. He trimmed his fingernails and tipped eau
de cologne over a handkerchief. He took two more of the pills,
sitting bolt upright on the edge of the bed until their beneficial
result became apparent.

He glanced at his watch.

Now, he thought, and began to struggle into his overcoat.

By the time he reached The Laurels he was feeling fine, fine.
He presented Ada with a box of American candies and, as an
afterthought, a resounding smack on the bottom which she
received with a grin that matched his own. Good old Ada. She
had always been his friend.

Jerking her head toward the living room Ada hissed: "She's in
there with yon Plum woman and young Ronnie. I'll soon get rid
of *them* for you." She threw open the door and gave him a push
in the back. Following his rather precipitant entry she folded
her hands at her waist and confronted Miss Plum with a stony
glare. "There's a good fire in t'morning room," she announced
implacably.

The little dark creature immediately scuttled from the room,
throwing George a wide-eyed glance of pure terror as she passed.

Or was it terror? He turned his head; and she had paused on
the threshold, was staring at him over her narrow shoulder, her
eyes strangely glowing in the half-light of the doorway.

"Nay, now," he protested genially. "I'm not going to eat you!"

She gave a little gasp and vanished.

The boy departed more slowly, eying him with a deliber-
ate disdain. What's biting *him*? George wondered. He knew an
almost irresistible urge to assist the young rascal's strut with the
toe of his shoe, but remembered in time that this was England;
this was the decorous, civilized home of his little English rose. . . .

There she stood on the hearthrug, smiling shyly, blushing
most becomingly. Forty if she was a day, and looking not a day
more than twenty-five, so help him.

"Who's the boy friend?" he inquired, advancing on her with
a swagger that denied his sober raiment.

Fully expecting to engulf her in an embrace, George was
astonished to find himself sitting in an armchair on one side
of the blazing fire while Alison perched smiling on the other,
urging him to smoke, offering him the choice of sherry or gin
and tonic.

He chose sherry. She brought it to him with a pretty gesture
and accepted a light for her cigarette.

"The boy friend, as you call him, is Ronnie Sturgess, our
vicar's son. He is not yet fifteen in spite of his size. I think he has
a crush on Miss Plum."

"And who's Miss Plum when she's at home?"

Alison shook her head at him.

"You went to church with Miss Plum this morning, George,
surely you cannot have forgotten. And you have just given your
assurance that you have no intention of eating her. Probably at
this moment she is weeping on Ronnie's shoulder because you
found her unworthy of being eaten. She is extremely sensitive."

"Yes, but who is she? I mean to say, why is she here?"

Alison delicately removed ash from her cigarette.

"It is difficult to answer the first question. Let us say that
Miss Plum is a . . . a fugitive from life. I found her in the Recreation Ground at Huffley, committing suicide; I brought her here
because, at the time, there seemed nothing else to be done."

George set down his wine glass with a thump.

"*Committing suicide? . . .* How?"

"In the duck pond," Alison replied. "Let me give you some
more sherry."

George snorted his derision. "You couldn't drown a kitten in yon duck pond!"

"Oh, yes, you could. Unless it was an exceptionally robust and unwilling kitten. Miss Plum is neither."

In a few words Alison outlined the story of Miss Plum; the help she had been and the hindrance she had been and the delicate position in regard to her future in which they were now placed. George sipped impatiently at his sherry.

"I shouldn't have thought there was any problem, living in this welfare state of yours."

"Unfortunately, Miss Plum appears to have eluded the welfare state and all its benefits in an astonishing way."

"We'll soon do something about that!"

"Something must certainly be done," Alison agreed. "But not before Christmas, George. It wouldn't be human. And George . . ." She leaned forward gazing earnestly at him. "Her name is Victoria, and I want you please not to laugh or make a joke about it. People have made jokes about it all her life and it's given her a terrible inferiority complex. Actually, I believe that is what lies at the root of all her troubles. It may seem a molehill to you and me, but it is a mountain to Miss Plum: an unconquerable mountain. Please promise me that you won't laugh."

"Victoria. Victoria Plum . . . I don't see anything to laugh *at*," George said. "It's not the sort of joke that sounds funny to me. The sort of joke I laugh at is the one about the three travelling salesmen who were given adjoining rooms in a New York hotel. . . . But I expect that's not the sort of joke *you* laugh at . . ."

"Perhaps not," Alison agreed sedately.

"And I wouldn't want you to, Alison."

"No, George."

She gave him some more sherry and resumed her perch on the other side of the hearth, patting her neat hair with a tiny tinkle of bracelets and avoiding his eyes.

George gazed helplessly at his little English rose.

For the first time in his life he did not know what to say to a woman; how to act; what to expect.

Here they were, together again after twenty years; alone, adult and responsible to nobody but themselves and each other. They sat on opposite sides of the hearth, and all they could find to talk about was this Miss Plum.

Was he a man or a mouse? he wondered indignantly.

He rose to his feet and stretched. His limbs felt light and fluid, his head clear: that was very good sherry, not the sweet muck he had expected in a woman's household.

"Alison," he said.

He had meant to speak in deep, tender tones resonant with feeling, but his voice came out in a high squeak, very disconcerting. He tried again. *"Alison! . . ."*

Taking her hands he pulled her upward and forward. Her head drooped and he found only the lobe of an ear to kiss, but this he kissed with determination.

"Alison! . . ."

There was a thump on the door which burst open to reveal Ada standing in the aperture, cheeks scarlet from the heat of the oven and eyes glazed with triumph.

"If you want yer dinners," she announced harshly, "you'd best come and get it while it's hot."

CHAPTER EIGHT

1.

IT WASN'T so foul up at old Hartley's, after all, Ronnie decided.

Sprawled luxuriously amongst foam rubber cushions before a brightly blazing fire, his stomach comfortably distended with the appetizing supper Stanley had provided, Ronnie was convinced that this was the life. Make a lot of money and spend it on yourself. Be a bachelor gay, and to hell with all women (except, of course, when you were being especially gay.)

Gazing around the pleasant room he realized that Stanley did himself very proud indeed. The heavy velvet curtains, the softly shaded lights, the cushions of velvet and silk, the delicate china, the gleam of fluted silver—all this was surely not the result of merely being a bank manager in a provincial town. Stocks and shares—that's what it would be. Buying cheap and selling out—bingo!—just at the right moment. That's how it was done. There was a fellow at school whose father made thousands overnight. Of course, he sometimes lost thousands, too, but that was the fun of the game, Dysart said.

Dysart always seemed to be in the money, anyway. His people were going to Austria next summer and Dysart had promised that if Ronnie would do all his latin prep for him, he'd wangle an invitation for him to join the party. It might be possible to get some tips from Dysart's old man. An earnest, respectful attitude. "I see, sir. Yes, sir. No, sir, of course not. I say, sir, how absolutely wizard!" All that old stuff. Ronnie had found that it usually paid off pretty well.

It had gone down well with Cooper's old man in Italy, last Easter. The Coopers were in oil and, at that time, Ronnie had rather fancied himself in oil.

The Italy adventure had been all right, but it had been spoiled for Ronnie because the Coopers had imagined that he would yearn to attend the Protestant church twice each Sunday, on account of Pop being a parson.

Of course, Pop was nuts on this idea of Ronnie being a parson too. Me, a parson—give me strength! thought Ronnie. Don't make me laugh!

He did laugh a little, and Stanley broke off his conversation with Hubert to inquire indulgently: "Are we to be let in on the joke?"

"No," said Ronnie. And as an afterthought added: "I don't think either of you is old enough."

In the ensuing merriment the conversation became more general. Ronnie found it rather pleasant to be included in male, adult talk that touched lightly on politics, art, travel, books and education. He spoke with modest authority on Rome and Florence, secure in the knowledge that Stanley had never been out of England, and Hubert no farther than France—and that many years ago, when he had gone hiking through Normandy with other impecunious undergraduates. He was deferential on politics, humorous on education, admittedly ignorant on the subjects of art and literature. He made quite an impression. Even Stanley mellowed toward him.

What a dear boy he is, Hubert thought fondly. What a good boy. How I have misjudged him!—And the thought of how proud Edna would have been of their son made him blink mistily and miss the ash tray Stanley had placed at his disposal by at least three inches.

Almonds and raisins were produced; Chinese figs and an expensive brand of crystallized fruits. The two older men barely touched these delicacies, but Ronnie tucked in with a will.

At ease on his foam rubber cushions, jaws working slowly but rhythmically, Ronnie wondered what Victoria was doing now.

If it were true (though to him it seemed quite incredible) that the old boy with the tie and the face fungus had actually come back after all these years to marry Alison Penny, then it was more than probable that Victoria was now in bed, crying her eyes out.

He felt sorry for her in a remote kind of way; but not so sorry as he had been. She did cry so frequently and in such quantity! When they had been flushed out of the living room by that old gorgon of an Ada, she had cried all over his nice clean shirt, sniffing, moreover, in a quite revolting manner. When he had attempted to release himself, she had clung all the harder, wailing that he was the only one who really understood, and what she would do without him she really did not know. It had nearly scared the pants off Ronnie.

Silly old slut, he thought gallantly, wedging an outsize piece of crystallized pineapple into his mouth with some difficulty.

The old boys were droning away about parish affairs. They were drinking port. Resentfully he felt they might have offered him a glass, seeing it was Christmas. He wondered if he should smoke, but decided not to because that would stop him eating.

The Old Folks' Christmas Party. The church roof repairs. The shocking condition of the hassocks. Old Mrs. Somebody and old Mr. Somebody-else. . . . The voices droned on and on, weaving a web of comfortable boredom over and around him. He felt sleepy and stupid and rather sick.

The voices dropped to a lower, more confidential note. They were leaning together as if they didn't want him to hear; but of course he knew quite well they were talking about old Alison Penny and the fellow with the beard. He thought they both looked rather glum, and this faintly tickled him. What would have happened if George hadn't suddenly turned up and put a spoke in both their wheels? . . . Now they were talking about Victoria, and still looking glum. He heard old Hartley say: "I don't see what either of us can do: it's out of our hands now, I imagine. And anyway, she had promised to help me at the Old Folks' Party." And Pop said: "She asked me to teach her to skate. And she was anxious to help with the Mothers' Union tea. It's all rather difficult."

Silly old dodderers, Ronnie thought. He gave a jaw-cracking yawn and shut his eyes.

A clock chimed eleven.

Pop was saying once again that it was time they were off and old Hartley was protesting stoutly that the night was yet young (though not quite so stoutly, Ronnie fancied, as before.)

He didn't want to move out of this comfortable room. He didn't want to climb into Pop's old rattletrap and go skidding and honking back to the cold, dark, dreary vicarage behind its gaunt palisade of poplars thrusting warning fingers against the sky. There was no warmth at home, no comfort, no life. And there was a whole blooming six weeks of it before he could get back to the normality of school.

If only his mother hadn't died, he thought. If only there were a woman to come home to; a woman to coddle him and fuss over him and give him the things he liked to eat; to sit on the end of his bed listening admiringly to his accounts of cricket matches and cross-country runs, and to get all het up about the awful school meals. . . . A woman of some sort—almost of any sort— who would turn up for Speech Day in an awful hat and take him out to lunch. (Why did the nicest ones always wear awful hats? he wondered: but it was a fact that they did.)

He wondered if it would be a good idea for Pop to marry again.

Alison Penny?

No. Because of the fellow with the tie and the face fungus. Miss Plum? . . . *Then, I'd have to call her Mother*, thought Ronnie sourly. He didn't like the idea at all. Rather loathsome, actually, when you dwelt on it. Old Pop and Victoria. . . . And she'd cry all over the vicarage at the drop of a hat. No; better an empty house than a house with Victoria in it for keeps. It wasn't so bad in summer. And in a year or two he'd be out of it, anyway. Out in the world on his own, making thousands overnight on the Stock Exchange, or striking oil somewhere in the Middle East, or running a chain of stores. Being a bachelor gay with lots of beautiful dolls. That was the life! The sooner the better!

"Well," Pop was saying, "now we really must be off."

This time Stanley made no protest. In no time at all Pop was outside working away at the starting handle, while Ronnie was levering up positively his last piece of crystallized pineapple.

2.

At The Laurels every room was brightly illuminated. This was the custom of the house on Christmas Day, dating from the times when Mummy and Daddy had entertained on a lavish scale which had made such an extravagance necessary. Alison had taken a nostalgic pleasure in keeping up the custom.

Ada took a very poor view of such wicked waste of electricity. "It were different in the old day, when we'd the gas," she would complain. "You can turn t'gas down low and leave it. But all this electric goin' to waste, an' nobbut you an' me in t'place— it don't mek sense!" She and Alison had a little tussle about it every year, but Alison always won.

"This year you cannot bring up that old argument," Alison had pointed out triumphantly, "for we have Miss Plum with us. And we have George."

Ada said relentlessly: "George is stoppin' at The Goat, and he's got no call to go upstairs without he wants to go to t'lavatory. And me and Miss Plum sleeps at the back, anyroad."

Nonetheless, all the rooms in the house were ablaze with light as usual, giving pleasure and comfort to such few as were obliged to be abroad on this night, and there was nothing Ada could do about it.

Another rule of the house, and one equally resented by Ada was that everyone should lend a hand on Christmas Day, setting tables, clearing away and helping to wash up. This inevitably caused a major confusion which was the source of merriment to guests and of an almost homicidal impulse to Ada, who liked her kitchen to herself and bitterly resented intrusion.

Also, as if these idiocies were not enough, she was then required to spend the rest of the evening in the living room, joining in whatever silly games they chose to play or, as of later years, watching a lot of nonsense on TV, when she would have given her best hat to snooze beside the kitchen fire in her own comfortable rocking chair.

Christmas comes but once a year, thought Ada with deep satisfaction. And this year, anyroad, she thought, her an' George'll want to be on their own. I shall have to put up with yon Plum; but there's plenty of Christmas magazines—we shan't even need to speak.

But even in this she was frustrated, for Alison declared that nobody must miss the television program which promised to be better than ever this year. Ada muttered that there were jobs she wanted to do, and Alison said, "Nonsense!" Miss Plum pleaded a headache and was given two aspirins and a pep talk. George mentioned that television always sent him to sleep and Alison gave a brisk promise to wake him up. There's no doing owt with her, Ada thought gloomily. Her an' George should ought to be on their own, talkin' things over an' gettin' things straight. Twenty years!—and here we are all sittin' together chewing chocolates an' watching a lot of brazen besoms kicking their legs up. It ain't natural. . . .

3.

But everything comes to an end, and eventually this evening came to an end also. The television was switched off. Miss Plum skedaddled upstairs with a hot-water bottle and two more aspirins. Ada banged the kitchen door shut. And Alison was left alone with George, with everything still to be said and neither of them knowing how to say it.

Alison patted a polite yawn and exclaimed: "Good gracious— *look* at the time!"

"They've given me a key," George said flatly.

"All the same," said Alison. She began to plump up the cushions and push the furniture about.

"Alison."

"Yes, George?"

"When are we going to be alone? When are we going to talk? I mean really *talk*. About us. About our future. . . ."

"Surely there's plenty of time for that?"

"We've wasted twenty years out of our lives already. There's not all that much time left."

"And whose fault is that?" Alison's tone had an astringent quality that George resented.

"Yours," he said bluntly.

"Mine!" She raised a brightly flushed face.

"It was you turned me down, Alison. You hadn't got the guts to cut loose and take a chance on happiness. You never really believed in me. You never really loved me."

She stood up straight, clasping her hands beneath her chin and gazing at him with troubled eyes.

"I did love you, George. I loved you very much. But I was so young, so sheltered, so ignorant of life. . . . You asked too much of me."

"You loved your snug little rut better than me," he said inexorably.

She blinked a little, clutching her hands closer beneath her chin.

"Did I? . . . Yes, I think that may be true. But it would not have been true if you had stayed in England. Sooner or later I think I should have come to you and lived whatever sort of life you chose to make for us . . . Mummy and Daddy would have given in eventually—of that I am certain. We should all have been happy together if you hadn't wanted to go all those thousands of miles away. If only you'd been content to go on working on the farm."

"There was no future in working on the farm. What had I to offer you? At best a tenant farmer's cottage without gas or electricity, and all the water to be carried from the pump!"

"I was young and strong, George. It wouldn't have hurt me."

"Everybody looking down on you, sniggering in their sleeves because you'd married a farmhand."

"They would soon have tired of that."

"Cut off from your folks. . . ."

"Never!" cried Alison with conviction. "Mummy and Daddy wanted me to be happy. But they had to be sure. Once they were convinced that marriage with you was in my best interests, they would have come around and we could have been happy all together. Happy and safe."

George looked at her strangely.

"Love isn't safe," he said heavily. "Love is a blinding flash in the dark. It is a leap over a cliff. It is a breathless dive to the bottom of the ocean. . . ."

His words beat down upon her like stones. She felt the impact of weight, of pain. Her hands thrust outward as if to ward off the falling stones.

She said uncertainly: "Doesn't it all depend on what you mean by love?"

He came closer; gripped her shoulders; tipped her chin so that her eyes were forced to meet his.

"What did *you* mean by love, Alison, twenty years ago?"

He felt her withdrawal; felt the small bones of her shoulders melting beneath his hands; sensed the faltering of her spirit. She gave a sigh.

"I don't think I know, George . . . Prince Charming, perhaps. Nymphs and shepherds. Walking hand-in-hand through clover meadows. . . . Lots of white lace, and rose petals showering, and a cold new ring slipping around on my finger. . . ."

"You never thought further than that?"

"I wasn't brought up to think further than that. Well . . . maybe I sometimes saw myself playing dolls' house in a frilly apron, flicking a feather duster around and filling vases with sweet peas. I believe I sometimes went so far as pushing a very clean little baby in a white pram along the lane to visit Mummy and Daddy. I wore a pink frock and the hedges were full of wild roses. . . ."

"It never occurred to you to think about the baby *before* it was in its pram—did it?"

Alison gave him her candid gaze.

"You know, George, I don't honestly believe it ever did. It sounds incredible, doesn't it? After all, it's only twenty years ago. I'm making myself sound like something out of a novel by Mrs. Henry Wood, and you must find it very hard to understand."

He took his hands from her shoulders, lit a cigarette and began to pace up and down the room.

"My letters must have shocked you," he said.

"Oh, they did," she replied honestly. (They had also delighted her with a secret, perilous delight, but she did not think it necessary to tell him that.)

"They must have shocked your parents even more," he grinned.

"Daddy and Mummy never asked to see them. I would not have allowed them to even if they had. You see, George, when you went away and left me I began to grow up."

"Not before time." He halted before her, drawing smoke deep into his lungs and expelling it in a thin stream. He said abruptly: "Why did you never marry, Alison?"

She clasped her hands behind her back in a schoolgirlish fashion he found oddly touching.

"Nobody ever asked me. Had they done so, I should have refused."

"Why?"

"At first because I still loved you. I still hoped you would come back and everything would come right. . . . That was how the fairy tales always ended, you see."

"And afterward?" he persisted. "Afterward you stopped loving me?"

"Yes," she said gently. "Yes, I think so, George. In a sort of way, I mean . . . I had such a happy home, and my friends, and my church work, and interests in the village. . . . My life seemed full. And somehow time slipped by so quickly . . . I am not the adventurous type, George. I like to feel comfortable and safe. And cherished. . . ."

The clock chimed again but neither heeded.

George threw away his cigarette. He stood before her lumpishly, arms hanging at his sides and head thrust forward.

"I will cherish you," he said slowly. "I will give you comfort and safety, and other things as well. I've got plenty of money. I'm going to buy a yacht. We can go pretty well anywhere you fancy. All the places you've read about and never hoped to see. You can have all the clothes you want, all the fun you've missed. Something different happening every day. . . . We're not young any more, but we're not old, either. We'll make up to each other for all the wasted time." He paused, then continued more urgently: "Don't tell me you've never dreamed about the forests of Brazil, or the small, rare flowers of the Dolomites, or the Tyrol in spring . . . Venice in moonlight. Paris. Madrid. . . . You can see all the churches and picture galleries you ever heard of. We'll go to Switzerland for the winter sports and sail down the Dalmatian coast and laze about on little islands soaking in the sun. We'll fly to New York, San Francisco, California—"

He dug his hands into his pockets, unconsciously rattling the loose money, going up and down on his toes as he stood before her, boasting to hide his humility.

In spite of herself excitement rose in Alison, flushing her cheeks and making her heart beat more quickly.

Once she had been an inveterate collector of travel brochures; poring over them with pleasure, planning itineraries, doing little sums in margins—even going so far as to obtain a passport containing a horrifying picture of herself looking as if she had just committed a murder and thoroughly enjoyed it. Nothing had ever come of it. She went for two weeks to Bournemouth each July and that, apart from an occasional week end with a distant cousin in Leeds, comprised the sum total of her travels.

"We'll be married right away," he was saying. His voice was harsh and loud, as if he felt the need to shout. "I'll go up to London tomorrow and fix things up: it's easy if you've got enough cash. We'll get married as soon as possible—say a week's time. What about the Thursday? Thursday suit you?"

Alison's mind functioned swiftly, instinctively.

"Not Thursday," she said. "Thursday is the Women's Institute."

He stood quite still, staring at her.

He thought he could not have heard aright—and then he knew that he had.

"Thursday," he repeated slowly, "is the Women's Institute . . ."

He gave a sudden bark of laughter. He turned on his heel and went out of the room, grabbed his hat and coat and slammed the front door behind him.

The ice-cold night gripped him by the throat, stifling laughter; sent him slithering down the slope to the gate. Hanging on to the gate he gazed up at the façade of the house, every room illuminated in honour of the Festive Season.

Even as he gazed the lights began to go out; one room after another, until only one room was left lit up.

Thursday is the Women's Institute—"My god!" he said incredulously.

He began to stump over the frozen snow toward the pub.

4.

The lights in the house went out one after another, until only one light was left burning.

Alison sat beneath it at her dressing table, staring into the mirror.

She thought her face looked strange, small and queerly pinched. Red patches burned on each cheek as if they had been painted on; like a Dutch doll she had once owned but never greatly cared for. She unplaited her hair and began to brush it. One hundred strokes. Twenty-five each side, twenty-five at the back and twenty-five at the front. Slowly and rhythmically, very thoroughly. There were quite a lot of grey hairs, especially at the sides.

But for once she forgot to count, and after a while the brush dropped from her fingers.

She was tired, so tired; and she was frightened; and she was ashamed of her gaucherie. She heard her voice again: prim, stupidly consequential. *Thursday is the Women's Institute. . . .*

She buried her face in tense hands; covered up the pinched mouth, the frightened eyes, the Dutch-doll scarlet, the stupid, staring, Dutch-doll wooden idiocy that was her face.

She thought: in those five words I summed up my whole attitude to life. . . .

She went into the bathroom and washed her burning cheeks; scrubbed violently at her teeth, as if she would scrub away the feel of her words, even the memory of them. She climbed into bed and switched off the light, staring into darkness because her eyes refused to remain shut.

Of course she wanted to see the Dolomites—magic name that she had dreamed about. Venice in moonlight. The sky line of New York harbour, staggering, incredible. . . .

Excitement. Change. Cupboards full of pretty clothes. A yacht of her own. A husband of her own.

All the fun she had missed. . . .

But I have had plenty of fun, she thought. Picnics and coach trips: parties at friends' houses; camping with the Cubs; my two weeks at Bournemouth; the choir outings. All these things have been fun.

She stared into the darkness wide-eyed, resentful because these dear, familiar occasions had suddenly been made to seem shabby and inadequate.

Do I truly wish for a yacht? she thought. I am always seasick on a boat. Do I really want cupboards full of fashionable clothes? I have never been able to wear high heels. I suppose a mink coat would be nice; but I can't wear a mink coat all the time, and my squirrel is still quite passable. . . . How do I know that George really has all this money? I've only got his word for it. How much can I believe? I have not seen him for twenty years and I don't know him: I don't know anything about him. . . .

She remembered George's letters; those shocking, exciting, revealing letters that lay in the cedarwood box tied up in white ribbon. He had never pretended to be faithful—and how could one blame him for that? He had often admitted to being broke. He had tramped the roads of Europe, hungry, even dirty, waiting for his luck to change, taking any job that came his way, however menial.

It might be like that again, she thought. And she had a horrific vision of herself trailing along a blistering highway a few paces behind George; scuffing up dust with broken shoes through which poked unwashed toes. . . .

What was it George had said about love? *A leap over a cliff. A breathless dive to the bottom of the ocean.* . . .

No, that was not true, she thought, shrinking. Not love as she knew it, as she had wanted it. Love should be gentleness and tolerance and a sweet cherishing. That was the only kind of love she could ever have given—or accepted.

She tossed over on her other side, buried her face in the pillow and brought her knees up high.

What was George doing now?

Was he already throwing his belongings into suitcases ready for tomorrow's departure? Was he laughing? Was his laughter wry and disillusioned or ringing with thankfulness for a timely escape?

Had she seen the last of George?

She thought suddenly: I wonder what *did* happen to the three travelling salesmen in the New York hotel? . . .

I must sleep, she thought. No good purpose is served by worrying. She straightened her limbs, turned the pillow over and lay quietly, trying to relax tense muscles.

I must slee-eep, she thought resolutely. Slee-eep. Slee-ee-eep. I must slee-eep. . . . The formula had always worked on the rare occasions when she had been wakeful.

I must slee-eep, she thought.

And she was picking flowers on a canal in Venice: they came up through the green water with a delicious *plop* and she threw them at George, who was standing in New York harbour holding a torch in one hand and a mink coat in the other. "That's right," George shouted, "have all the fun you've missed!" And they climbed onto the tilting deck of a yacht whose white sails spread sideways like a bird's wings, and they went dipping and soaring over the Austrian Tyrol at a great rate. Ada was on board and so were Hubert and Stanley, and three travelling salesmen who kept trying to tell her what happened to them in a New York hotel, but she put her hands over her ears, refusing to listen. . . .

But suddenly she was back in her bed at The Laurels, wide-awake and tense in every nerve and muscle.

Somebody was scratching at the door. Somebody wanted to come in, would have to be admitted.

"What is it?" she whispered.

"It's only me," said the voice of Miss Plum.

And then the door creaked, a colder air came in and the darkness thickened by the bed as Miss Plum flung herself upon her knees and groped for Alison's hand with both her own.

"Alison . . . Oh, Alison, dear!"

"Go back to bed," Alison ordered in a feeble attempt at her Cubs voice. "Miss Plum—go back to bed."

"Victoria," Miss Plum pleaded.

"Victoria—go back to bed. It is very late. It is almost morning, Victoria, and I am worn out. I cannot attend to you now."

She felt Victoria's lips upon her hand; barely resisted the impulse to snatch it sharply away.

"I only wanted to tell you, Alison, how happy for you I feel; how wonderful it seems to me that he should come back after all these years to make your life complete. . . . It is no more than you deserve. It is far, far less than you deserve. It's like a fairy-tale come true! I only wanted to tell you, Alison, that I am going away. I will be a burden on you no longer. You can live out your fairy tale to the full without having to worry about the Ugly Sister sitting in the corner, the old witch watching the spinning wheel . . . I only wanted to say good-by. Now; alone together in the darkness. To say thank you and good-by. Tomorrow, when you get up, Alison, I shall be gone."

"You will be nothing of the kind," Alison said peevishly, groping for the light switch and her bed jacket. Blue ducks with yellow beaks, she thought, as she thrust her arms into Ada's beautiful knitting. Ducks. Duck ponds. . . . Why am I thinking about duck ponds?

She fought sleep fiercely as recently she had wooed it. She said more kindly: "As soon as Christmas is over we will go to the Labour Exchange in Huffley. They will find you a job, fix you up with an insurance card and everything, and you will be properly provided for. You will be your own mistress and will be able to make a life for yourself that is useful and happy."

"Happy!" said Victoria, her voice muffled by the eiderdown. "How can I be happy away from you? How can I be happy alone?"

"We are all alone, Victoria. However we may be surrounded by friends, money, possessions, each one of us is alone from the moment we are born until the day we die. Life has taught me that if nothing else."

"I am not strong like you. I cannot be alone and live."

"You can and must, Victoria. You have never yet given your-self the chance to prove it. Always you have taken the easy way."

"Easy! You think my life has been easy!"

Alison blinked determinedly. She must not fall asleep now. She *must* not. She said carefully: "A stile is easy to climb, but the field beyond may be rough and full of thistles. If you have to climb a high wall you may find it leads to a well-tended pasture. . . . Once you learn to face difficulties, tackle problems alone, you will probably find life running smoother than you ever expected." Oh, dear, what a sermon! she thought. And I don't believe she's taken a word of it in. She'll go back to bed and cry and cry. And perhaps, before it is light, she really will go away. Perhaps she really means it.

She had a sudden, vivid and horrifying vision of Victoria stealing downstairs, unbolting and unchaining the front door and going out into the darkness without hope. Blackness of night; blackness of water, deep and still beneath its frozen covering. The crunch of feet on ice, the sharp explosion of ice breaking; the startled note of a bird twittering back into stillness; ripples on the blackness widening into eternity. . . .

Involuntarily she seized Victoria by the shoulders, and was shocked to find how cold she felt.

"You stupid child!" she exclaimed, "why are you not wearing your dressing gown? You are absolutely frozen. Do you want to be ill again? Here—come in with me. My bottle is still hot. Hold it against your tummy and try to relax."

She bent over Victoria, tucking the bedclothes firmly around her. The girl's body felt marble-cold against her own. In all her life Alison had never shared a bed with anyone and she had to steel herself not to shrink away to the edge of the mattress. Setting her teeth, she put her arms around Victoria, holding her closely against her own warmth. She thought: I am doing a good deed, but it is no credit to me because I am not doing it with love. But at least she will be unable to move without my knowing it. . . .

CHAPTER NINE

1.

HUBERT carved the ham thinly; Ronnie fitted the slices between buttered bread, lavishly applying mustard. Hubert hated mustard but he made no protest, knowing how Ronnie loved it. Edna had loved mustard, too. What did a little thing like that matter! Christmas was over for another year and he was experiencing the customary relief mixed with regret: regret that he had not done better; relief that he had not done worse. But on the whole, Hubert was happy. Ronnie was really being very good. They were getting on splendidly together.

On Boxing Day a thaw had set in, making the proposed expedition to the Tarn quite impossible. There would be no skating, anyway, and the track over the moor would be soggy and unattractive. It was definitely not weather for walking.

The village street was awash with a greyish sludge on which pedestrians skidded precariously as they picked their way from shop to shop, shivering and grumbling at the change in the weather, feeling the usual after-Christmas flatness, the warning touch of liver, the sharp twinge of gout, the dismal realization that they had spent far too much and now faced the inevitable lean weeks.

The poplars in the vicarage garden dripped monotonously, starkly rooted in their own tears. Gutters gurgled and over-flowed. Fires refused to draw. The bath water was never hot enough and the plumber, when approached, stated testily that he was working overtime already and that he only had the one pair of hands.

A tow-headed child arrived at the back door with the depress-ing news that Mrs. Hart was "queer" and would be unable to resume her duties at the vicarage for an unspecified period. After a nightmare battle with towering arrears of washing up, unmade beds and accumulated dust, Hubert had prevailed upon the sexton's wife to "oblige." The sexton's wife didn't know where anything was kept or how anything worked and her knowledge of the culinary art appeared to extend no further than a nice kipper or a nice chop. It would not have mattered so much if they had been nice, but they never were. Hubert and Ronnie ate mostly out of cans.

Once Hubert had the bright idea of buying fried fish and chips, unfortunately overlooking the fact that the fish-and-chip shop was run by the sister of the sexton's wife who often helped behind the counter in the rush hours. She was helping when Hubert arrived with his little bag, and she took a very poor view of the transaction. "What do you want with fish-an'-chips?" she demanded belligerently. "Didn't I leave you a nice chop apiece?"

It was a sad, sodden, mournful period following the brightness and gaiety of Christmas, but it ended as abruptly as it had started.

Overnight the frost returned, fiercer than before, more beautiful and awe-inspiring, if that were possible, than before. The land lay in an iron grasp and the Tarn was reported to be a solid sheet of ice such as had not been seen for many a year.

Hubert bought a can of oil and he and Ronnie cleaned up their skates.

2.

Ronnie popped a buttered crust into his mouth and began to wrap up the sandwiches in wax paper.

"It must be four years since we got any skating," he gloated. "Buck up, Pop. Something to do at last!"

Hubert blinked and swallowed. He said apologetically: "I expect you find the holidays a bit dull . . . I wish there were more young people in the neighbourhood. I'm afraid Greeth is becoming increasingly an old folks' place."

"Absolutely ghastly," Ronnie agreed. He rubbed his greasy hands on a towel and added with a show of nonchalance: "I'm expecting an invitation to Austria for the summer."

Hubert looked up, startled.

"From whom?"

"Dysart's folks. Dysart said he'd wangle it if I'd do his latin prep this term."

After a pause in which Hubert mustered all his meagre store of courage he said quietly: "You can't do that, Ronnie."

"Can't I! I can do it on my head! Dysart's the most awful fool, but I'm a bright boy at my lessons. Very bright. You'd be surprised!"

"You are not to do it, Ronnie. I forbid it." Hubert's voice cracked weakly on the word. "I will not allow my son to lie and cheat."

Ronnie swung around, dropping the towel upon the floor.

"Who are you calling a liar and a cheat?"

"You," Hubert said heavily, "if you do Dysart's prep. You, my son. The only creature I love in all the world. All I have left . . ."

They stood staring at each other across the kitchen table; across the package of ham sandwiches, the thermos of coffee, the two pairs of bright, gleaming skates.

Ronnie saw a thin, middle-aged parson with retreating hair, whose Adam's apple bobbed convulsively above his dog collar, whose eyes pleaded more than they condemned. Hubert saw a boy with Edna's mouth. The boys' eyes were hard as pebbles, the smooth brow furrowed in astonished anger. But the mouth was Edna's mouth; sweet and tender, a little tremulous, perhaps a little frightened?

They stood staring at each other; each seeking for words, neither finding them.

Hubert began fumbling with the haversack, the sandwiches, the thermos flask.

Ronnie picked up the towel and hung it behind the kitchen door.

"All right," he said cockily, "if *that's* what you think about me!"

Almost inaudibly Hubert replied: "I don't think that about you. Not really. Because I know you won't do it."

"But I want like hell to go to Austria."

"I cannot afford to send you to Austria."

"You don't have to worry about that. Dysart's old man stinks of money."

"We cannot accept charity, Ronnie."

"It won't *be* charity if I do Dysart's latin prep. I shall have paid my way." He opened a package of Player's and began to smoke defiantly. "Didn't you ever help a chap with his prep when you were at school?"

Hubert gazed at him perplexedly.

"I expect I did. Yes, I'm sure I did—often. But not for gain, Ronnie. . . . That's it, you see. What you propose to do is a—a sort of blackmail."

"So I'm a blackmailer now, as well as a liar and a cheat. I sound like a good candidate for Holy Orders, I must say!"

"And are you proposing to be a candidate for Holy Orders?"

"What, me . . . ?" Ronnie blew out a stream of smoke, straddling the hearthrug and digging his hands deep into his pockets. "D'you think I want to spend the whole of my life without a bean to spend; living in some damp old mausoleum of a vicarage? Holding old women's hands and eating buns with the Mothers' Union? Preaching to empty pews and poking my nose uninvited into other people's houses and falling flat on my face when some fat old Bishop deigns to come to tea? What do *you* think!"

Hubert began to pace up and down between the choked-up stove and the frost-flowered window. Presently he halted in front of his son. He laid his hands on Ronnie's shoulders.

"Look," he said, "we're getting this thing all mixed up. I don't think you are a liar, a cheat or a blackmailer. I don't believe there's anything wrong with you, Ronnie, beyond the fact that I've spoiled you dreadfully. Whatever your faults may be, mine is the blame . . . I do not deny that my dearest hope is for you to enter the Church. It was your mother's wish, also. We talked about it often. 'He might even become a Bishop,' she used to say, and her eyes would shine with pride. . . . She was a wonderful woman, your mother. I wish you could remember her as I do."

Ronnie stared at him helplessly. His shoulders felt the weight of his father's hands. His spirit bowed beneath the weight of his words.

"Oh, Pop," he muttered; and, to his own fury, began to cry.

"No!" Hubert cried sharply. "I was wrong to say that. *That* was blackmail—the worst kind. . . . Forget it, Ronnie, please. No one has the right to direct your life. That is something you must do for yourself. Whatever career you choose, I shall be satisfied so long as you meet life with courage and integrity. Of course I want my son to be successful—what father doesn't? But success without integrity is no more than failure. Without courage it is a burden. I rate courage very highly, Ronnie. I have longed for it— prayed for it—all my life and never achieved it. For you I desire it even more earnestly. Do what you must with your life, but do it with courage. . . ." He leaned forward and kissed the boy's cheek, feeling the down thick and soft under his lips. "We must get you a razor," he said laughing awkwardly, "or you'll be as bad as Miss Penny's mysterious friend."

Ronnie grabbed his skates from the table. He said shakily: "Let's get out of here, Pop, while we've got some strength left."

They went out into the bright, hard sunlight and began the long walk up to the Tarn.

3.

Almost the first skaters they saw were Alison and Ada, who were circling the ice slowly but competently, with hands clasped, and wearing the ecstatic expressions of those who experience joys they have almost forgotten; accomplishments they had feared lost.

"Aren't we being clever!" cried Alison. "We haven't done this for years. Look—no hands!" She twirled out of Ada's grasp, waved gaily and sat down hard with a small shriek.

Hubert made a gallant rush toward her. Ronnie guffawed. Ada sailed sublimely on alone like a ship in full sail, eyes glazed in a sort of rapture, wind-bitten cheeks red as apples.

"Isn't Ada *marvellous!*" Alison exclaimed, gasping and tottering in Hubert's arms. "It was she who taught me to skate— oh, years and years ago—but I've never reached her standard. Oh, isn't it fun! We shall all be as stiff as boards tomorrow, but isn't it *fun!* I must just sit down for a breather."

While she had her breather Hubert and Ronnie fastened on their skates and made a few preliminary lunges and circles, cannoning into each other with great good humour to the accompaniment of Alison's laughter and cries of encouragement.

Secure in his youthful litheness, Ronnie finally shot off on his own. Hubert hauled Alison to her feet and together they began a more cautious circumambulation.

The air was like wine. It went first to Hubert's head, then to his heart and finally to his feet. He began to show off a little, swinging Alison around, laughing at her shrill squeaks of protest. He felt like a boy, and she seemed no more than a girl; a gay and pretty girl with whom he was having the time of his life. Oh, yes, this was fun!

And Alison remembered: *"Have all the fun you've missed."* Oh, what nonsense that was! What could possibly be more fun than this? It all depended on what you meant by fun. . . .

"And where is our Miss Plum on this glorious day?" asked Hubert, attempting a fancy step, nearly coming to grief and achieving the perpendicular just in time.

"Our Miss Plum," said Alison crisply, "is cooking the supper for tonight. At least, I hope she is. I'm afraid it won't be a very *good* supper; but I was quite determined that Ada should have this chance to enjoy herself. She really is astonishingly light on her feet. Just look at her now!"

Hubert peered in Ada's direction. What he said was: "Miss Plum wanted to learn to skate. She asked me to give her a lesson. Perhaps tomorrow?"

"Perhaps," Alison agreed coolly.

Hubert coughed nervously.

"And have you come to any conclusion yet about Miss Plum? I remember you consulted myself and Stanley about her some time ago."

"And a fat lot of good you were, the pair of you!" Alison flashed back in such downright tones that Hubert stumbled in his smooth progress, nearly bringing them both to the ground.

"Indeed," he faltered, "I fear we were of little help. But it was an unusual case. Most unusual. One hesitated. . . ."

"And was lost. I know. That is what I have been doing myself, ever since I found her—hesitating and losing . . . I meant to take her into Huffley and get her fixed up with the Labour Exchange. But with the Tarn just right for skating and Ada so eager for the chance, I put it off once again. It was foolish of me, no doubt."

"But kind," Hubert commented gently.

In a much milder voice Alison said: "Make no mistake, Hubert, I am not being kind about Miss Plum; only weak—and weakness is no virtue as you very well know. . . I want to forget

Miss Plum, Hubert, just for today. Shall we try going a little faster? We seem to have our sea legs by now."

They went a little faster. They went very fast indeed. They met Ada, who grinned and made a circle around them and shot off again, still grinning. The Tarn began to fill up with skaters, skilful and otherwise. A hot-chestnut vender appeared and did a roaring trade. The air was alive with laughter and shouting and the pleasant whine of steel upon ice.

Stanley was glimpsed standing upon the verge and beating gloved hands together. Stanley had never learned to skate and did not now propose to do so, but he surveyed with tolerance the general gaiety. People waved to him and he waved back rather condescendingly, as if to say. "Carry on with your childish pastime. Carry on, if this is what pleases you . . ."

By mid-day the whole of Greeth appeared to be circling and staggering upon the ice—to say nothing of the half of Huffley.

The plumber, who should have been exploring the faults in the vicarage hot-water system, was observed executing figures of eight with his fat little wife. Mrs. Hart, too "queer" to fulfill her duties as housekeeper, was ploughing a lonely furrow around the extreme edge of the Tarn, her face set in a fearful foreboding. Farm-hands who should have been farming and farmers who should have been seeing that they did so, swooped to and fro, apparently oblivious of each other. The sexton was flat on his back with his legs in the air. The grocer's mother-in-law, who was old enough to know better, went around and around with her mouth wide open, obviously not knowing how to stop. Dozens of people who were themselves too timid to skate lined the banks to jeer at or encourage those who were determined to seize this opportunity or die in the attempt.

Hubert and Ronnie, Alison, Ada and Stanley ate their lunch together in a gay little group.

Ada had baked Cornish pasties of a superb succulence. Stanley, with the air of a conjurer producing rabbits out of a hat, contributed a rich fruit cake and a dozen of the Cox's Orange Pippins that were his pride. He also bestowed upon Ronnie the little that was left of the box of crystallized pineapple, to that young gentleman's infinite content. Hubert's ham sandwiches were praised even while eyes watered from Ronnie's mustard.

They had fun. They all ate too much, clowned like irresponsible children, laughed at nothing, laughing because they had laughed at nothing. Alison cried: "Oh, I haven't had such fun for years!" And Ada came in heavily with: "The best things in life are free."

In the midst of the merriment Stanley fixed Alison with his bank manager's eye and asked: "And where is your guest today?"

"My guest?" Alison repeated, startled. "Oh, you mean Miss Plum? She is taking over Ada's duties for today. Ada can skate, you see, and Miss Plum cannot."

"I was not referring to Miss Plum," Stanley said carefully, "but to the gentleman who shared your pew on Christmas Day."

"Oh, *him*!" Alison was less concerned with grammar than with accuracy, and very little with either. "George is just somebody I knew—oh, twenty years ago. He happened to be staying at The Goat over Christmas."

"And still remains," Stanley amended, "as I observed on my way here."

"Really?" Alison said coolly.

Although she had not seen George since their disastrous parting, she was perfectly aware that he was still at The Goat, and needed no telling from Stanley. She did not propose to discuss George with Stanley or with anybody else for that matter, and she changed the subject adroitly. Stanley, still pulling his bank manager's face, as adroitly brought it back again.

"Twenty years is a long time."

"It is indeed. Will you take any more coffee, Stanley? Hubert? Anybody?"

Nobody wished for more coffee. The remains of the lunch were packed up, cigarettes lit, and limbs already stiffening eased up from folded rugs with many groans of pain and dismayed forecasts of tomorrow's sufferings.

"Twenty years," Stanley repeated heavily. "Yes, that is a very long time to be away from one's home and friends."

"I'm off," Ronnie cried. "Come on, Ada, I'll beat you to the end of the Tarn. Let's have sixpence on it!"

"We'll do nowt o' t'sort," Ada said flatly. "I've forgotten more about skating than what you'll ever learn, but that don't give me a young back, nor it don't do nothing for me fallen arches. I'm going around at me own pace, if it's all t'same to you."

"Doubtless we shall be seeing him later," Stanley continued, with the dogged persistence that had got him where he was today.

"I think it very unlikely," Alison said. "George is not fond of exercise, nor does he care for our cold weather. And it really has turned very cold now, hasn't it? I will take a few more turns and then I must be thinking of getting home. Don't stand about too long, Stanley. It's easy to take a chill."

She sent him a compact little smile and, raising her muff to her chin, glided off amongst the circling, swooping skaters and out of his sight. Hubert, with a valedictory word and wave, plunged after her, and Stanley was left alone to stamp his feet or to pick up his picnic basket and trudge the long way back to his home, as he chose.

He chose the latter, for it had certainly grown extremely cold, and there was no longer any sun to brighten the scene. The skaters glided eerily amongst floating shreds of grey mist that thickened beyond the far edge of the Tarn, so that frozen land became indistinguishable from frozen sky. By evening, no doubt, there would be bonfires leaping and lanterns hanging from trees; and there would be potatoes roasting and young men playing piano accordions and children dashing about with shrill cries and flickering torches. All very gay indeed, if you liked that sort of thing. To Stanley, the thought of his armchair with the foam-rubber cushions, the pheasant he, personally, had prepared for his dinner, the correctly angled lamps and the two new library books lying ready on the occasional table by the fire, presented far greater attractions, and he stepped out vigorously with a good deal of pleasurable anticipation.

4.

There seemed little point in going the long way around by the village, even though that would take him past The Goat, and possibly give him another glimpse of Alison's mysterious acquaintance. If Alison did not wish her friends to meet this long-lost George, that was her own affair and possibly she had good reasons for such secrecy. Far be it from Stanley to poke and pry. . . . No, he would go home the shorter way, which would take him past The Laurels. He might even call there for a few minutes and drink a cup of tea with Miss Plum, who would surely welcome such a break in her lonely day, and would give his feet a rest, too.

At the gate of The Laurels he paused, a little daunted by its unwelcoming façade starkly grey against the darkening sky.

No light shone in any window. No smoke beckoned from any chimney. No sound of living lifted the frozen hand of silence laid on stone and wood and darkly glittering pane, on flattened earth and rime-encrusted border and the bare bones of trees whose outstretched arms lifted warning against the intruder's approach.

Was Miss Plum, then, not at home? Was she asleep? Ill? It was to be hoped not, for Alison and Ada would soon be coming home, tired out after their unusual exercise and in need of hot baths, hot food and the welcoming flicker of fires. All these things it was Miss Plum's duty to provide. She had been left at home for that very purpose and should now be at the apogee of her activities. The *apogee* of her activities, Stanley repeated to himself with satisfaction. It was a word to which he was much addicted; and the fact that few of his hearers knew what it meant did nothing to lessen his delight in it. The word, however, did not apply at this moment, for there appeared to be no activity of any kind in The Laurels.

Cautiously Stanley climbed the steep, slippery path, hesitated before the door and finally, and rather gingerly, placed a tentative finger on the bell push.

Then, without ringing, he took his finger off again. For he heard the slam of a door and the thud of feet on the path leading to the back premises.

The bulky figure of a man came around the corner, hesitated on seeing Stanley, then made to pass on.

It was, without doubt, Alison's friend, George. There was no mistaking that beard, those outlandish garments.

"Good evening," Stanley said, a little stiffly.

"Hi." The word snapped out over a hunched shoulder. With it came the strong odour of whisky.

"Is anyone at home?" Stanley inquired to the retreating back.

"Why don't you ring and find out?"

"I was just about to do so."

"Then do so, and be damned to you."

The front gate slammed. Stanley was left standing alone on the doorstep, astonished and affronted beyond measure by the brief encounter.

Naturally, one would not expect refinement from the wearer of those terrible shoes, those revolting checks; but that was no excuse for bad language, for aggressiveness quite unprovoked.

A queer sort of friend for Alison to have kept for twenty years, thought Stanley indignantly, approaching the bell push once again, and this time pressing it good and hard.

Almost immediately the door opened a little way and in the narrow aperture the face of Miss Plum materialized ghost-like, wide-eyed in apprehension.

"Oh," she whispered, "it's only you. I thought . . ."

"Only me," Stanley assured her. "I just looked in as I was passing. But if it is inconvenient . . ."

"Oh, yes. I mean no, of course. Do come in. I'm afraid I'm in a dreadful muddle. Everything's gone wrong. It's been one of those days—you know?" She hiccuped, put her hand to her mouth and said, "Pardon!"

"They happen to all of us," Stanley said kindly. He stepped inside and switched on the hall light. "Perhaps," he added, chafing chilled hands, "a nice strong cup of tea, eh? Nothing like a nice cup of tea when things get on top of us."

Miss Plum stared at him bleakly.

"The kitchen stove went out," she whimpered. "I don't know what's the matter with it. I don't understand those sort of stoves. They're all right so long as they keep in, but once you let them go out. . . . So then I tried to use the gas stove, but it works on a meter and I hadn't got a shilling. I lit the primus, and it flared up suddenly and frightened me out of my wits. Flared right up to the ceiling, it did! Oh, it's been a simply *awful* day! I'm supposed to have a hot dinner ready for them—and I haven't even started yet!" She began to cry weakly, dabbing at her face with a limp rag of handkerchief and sniffing loudly. She swayed a little and hiccuped again, and Stanley glanced at her sharply.

With a sigh of resignation he removed his outer garments and hung them on a peg. He placed his galoshes beneath the hall chair. He wished most heartily that he had gone straight home, but it was too late now. Obviously, one could not just exclaim: "Too bad!" and walk out, leaving Miss Plum to her tears and her muddle. One was, one hoped, a gentleman. Also, though Stanley had not the least intention of cleaning out kitchen stoves and relighting them, he had no objection to lending Miss Plum a shilling for the gas meter and giving her some timely advice on how to provide a quick, hot and nourishing meal by the simple method of opening cans.

In principle Stanley disapproved of eating out of cans, regarding the habit as both extravagant and slothful. But in times of crisis one set aside such scruples and made the best of things. Alison obviously had the same idea, for the larder was stocked with canned food of every description.

Presenting the still-sniffing Miss Plum with a shilling, Stanley bade her brew a pot of strong tea immediately, while he planned his menu and made a selection of cans. "And while the kettle comes to the boil, it might be well to tidy the place up a little," he added, glancing pointedly at a nearly empty bottle of whisky that stood upon the dresser with two used tumblers. "Since the party seems to be over. . . ."

Miss Plum looked, if possible, even more stricken.

"I can't bear the taste of it, really, only he kept on at me. He said he didn't like drinking alone."

"Who did?"

"Miss Penny's friend, who's staying at The Goat. He called to see her and when he found she'd gone skating he seemed so put out. He asked for a drink, so what could I do?"

"You could have borrowed a shilling from him and given him a cup of tea, which is the proper drink at this hour of the day," Stanley pointed out with some asperity.

"I wish I was dead," said Miss Plum. She gave another hiccup and sat down abruptly on a chair. She looked very peculiar indeed, and Stanley regarded her with alarm and distaste.

Here was a pretty kettle of fish! He could only hope the hot tea would revive her before Alison and Ada returned, or the situation would take a bit of explaining.

"There," he said, pouring out a large, strong cupful, so hot that her eyes watered as she drank, "that should pull you together. I advise you to go upstairs and have a good wash in cold water and lie down. I will hold the fort here meanwhile." He propelled her firmly along the passage. "Perhaps I had better assist you up the stairs?"

"I can manage," she said, clinging to the banisters like grim death.

"Are you sure? Then I will take a look at the living room fire."

"That went out, too," said Miss Plum.

CHAPTER X

1.

ONE of Stanley's favourite maxims had always been that it is useless to cry over spilled milk.

Accordingly, although his feelings toward Miss Plum, if they had ever approached warmth, were certainly warm no longer, he lost no time in tackling the living-room grate which was choked with ashes and charred pieces of wood, and soon succeeded in creating a brisk blaze which he banked up in his methodical fashion until a good steady fire was assured. He brushed the hearth, drew the curtains and switched on all the lights. Then he returned to the kitchen, washed his hands, drank another cup of tea and began to prepare the meal he had planned.

As this consisted mainly of emptying cans into saucepans, the work was soon finished and he stood looking around the cluttered place, rather undecided what he should do next.

The thought of the plump pheasant which he had prepared with such loving care and which Mrs. Platt should soon be placing in the oven, caused his mouth to water and took him halfway to the door. But then the thought of Miss Plum lying prone on her bed and very likely being sick brought him back again. Was it safe to leave her? Suppose she should fall down the stairs? Suppose she took advantage of his shilling to put her head in the gas oven!

Even if she remained in her room, as he devoutly hoped she would, she was in no state to make coherent explanations to Alison on her return, which must surely be soon.

And it would not be unpleasant, he felt, to witness the surprise and gratitude of the two women when they discovered that it was his efforts and his alone that had assured them of an appetizing meal and a good hot fire.

Impulsively he decided not to mention the shilling at all.

It was too bad about the lack of hot water; but quite probably there was an immersion heater in the bathroom which could be switched on in time for baths before bed. He was half inclined to go up and see for himself, but decided that the risk of running into Miss Plum in some embarrassing situation made this inadvisable.

He picked up the whisky bottle and put it in a cupboard filled with pots of home-made jams, bottled fruits and jars of chutney.

It looked wrong there. It looked guilty. As if it had been popped in quickly on somebody's unexpected arrival. . . .

He put it back on the dresser along with the two tumblers. He did not regret having helped Miss Plum in her hour of need, but he had no intention of helping George. Alison was well aware of his own temperate habits and would be unlikely to suspect him of drinking at four o'clock in the afternoon. But Ada, he knew instinctively, had no liking for him and might succeed in causing unpleasantness if she found the bottle hidden away in the jam cupboard. It was astonishing, the influence such old servants wielded over their employers.

Really, it was a most difficult and undignified situation into which he was plunged by his own well-meant actions.

How could one stoop to saying: "It was not I who drank whisky with Miss Plum; it was your old friend, George."

Impossible. Quite unthinkable—Yet suppose Miss Plum concealed the fact of George's visit—and what more likely? And suppose George did not mention it, either? . . .

A light sweat beaded Stanley's brow and his stomach knew a hollowness quite unconnected with the pheasant which soon would be deliciously browning in his own safe, tidy kitchen where he longed with passion to be.

He hoped Miss Plum was recovering by now.

He went to the foot of the stairs and listened. All was quiet up there. All was dark. The darkness and the quietness held an uneasy quality that caused him to wonder if he ought to go up and tap on her door.

Suppose she had suffered one of her suicidal impulses and had flung herself from her bedroom window! Even now she might be writhing upon the frozen ground in some horrible pattern of pain. Or lying still with broken neck, her tears and incompetence ended forever. . . .

One half of Stanley's mind refused to accept the possibility. The other half felt quite faint with fright. Illness of any kind revolted him; the sight of blood made him sick. He had a horror of street accidents: the sound of an ambulance bell, the glimpse of a crowd milling about something lying on the ground, always caused him to walk rapidly in the opposite direction.

Yet now it seemed there was no way out of it: he had to satisfy himself that Miss Plum was not lying dead amongst the frozen cabbage stalks in the kitchen garden, above which he judged her bedroom to be.

He began to pull on his cardigan, his overcoat, his hat and muffler, even his thick gloves—for there was no point in giving himself a chill, whatever the urgency. He was, in fact, reaching for his galoshes when he heard the blessed sound of voices approaching up the garden path. A moment later Alison had opened the front door and she and Ada were regarding him in mild astonishment.

"Why, *Stanley*!" Alison cried, "this is an unexpected pleasure. Are you coming or going, if you see what I mean?"

Despite his agitation, Stanley noticed how young and pretty Alison looked. Her cheeks were rosy, her hair dishevelled, her small teeth shone very white as she laughed up at him; and he felt a glow of pleasure in the thought of all the services he had rendered her.

As briefly as possible he recounted the circumstances of his visit, omitting any mention of George or the true nature of Miss Plum's indisposition. Almost before he had finished his story Ada had stumped upstairs, switching on lights as she went, and could be heard thumping on Miss Plum's bedroom door.

Alison led the way back into the kitchen, where she exclaimed over the dead fire, the ceiling blackened by the flare-up of the primus stove, and the evidences of Stanley's attempts to provide a meal. Mushroom soup in one saucepan, peas in another, chicken breasts in a third. Raspberries ready in a glass dish with a little jug of evaporated milk beside it.

"How kind of you, Stanley!" she cried. "How very *thoughtful*. I am so sorry you were let in for all this. And lighting the living room fire as well! You really shouldn't, you know. . . Oh, dear, one really cannot rely upon Victoria for *anything*. She was perfectly well when we left home this morning, and all she had to do was to keep the house warm and pop the shepherd's pie in the oven. You'd think anyone could manage that, wouldn't you? And even if the kitchen fire did go out, she could have used the gas stove."

After a brief struggle with himself, Stanley gave in.

"It seems she needed a shilling for the meter. Fortunately I was able to supply that."

"Then you must be paid back immediately," Alison cried, pulling a little purse from her muff and poking feverishly amongst its contents.

"Alison—*please!*" Stanley protested. A shilling rolled across the table in his direction. He handed it back with the slightest of gallant gestures, the merest lift of whimsical eyebrows.

At this moment Ada followed them into the kitchen. She breathed rather loudly and her lips were compressed into a thin, straight line.

Alison said anxiously: "What is wrong with Miss Plum, Ada?"

"It's not for me to say," Ada replied, voice and face portentous; "but, seeing as you've asked, it looks to me like she's the worse for drink." Her dour gaze found and rested upon the whisky bottle and the two dirty tumblers. Alison's glance followed hers. Stanley felt compelled to turn and join them in their horrified regard.

"Oh, Ada, no! Miss Plum is no drinker, at least."

"Yon bottle were three parts full yesterday. If she's not drunk it, who has?"

Who, indeed?

The base of Stanley's scalp pricked as he sensed rather than saw Ada s inimical glance turned upon him.

Alison said in a worried voice: "Is this true, Stanley? Is Victoria really *drunk*?"

Stanley pressed judicial lips together.

"Not *drunk*, Alison. I would not say that Miss Plum was actually drunk. One must keep in mind that a very little whisky would be enough to upset a person who was unaccustomed to it."

Ada repeated implacably: "Yon bottle were three parts full nobbut yesterday."

"But," Stanley countered, carrying the war bang into the enemy's camp, "as you see, there are *two* tumblers."

"So I noticed," Ada replied tersely.

With a dignity stemming from a clear conscience, Stanley ignored her and, turning to Alison, took her hand and patted it soothingly.

"You must not allow this unfortunate incident to distress you, dear Alison. I feel sure it will not occur again. Miss Plum has had her lesson."

"It's not Miss Plum I'm worrying about," Alison said a little sharply. "It is the knowledge that someone else has been here drinking with her, without my knowledge or consent. It—it frightens me! I shall never again feel able to leave her alone in the house."

Ada removed her coat, rolled back her sleeves and began to rake the cold ashes out of the stove.

"Happen you'll get rid of her now, like I've bin telling you to ever since she came," she remarked with sour satisfaction.

"Well," said Stanley, "I really must be off. Mrs. Platt will wonder what has become of me. Unless, of course, I can be of any further assistance?"

"No, no. You have done far too much already," Alison said warmly. "I cannot thank you enough. And such a beautiful fire in the living room! So very kind . . ."

"It was nothing," Stanley said modestly.

He had got as far as the gate when the door opened again and Ada's voice hailed him.

"You forgot yer galoshes," she shouted.

She stood stolidly in the porch, holding the things at arm's length, and Stanley was obliged to climb back up the slippery path to retrieve them. She made no move to admit him. For a moment he wondered rather wildly whether to sit down on the doorstep and put them on, or whether to carry them and risk getting his feet wet.

He decided on the latter plan, as being more dignified. He would take a hot bath as soon as he got home and perhaps, as an extra precaution, a glass of hot milk on retiring. Hot milk with a spoonful of whisky in it. For though he was a temperate man—indeed, practically a total abstainer—Stanley always kept spirits in the house for medicinal purposes.

He set off home at a brisk trot, the galoshes clasped to his bosom, his mind upon the pheasant which, he devoutly trusted, would not be overdone.

2.

The two women ate their supper together by the fire in the living room, which was the only warm room in the house. They were both exceedingly hungry and did full justice to Stanley's choice of cans. Even Ada had to admit that you might do worse if you were pushed to it.

"It was really providential that Mr. Hartley should call at that moment," Alison exclaimed. "He saved the situation."

"Providential, happen. But a bit peculiar when you come to reckon it up, seeing as he'd nobbut just left you up at the Tarn."

"He wanted a word with Miss Plum about the Old Folks' Christmas Party. I believe she had promised to assist him in some way. And he said, quite frankly, that he hoped to get a cup of nice hot tea. . . . Poor man, all he got was trouble."

Ada sniffed.

"It's not all that much trouble to open four tins."

"And look at this gorgeous fire he made for us, too."

"Let's hope he never cracked his corsets doing it."

"Really, Ada, poor Mr. Hartley can do nothing right in your eyes!" She stood up, letting out a sharp groan. "Goodness, how stiff I am! I'm longing for a hot bath. Did you think to switch on the immersion heater?"

"I did. Water's pretty near boiling already. I shan't be sorry to get to bed meself. I reckon we're past skating and all such larks."

"We are nothing of the kind," Alison said indignantly. "I am looking forward to another good day tomorrow."

Pushing the last raspberry around her plate, Ada reminded Alison that she had arranged to take Miss Plum to the Labour Exchange tomorrow.

"Oh, dear. So I had."

"And I've got me kitchen ceiling to whitewash."

"Poor you!"

Avoiding each other's eyes they gathered up the dirty dishes, carried them into the kitchen and began to wash up in gloomy silence.

"It seems such a pity," Alison grumbled presently. "We don't get real skating weather once in ten years. It might never happen again in our lifetime, for all we know."

"Aye," Ada agreed heavily.

"And after all, it doesn't really matter about the ceiling—not for a few days. Nobody sees it but us."

"True enough. And you've put off going to t'Labour Exchange so often, once more can't mek all that difference."

"We'll go," Alison decided. "Hang the Labour Exchange—and the ceiling! Hang everything! . . . We're going skating tomorrow, Ada. And every day while the ice holds."

"What about *her*? I'm not leaving her alone in the house again."

"She will have to come with us."

"She can't skate."

"Then she can watch."

"She'll tek a chill, standing about all day."

Exasperated, Alison cried: "Whose side are you on, Ada? Someone will lend her some skates. Someone will offer to teach her to skate—you see if they don't. Miss Plum always lands on her feet."

Ada fetched the two tumblers from the dresser and washed them fanatically, as though they had contained arsenic. She said abruptly: "It were never that Hartley as drank it. He wouldn't have the guts!"

"Of *course* it was not Mr. Hartley!"

"Then who was it?"

"How should I know!" Alison said crossly. "Oh, dear, what a horrid ending to a lovely day. It's just spoiled everything."

"You've got to find out, you know," Ada persisted. "You've got to talk to her an' get it over with. Mek up yer mind to it, luv; it might as well be soon as late. I'll finish off here."

"Do you suppose she is . . . well enough for talking now?"

"No harm in going up to see."

"Oh, dear," said Alison, clutching the vegetable dish she was drying as if it were a shield. "Ada, do you really think it necessary tonight? I am so awfully tired, and if she starts to cry again I don't believe I can bear it." Suddenly she looked her age to the full: the bright colour faded, the lines about her eyes showing up sharply. She looked small and defenceless and rather frightened, and Ada's faithful heart yearned over her.

"Never heed, luv," she said more gently, "there's worse troubles at sea."

Alison stared intently at the tips of her fingers. Then suddenly she pulled herself together and went quickly out of the kitchen, Ada's compassion followed her.

"Nay!" muttered Ada. She gave a short, exasperated laugh and then a sigh. She wrung the wet dishcloth venomously, as if it were somebody's neck. "Men! They're more trouble than what they're worth."

3.

"I couldn't help it," whimpered Miss Plum. From behind a barricade of bedclothes her eyes shone round and dark, like a frightened hare's.

Alison said coldly: "You never can help anything, can you? You forget to attend to fires, so they go out, but you can't help it. You over-pump the primus and it flares up, but *you* can't help it. You dislike alcohol and know that you have no head for it, but when you are invited to drink whisky you can't help it . . ." She drew a long breath and expelled it slowly, scornfully. Count ten, Daddy had always cautioned. But she had counted ten so often for the sake of Victoria's feelings. Far too often.

The room had a faint, unpleasant smell. She went to the window and flung it wide open, standing for a moment to drink in the clean, bitter frost-smell of the night. It was dark out there; silent save for the small stir and scrape of leafless branches and the sudden harshness of an owl's cry. She breathed deeply, trying to calm herself, to balance anger with common sense and understanding. But it didn't work. She knew that she didn't really want it to work.

Behind her in the frowzy bed, Miss Plum whined about the draught, about her cold hot-water bottle, about her headache.

Alison went and stood beside the bed, looking down on the disordered covers, the wild eyes and hair appearing above them, the thin outline of the body beneath them. She looked down without pity.

"Get up," she said harshly. "Wash yourself and make your bed. Refill your hot-water bottle. Take some aspirins. You know where they are kept. You know where everything m this house is kept, don't you? Get up and look after yourself. You are not ill. Merely drunk. That is something I will not tolerate in my house."

"I couldn't help it, Alison—really I couldn't."

"Your life," Alison continued implacably, "has been one long series of misfortunes and hardships, none of which you have been able to help. You have not attempted, even in the most elementary fashion, to deal with any of them yourself. You have just sat down and cried and cried until somebody came along and helped you. . . . The only definite decision you ever made in the whole of your miserable life, was to end it. . . . And you didn't make a success even of that."

"It was you! You!" Miss Plum's voice came out in a thin, high scream. "You stopped me from doing it!"

"Yes," Alison replied after a brief pause. "Yes, I did, didn't I? Please accept my apologies."

She went slowly along the corridor and shut herself into her own room, turning the key against intrusion. She switched on light and heat, drew the curtains, moving without conscious volition about the room; touching a cushion here, an ornament there; turning back the bedspread, taking a clean nightgown from a drawer; trying to control her trembling limbs, her racing heart, the throbbing sense of fullness in her throat by such ordinary, familiar actions.

She thought: in all my life I have never before spoken such terrible words. In all my life I have never felt anger such as this.

I didn't know I was capable of such anger. I suppose this is what murderers must feel like, before . . .

She pulled the pins out of her hair and the two plaits slipped down like brown ropes, one across either shoulder. She began to brush her hair with the slow, methodical strokes of long habit. Staring into the mirror she watched her arm go up and down, up and down. Her hair shone in the lamplight. It crackled as the brush swept down the strands, clinging to the bristles as if to a magnet.

I've got good hair, she thought dispassionately, without pride or pleasure. My eyes aren't bad, either, nor my skin. My teeth are my own. Automatically her tongue explored the small cavity in the left molar, and she made a mental note to phone the dentist in the morning.

Twenty-five each side, twenty-five at the front, twenty-five at the back. . . .

She plaited her hair loosely and tied it with a blue ribbon. She undressed, legs and back protesting each time she bent. She thought: surely I ought not to be so stiff? I don't take enough exercise. Perhaps I should take up golf. . . . She examined her body in the mirror; turning from side to side, bending, stretching, standing on tiptoe, running her hands over the warm skin, tightening the muscles of her abdomen and letting them go slack again. Ada was right: she had got fatter recently. The cherished fragility following her illness had been, alas, only temporary.

Fair, fat and forty . . . I shall be just like Aunt Gladys when I'm old, she thought. I don't mind, really. Why does everybody make such a fuss about getting old, about getting bald and deaf? There's nothing one can do about it, and it doesn't matter in the least. Nothing matters. We are no more than specks in an infinite space, whirling through an immeasurable span of time. I do not matter. Neither does Victoria. Nor George. There is nothing for me to be angry about. . . .

Outside the door Ada's voice inquired: "Haven't you had your bath yet, luv?"

"Go ahead and have yours, Ada. I'm not quite ready."

There was a pause, then the doorknob turned stealthily, fruitlessly.

"Are you all right, luv?" The voice was troubled, and Alison knew she was being unkind in locking Ada out. But she only answered: "Perfectly all right, thanks. Good night."

"Good night, luv."

She heard the slippered feet slap down the corridor, heard the bathroom door shut and water gush from taps.

Putting on her dressing gown she sat on the edge of the bed and gazed around this room that had been her refuge since she was a small child. It had witnessed her foolish tears and tiny triumphs, her young-girl's heartbreak, her growth into womanhood. Here she had hidden from parental wrath and importunities and the over-zealous vigilance of Ada. Here she had lain in sickness and convalescence; dressed for parties, bright-eyed with excitement; mourned the loss of loved ones; prayed with hope and accepted with resignation and had finally achieved the tranquillity that for years had sufficed her.

She loved this room. The thick grey carpet, so soft to bare feet. The pink-flowered curtains glowing in rosy light: they were exactly like the ones Mummy had made for her when first she slept alone here as a small child. She had gone to considerable trouble to obtain the same material and pattern whenever new ones had been required. The tiny statue of Eros that stood on the highboy, pointing his arrow at her heart in a coy, futile gesture. She had seen him in a shop window during one of their Bournemouth holidays and most of her spending money for the two weeks had been spent on his purchase. Mummy had thought it wasn't a very *nice* ornament for a young girl's bedroom; but Daddy, unexpectedly, had taken her side, and she had been allowed to keep it.

The books she had loved as a child stood in shabby ranks on the white-painted shelves. *Black Beauty. The Wide, Wide World. What Katy Did. Alice in Wonderland. The Jungle Books. A Girl Of The Limberlost.* Some were neatly mended with adhesive tape, others held together in covers of brown paper with their titles written in a round, girlish hand. Some of her schoolbooks were there, too. *First Steps in Algebra.* Alison Penny. Form III. Huffley High School for Girls. *Contes Et Lègendes.* Alison Penny. Form II. With little drawings scribbled in the margins and one page obliterated by ink. ("Disgraceful, Alison! Take an order mark and be more careful in the future.") *A History of England.* Alison Penny. Form VI. She had worn her plait doubled up under a black bow, a prefect's badge pinned on her gym tunic, and a dedicated look; secretly determined to enter a convent at the earliest possible moment.

There were even two of her toys on the bottom shelf: a Teddy bear minus an arm and an ear and a little grey plush donkey with scarlet saddle and bridle, beautifully made and in perfect condition. These she could never quite bring herself to give away to any covetous child, to any rummage sale, however worthy the cause.

And of course there were the letters, tied up with ribbon and locked away in the cedarwood box in the bureau drawer.

George's letters, that had ended her childhood. . . .

4.

She heard Ada come out of the bathroom and shut her bedroom door.

Now she would have her own bath and a good night's sleep; and tomorrow, maybe, this terrible anger that consumed her would be spent and gone.

She lay for a long time in the steamy, scented water, feeling the tortured muscles relax, the stiffened limbs eased of pain. She thought: it is George I should be angry with, not Victoria. For Victoria is a poor thing with no knowledge of life and how to deal with it; but George is a man of great experience, who has lived life to the full in many countries, amongst all sorts of conditions of people; and he must have known perfectly well that he was behaving quite unspeakably. He is certainly the one to blame. . . .

Still she found herself seeking excuses for George.

She had treated George badly, promising to marry him and then breaking her promise because Daddy and Mummy had known best. And when, after all the years, he had returned and asked her once again to marry him, all she could say was "Thursday is the Women's Institute."

She began to rub herself dry in the huge, soft towel with A.P. embroidered in one corner in Ada's neat stitching.

Men were different from women; not so meek yet, at the same time, curiously enough, less tough. Women accepted sorrow and defeat. The cruel wind battered at them and they bowed to the wind; and when calmness came again they lifted their heads, bruised but unbroken. Not so men, who stormed and argued and kicked against the pricks, and often went to pieces altogether. . . .

Lying in her warm, comfortable bed, she wondered about George's visit.

Had he intended to ask her once again to marry him? Maybe he had come to say good-by? Or perhaps to apologize for going off in such a temper?

Naturally, he would have been disappointed not to find her at home—even piqued to learn that she was up at the Tarn, enjoying herself. . . .

He could have followed her up to the Tarn. He could have sought her out and joined in the fun. Even if he could not skate, even though he disliked walking, it would have been the natural thing for any man to do in the circumstances.

Instead, he had sat in the kitchen with Victoria; had demanded whisky and insisted that Victoria should join him in drinking it. They had sat together in that deplorable muddle, without comfort or warmth, and between them they had got through the best part of a bottle of whisky. . . . He had made no effort to help the girl; to rekindle the stove or deal with the primus, or even to put a coin in the gas meter. He had just sat there drinking, and persuading Victoria to drink—despite her protests that she truly disliked it.

The whole affair seemed quite incredible to Alison. Yet she believed it.

She even believed that George had tried to make love to Victoria, seizing her in his arms and forcing kisses upon her; obliging her to fight and struggle—even to scream loudly for help—before he released her.

That was Miss Plum's story, and Alison believed it. She knew Miss Plum, and she knew George.

Why, then, should she feel for Miss Plum such a bitter searing anger and for George merely an impatience such as one might feel for a naughty child?

She dozed a little and woke again to a sudden violent rejection of Miss Plum's innocence.

There was something *about* Miss Plum.

She was no siren. She had few charms either of face, figure or manner. The large, dark eyes, the dark hair springing from the widow's peak above them were not without attraction; but the hair was ill-groomed, the eyes too often red with weeping or popping with fright.

Yet there was *something*. Something that appealed to all the men. Some power Miss Plum possessed and exerted without having to speak a single word or move a finger.

She remembered Stanley's tea party—how long ago it seemed!—When both he and Hubert strongly advised how to get rid of Miss Plum at the earliest possible moment. They had promised to help if need be. Yet only a short time afterward, sitting at her own fireside, Hubert had suggested that Miss Plum should take over the Cubs; while Stanley had been so engrossed in conversation with her that Alison had found it difficult to get a word in edgeways. Hubert had promised to teach her to skate. Stanley had asked her to help with the Old Folks' Party. Both expressed surprise and disappointment if Alison appeared in public without Miss Plum.

And then Ronnie—even Ronnie!—mooning about after the girl in that stupid fashion; shopping with her in Huffley, carrying her packages, beating up unruly Cubs in her defense; practically accusing Alison of physical cruelty in not offering Miss Plum a permanent home. Ronnie's devotion had been short-lived—but it *had* lived.

And now George. . . .

Was the possession of such power compatible with true innocence? Alison tried hard to believe it, and could not.

Tossing and turning, she slept and woke and slept again. And presently she became aware of Ada standing beside her bed, Ada's hand gripping her shoulder, shaking her out of sleep.

Shielding her eyes from the sudden dazzle of light she muttered peevishly: "Whatever is the matter, Ada! It can't be time to get up yet."

"Never heed the time, you've got to get up." Bulky in flannel dressing gown, unfamiliar in steel curlers, Ada stood by the bed, an implacable hand refusing to let her slide back into sleep again. "Come on, luv, wake up. Summat's amiss."

"Oh, Ada—whatever is it *now*?"

"Miss Plum's gone," said Ada.

CHAPTER ELEVEN

1.

STANLEY was having breakfast in bed.

Seldom did he so indulge himself; but this morning he had awakened with a slight sense of constriction in the chest and, on getting out of bed, he had sneezed three times so, as a precaution, he had decided to take things easy.

Mrs. Platt had brought him tea and toast and honey, his warmest dressing gown and the morning papers, and had done something clever with his pillows. The electric heater gave out a pleasant warmth and a slight mist beyond the windows merely emphasized the comfort within.

Stanley did not think he was actually ill. His throat was not sore, neither did his head ache. The sneezing had subsided and the slight discomfort in his chest could quite possibly be the result of last night's pheasant which had, as he had feared, proved dry and unpalatable. He took his temperature, just in case and, as usual, it was slightly under the normal. There was no apparent reason why he should stay in bed.

Yet it was very pleasant in the warm, quiet room and he fancied it would do him no harm to indulge in an extra hour of relaxation for once. Yesterday had been both strenuous and upsetting. There had been the long walk up to the Tarn, and all that standing about on the chilly bank talking with one or another; the walk back and all the work he had done at The Laurels; the distasteful necessity of dealing first with Miss Plum's indisposition then with Alison's agitation and Ada's hostility. Then the walk home carrying his galoshes, picking his way through patches of slush which, if they had not actually wet his feet, had certainly made them extremely cold. And the final disaster of his ruined dinner.

But no—even that had not been the end of it. For there had been a slight unpleasantness with Mrs. Platt, who had whisked the frizzled pheasant away with none of her usual meekness, saying quite disagreeably that nobody could be expected to serve up decent food if folks came in at all hours. She had added, rather ambiguously, that punctuality was the courtesy of kings, and had flounced—positively flounced!—from the room.

On the whole, an undesirable sort of day, best forgotten.

For the first time in their relationship Stanley had hesitated to suggest any departure from their accustomed routine; almost deciding to breakfast downstairs, despite the sneezes and the tightness in his chest. Mrs. Platt suited him very well. For the most part their days passed harmoniously and he was well aware that she would be difficult to replace. If she were going to start *flouncing*, Stanley reflected anxiously, he really had no idea what line he should take.

But Mrs. Platt had agreed to his request with all her customary placidity—even suggesting that it might be wise to spend the entire day in bed, thus nipping in the bud any threat to his health. Stanley had compromised by promising not to rise until lunch time, and had proceeded to devour an excellent breakfast, relieved beyond measure that the threatened storm had blown over.

He was not best pleased, therefore, when Mrs. Platt almost immediately re-entered to announce that the vicar was in the hall and demanding to see Mr. Hartley without delay.

"At this hour?" Stanley protested. "What does he want?"

"That I couldn't say, sir." Mrs. Platt smoothed her apron. "He seems to be in a bit of a dither."

"Very well. Ask him to come up—if he does not mind the risk of infection."

Hubert entered so promptly as to suggest that he had already been hovering outside the door.

"Good heavens—you're not ill, are you?" he cried, surveying Stanley's recumbent form in dismay. In the warmth and elegance of the room he struck a discordant note with his bony, wind-reddened hands, his shabby overcoat minus a button, his obvious need of a shave. "Phew! My word, you've got a fog in here. It feels like the tropical house at Kew. I'll open a window for you."

"Leave the windows alone," Stanley said sharply. "I am not so incapacitated that I cannot open a window if I find it necessary. The room seems warm to you merely by contrast with the intense cold outside."

"You're not getting flu again, are you?"

"I hope not," Stanley replied cautiously. "I think it is merely a slight indisposition, probably caused by overtiring myself yesterday. Mrs. Platt thinks it wise for me to remain in bed until lunch time, and I allowed myself to be persuaded. You know how women fuss. However, do not come too near me, just in case. Better be safe than sorry, as they say."

"Oh good heavens!" Hubert exclaimed. "I was counting on your help, and here you are stuffing yourself in bed. It's already nine-thirty and she's been gone for hours. Anything may have happened. Alison's nearly distracted—and here you are, stuffing yourself in bed . . ."

"Sit down, Hubert," Stanley commanded. "Sit down, man and stop fidgeting, and try to be coherent. *Why* is Alison distracted, and *who* has gone, and in *what* way am I expected to help? Let me give you a cup of tea. It will calm you."

"I can't stop for cups of tea," Hubert said irritably. "We're all out searching for Miss Plum. She's been gone for hours—nobody has the slightest idea where. Ada found her room empty quite early this morning. Alison phoned me. She and Ada and Ronnie and I have been out ever since daylight. If you're not going to have flu you'd better get some clothes on and lend a hand."

Stanley buttered another piece of toast.

"The police," he inquired with composure, "have, naturally, been notified?"

"No, they haven't," Hubert said shortly. "Alison doesn't want the police brought in unless it's absolutely necessary." He lit a cigarette and threw the match in the general direction of the fireplace, which it missed by inches, falling on the edge of the handmade white woollen hearthrug, where it sizzled merrily. "Oh, goodness!" he muttered. He stamped heavily on the rug, leaving the damp, soggy imprint of a shoe on its immaculate surface.

"Look out!" Stanley shrilled, starting up in bed so violently that all his breakfast equipage slid to one end of the tray. "Really, Hubert—will you never learn to keep your smoking under control? Just look at my rug! It came from the cleaners' only last week, and now your filthy footmarks all over it. . . . Scorched, too—I can smell it from here! In any case, it's hardly the thing for a parson to burst into a sickroom puffing smoke like a railway engine. My throat feels dry already. Most inconsiderate . . ."

"Sorry," Hubert said abjectly. He took the cigarette from his mouth, glanced wildly around for a non-existent ash tray, hesitated, and finally held it out to Stanley, who quickly dropped it into his saucer and poured tea on it. He fell back on his pillows with closed eyes.

"Little things like that upset me," he murmured faintly. "I fear my heart is not all it might be."

"Fiddlesticks," Hubert said crossly. "Moaning about a measly mark on your mat, when a fellow creature is at large in this bitter weather, lost and unhappy! Aren't you going to get up and help Alison find her?"

Still with closed eyes, Stanley said judicially: "I find the expression *at large* inconsistent with reality. Miss Plum is neither a convicted criminal nor a certified lunatic. She is over twenty-one and is merely a visitor in Alison's house. If she chooses to leave that house, I can see no reason why she should not do so. Granted, her method of departure was a little . . . eccentric; a little ungrateful after all the kindness she has received. Whatever we may think of her manners, however, she had every right to walk out of The Laurels whenever she chose to do so."

Hubert gnawed at a thumbnail. Put that way, the whole set-up did sound rather silly.

"Alison was afraid she might try to drown herself," he admitted apologetically. "She tried once before, you remember."

"But not very *hard*, if I remember correctly. And unless Miss Plum is a great deal more determined this time, and is moreover remarkably handy with a pick, she will find it difficult to drown herself anywhere north of the Trent for several days. Long before that she will have given up the idea, for she is a woman totally devoid of resource."

"Still . . . there are other ways. . ."

Stanley opened his eyes and gazed at the vicar as if he had just asked for an overdraft on a non-existent bank account.

"If," he said severely, "you feel that there is the slightest chance that the woman may attempt suicide again, it is your plain duty to inform the police without delay, however distasteful that may be. *Without delay*," he repeated, wagging a pontifical finger. "Let the police search for Miss Plum. That is their job, for which purpose they are supplied in immense quantities, equipped with fast cars, radios, fierce Alsatian dogs and I don't know what—all of which, remember, comes out of your pocket and mine—and they will pick her up in no time at all. As far as I am concerned," he concluded, settling himself more comfortably, "I have had quite as much of Miss Plum as I can stand."

Hubert opened the door and stood, undecided, twiddling the knob backward and forward, frowning at his feet. He said reluctantly: "One cannot altogether rule out the idea of foul play. From something Ada let drop, I gather that Miss Plum was not alone in the house yesterday, and that a considerable amount of whisky was drunk . . . I must say I find it hard to credit; such a quiet, unassuming little woman, and so anxious to be helpful. Still, one can understand two women living alone being scared to death at the thought. Alison refuses to talk about it but I can see she is terribly upset."

Stanley said with matchless forbearance: "Either in or out, if you please, Hubert. The draught from the door is quite excruciating. And do stop fiddling with that knob! I do not anticipate for one moment that Miss Plum has been murdered, though I should have some slight sympathy with her assassin if she had. I could enlighten you to an astonishing extent on the subject of Miss Plum's behaviour of yesterday, but if Alison does not wish it discussed, my lips are sealed. The sooner you get the police on the job the better it will be for everyone concerned, including Miss Plum. Give Alison my regards, if you please." He opened *The Times* at the financial page and began to read with attention.

Hubert went downstairs and let himself out of the house into the raw coldness of the morning.

He couldn't help feeling that Stanley was right.

No sooner had the front door slammed than Stanley was out of bed and on his knees examining the damage to his rug.

With loving care and a pair of nail scissors he snipped away the charred portions of wool, and the damage was not so extensive as he had feared. Even the dirty footprint showed less now that it had dried a little. He decided that if he allowed it to dry thoroughly before applying fuller's earth, it might, after all, be unnecessary to send it to the cleaner's again.

He stroked the thick, springing surface, admiring his own handiwork. It had taken him all of three months to make the rug and he had enjoyed doing it. He was glad he had kept it in his bedroom. One could hardly prevent visitors from indulging their deplorable habits downstairs; but one could and would make certain that none, in future, violated his privacy up here. . . .

"No!" Alison said with decision. "No, I will not have it—not unless all else fails."

"I can't help feeling Stanley is right," Hubert said, fingering his unshaven chin.

"I'm dead sure he is," Ada said. "For once in his life," she added under her breath.

"Me, too," contributed Ronnie with his mouth full of bread and dripping. Saving Victoria's life had soon ceased to hold any charms for Ronnie and he was raring to be off skating. "Besides I mean to say, how *could* she?" Conscious of having blundered, he stood first on one foot, then on the other, avoiding reproachful glances and applying himself steadily to a long-deferred breakfast.

They were in the vicarage kitchen, gathered around the table upon which reposed the remains of the ham, half a loaf of stale bread, a bottle of milk whose cardboard stopper had been mutilated by a titmouse, a pot of dripping and another of jam with knives sticking out of them, and a large pot of tea.

Ever since she had clapped eyes on this deplorable sight Ada had been itching to lay hands on a tablecloth, plates and cutlery, a jam dish and a sugar basin, and make the table look presentable. But she knew better than to stick her neck out in another woman's kitchen. True, Mrs. Hart was not present (being still too "queer" to attempt anything more strenuous than another full day's skating) but Ada knew perfectly well that if she so much as washed up a teaspoon Mrs. Hart, in some mysterious fashion, would hear of it and take offence. So she drank her tea which, she conceded gloomily, was at least hot and wet, and saw that Alison ate something, refilled her cup, watching the beloved face with more anxiety than she would have admitted.

She looks right done up, poor lamb, she thought.

Indeed, Alison felt almost at the end of her tether. Her joints and muscles still ached from yesterday's exercise; her spirit was still bruised from the bitter tide of anger that had battered her. She had slept little and had been out since daybreak searching for someone she had heartily wished never to see again in the whole of her life.

In theory she agreed with Stanley that Miss Plum was perfectly at liberty to walk out of The Laurels at any time. Had it been any other, Alison would merely have expressed indignation at the lack of gratitude and good manners, and let it go at that.

But Miss Plum could not be judged by ordinary standards. In spite of everything Alison could not help being fearful for her, distressed at the thought of the foolish creature wandering along the icy roads, possibly losing herself on the moor, which was treacherous in places, or amongst the strange, indifferent faces in some unfriendly town.

Ada said: "Yer tea's gone cold, luv. Give me yer cup and I'll pour you some fresh. And try and eat yer sandwich. Come on now, luv, you'll be no help to Miss Plum nor to anyone else without you've got summat in yer stomach."

Ronnie said with what he hoped was a guileless face: "Why I don't we all go up to the Tarn together? We could skate in different directions and make a proper do of it. No stone unturned, no avenue unexplored, and all that."

"There'll be plenty skating by this time," Ada said. "If she's up there she'll have bin found by now."

"Had she any money?" Hubert asked Alison.

"A little, I imagine. Possibly about five pounds, not more "

"And she took her clothes?"

"She took everything that belonged to her. It wasn't much."

"Well, I suppose we can take that as a hopeful sign. She would hardly trouble to hump a suitcase if she intended to do away with herself. I confess I don't understand your objection to calling in the police."

Alison gestured wearily.

"The police would ask a lot of awkward questions. They would want to know *why* we were panicking about her."

"You need not tell them."

"But we cannot ask for an official search without good reason, Hubert. If we are afraid for her safety, we must tell them why. If we are not—why ask for help? . . . Also, if—when—they found Miss Plum, they would certainly question *her*. And if I know her, she would immediately burst into tears and blurt out the whole story, right from the day I found her in the Recreation Ground." She sipped some tea and went on: "I don't know the legal position in regard to people who—who have Miss Plum's unfortunate tendencies, but I imagine someone would have to make themselves responsible for her; and I cannot do that any longer. Truly I cannot, Hubert."

"Why should you?" the vicar agreed. "You've done more than enough already."

"But then, you see, they might want to put her into some sort of institution."

"They're not all bad places nowadays, you know. I visit one quite often, and everything is bright and cheerful. Many of the patients don't want to go home. . . . And it would probably be for a short time only. It might do her a world of good."

Alison shook her head obstinately.

"It would finish Victoria off for good."

Hubert glanced covertly at his wrist watch. He had a meeting in Huffley at eleven o'clock, and he still had to shave and get the car to start. He thought Alison was being unreasonable, but there was nothing he could do about it if she refused to take all advice. She looked dead, poor girl, and no wonder. It was no joke wobbling up and down icy roads on a bicycle in a mist that chilled you to the bone however many clothes you wore. Actually, she had been quite wonderful. So had Ada, who hadn't ridden a bicycle for years until this morning.

"Why don't you both go home and lie down?" he urged. "Stay quietly at home for the rest of the day, and if we have no news of Miss Plum by tomorrow morning, we must think again."

3.

The back tyre of Ada's borrowed bicycle was flat.

Ronnie, full of the milk of human kindness now that he was free to skate, offered to mend it for her and return it on the following day. The offer was accepted.

"You ride on, luv," Ada told Alison. "No need for us both to walk And don't start doing anything, mind. There's the shepherd's pie, think on, and we never finished the raspberries. Get yersen a hot-water bottle and go to bed. World won't come to an end if we leave the work for once."

Alison mounted her bicycle and rode away, leaving Ada plodding stiffly in her wake.

The kitchen stove was roaring. She damped it down a little, put a hot-water bottle in Ada's bed and another in her own, took in the bottles of frozen milk, gave another glance around Miss Plum's bedroom; half hoping, half fearing that she might discover the girl cowering under the bedclothes; lay down on her own bed, drawing the eiderdown up to her chin, and immediately fell into a deep sleep.

Although she had promised herself she would go to bed the moment she reached home, when it came to the point Ada had never felt less like sleeping.

Tired as she was with all the skating and cycling and the shocking upset caused by Miss Plum's disappearance, she felt restless and unable to relax. She was a good bit older than Miss Alison, she reflected, but she was a good bit tougher, too. She could take it, and Miss Alison could not.

Besides, the greengrocer was sending an order up this morning, and it was the day for the fish man, too. You couldn't go flopping into bed with folks banging away at the door, and the shepherd's pie to heat up, and tomorrow's dinner to think of. . . .

A bit of a sit down-that was all she needed.

She opened the doors of the kitchen stove and sank into the little old rocking chair that she considered more comfortable than any of the big, soft chairs in the living room. The rocker fitted her back snugly; the head cushion was in the exactly right position; the smooth, swaying motion was infinitely soothing.

It was good to be back in her own kitchen. It might not display its usual spick-and-span order, but it was a palace after yon pigsty at the vicarage.

That Mrs. Hart wanted a good talking to, if ever a woman did; but she'd never get it from Mr. Sturgess. Poor little beggar, he'd never say boo to a goose! It'd take a woman to deal with Mrs. Hart.

The vicar needed a wife, that was a sure thing. Yon lad, too—he could do with a bit of mothering.

There'd been times when she'd wondered about the vicar and Miss Alison. . . .

And then there was that owd flabby-belly Hartley—though she'd never really believed Miss Alison would be daft enough to take up with one of his sort. Him and his corsets and his galoshes! Still, you never knew. There's nowt so queer as folks! she thought glumly.

And now, of course, there was George again. . . .

Ada sighed and poked the fire into a fiercer blaze. She remained bending forward, arms resting on knees, the long, steel poker still clutched in her hand. She stared into the glowing heart of the fire.

What would become of *her* if Miss Alison married?

Both the vicar and Mr. Hartley already had housekeepers and Ada wouldn't share a kitchen with any woman—that she wouldn't! As for George, she didn't reckon that George would ever settle down in England—or anywhere else, for that matter. If Miss Alison married George, they'd go gadding off to foreign parts, and that would be that. The Laurels would be sold up lock, stock, and barrel, and she'd have to find a new home for herself, make a new life. After all these years!

It didn't bear thinking about.

But she went on thinking about it. . . .

Ada liked George. She didn't approve of him, but she liked him.

Of course, he wasn't anywhere near good enough for Miss Alison; she'd yet to see the man that was. But George was, at least, a *man*. Not a very good man, perhaps; but the good men were not always the easiest to live with. The vicar was good; and he'd send you up a wall with his fidgets, and his butt ends flung all over t'place so as you'd never be sure as the house wasn't burning down about your ears. And you couldn't say George was *refined*. He hadn't come from a refined home—not that a fellow was necessarily any the worse for that-and his years of knocking around the world hadn't improved him seemingly.

But if you wanted refinement, you'd always got that Hartley. . . .

Ada brooded over this business of Miss Alison and George.

Ever since he'd come bursting in at Christmas, with his beard and his great booming laugh and his boxes of American candies, she'd been watching her darling's face for a sign, waiting for her to say a word. But not a word nor a sign had there been. Always the good hostess, of course, the considerate mistress, like her mother had taught her. Always the lady. But where were the happy blushes, the arms flung around her old Ada's neck while she poured out the happiness she had waited for and despaired of for twenty years?

Some might say you couldn't expect that sort of thing at her age, but Ada knew better. Ada knew that at heart Miss Alison was still a little girl. She could carry sorrow with courage and dignity—oh, aye, life had taught her that!—but against happiness she had no defenses. Happiness set Miss Alison's feet dancing and her eyes shining and her tongue chattering away fifteen to the dozen. If she had been happy at George's return, Ada would have known it soon enough.

The greengrocer's boy arrived. Ada stored away the contents of his basket without comment, barely troubling to glance at their quality. The boy departed whistling—a thing he rarely felt equal to by the time Ada had finished with him.

The fish man had little to offer but cod and kippers. He hovered on the doorstep, waiting for Ada to offer him his usual cup of tea; but she only said, "Good morning," and shut the door on him without another word. He went back to his truck beating frozen hands together and wondering what had bitten Ada; for they had known each other since childhood and he was accustomed to a warm by the kitchen fire and a bit of gossip.

Ada returned to her rocking chair and her thoughts.

George . . .

There had never been any doubt in her mind about who had got through that bottle of whisky. It had stuck out a mile. There couldn't have been much doubt in Miss Alison's mind, either. If she hadn't tumbled to it right away, she'd known for certain after her talk with Miss Plum. That was why her bedroom door had been locked.

Ada didn't know what story Miss Plum had told and she didn't suppose she ever would know, but she had a pretty shrewd notion of what would happen when George and a bottle of whisky and a poor wet fish like Miss Plum got together.

Her Albert had been just such another as George, she remembered with a twitch of her long upper lip. Couldn't keep his eyes off a pretty pair of ankles, even when he was walking arm-in-arm with herself. She'd smacked his face for it many a time, but there was no curing him. As a husband, Albert would have taken some managing; but at least he wouldn't have been dull. . . .

But it was different for a lady like Miss Alison, who would certainly never dream of smacking anyone's face, let alone her husband's. She would suffer in silence; trailing around one heathen country after another till her poor heart broke entirely. And no Ada to turn to for comfort. . . .

Happen they'd tek me along with 'em? she thought; but the thought quickly died. It wouldn't work. I'd never be able to keep me mouth shut if he got up to his games. I should smack his face meself, and that'd be the finish of it. . . .

No, if Miss Alison married George, it was the parting of the ways; the end of security and comfort; the start of a loneliness beyond imagining.

I suppose I could live with me cousin Annie, she thought drearily. I could get a part-time job in a factory. Or I could go out daily, cooking and that. I don't reckon I could settle to live in again, not in a strange house. If I had Annie's spare room it'd be somewhere to call me own, and she'd be glad of the money.

I reckon Miss Alison would give me this chair if I asked her. And there's the vases in me bedroom, and the china dog, and the patchwork quilt, and the clock she give me last birthday. I'd tek me can-opener, too. It would be a place of me own. . . .

And so, with most unaccustomed tears running down her cheeks, and the shepherd's pie quite forgotten, Ada rocked to and fro before the kitchen fire, facing the future, while Alison lay under her pretty eiderdown upstairs, sunk in the deep, dreamless sleep of exhaustion.

CHAPTER TWELVE

1.

THE landlord of The Goat stood in the deserted saloon bar, warming his backside before a frugal fire and gazing out of the window at the bleak, wintry scene.

It wanted ten minutes to opening time. He was cold, sleepy and peckish. Sleepy because his wife had nagged him far into the night; cold and peckish because, when she was in one of her moods, she cut down on fires and food. Breakfast had consisted of toast and margarine and lukewarm tea, and though it was past time for his morning break, none had been forthcoming. The fire was inadequate for this perishing draughty barn of a place. He had pondered the advisability or otherwise of replenishing it with a good-sized lump of coal, but had finally decided in favour of otherwise.

It was one of those days. And what did it matter, anyway, he thought glumly? Freeze to death, starve to death or be nagged to death—what did it matter? It'd be all the same in a hundred years.

Fed up, he thought. Fed up to the back teeth, that's what I am.

He hadn't got any back teeth, of course, or front ones either, if it came to that, because the army had taken them all away from him years ago and presented him with a full set of false ones which were even now steeping in a well-advertised brand of dentifrice beside his bed. He never wore them during the daytime. At night, when he put on a collar and tie just before opening time, embellished his thinning hair with brilliantine and brushed dandruff from his shoulders, he automatically put in his teeth. At night he was on parade; even if it was only the public bar of a second-rate pub in a godforsaken village.

At night the saloon bar was presided over by his wife, whose insignia of office was a tight dress of black satin topped by a long string of amber beads that swung and clattered as she moved about, reaching and stooping behind the bar. *Clatter, Pop. Gurgle. Thump. Ping of the bell. Well, thanks, I don't mind if I do. Cheers. That'll be two-and-six. Clatter.* And then the thin scream that she called laughter. And *clatter, clatter clatter.*

He would hear it all as he stood behind the public bar serving the old regulars with their mild-and-bitter and wishing to goodness he didn't have to be on the wagon because of his kidneys; wishing he were ten years younger and back in the army. A hard life but a good one. A man's life. When you didn't have a woman following you around all day telling you what to do and what not to do. You got on with your business and she got on with hers, and when you went home on leave it was a bit of all right. Even if you were in married quarters it was easy to dodge her if she started anything. . . .

His wife came into the saloon bar at that moment. Her hair, beneath the red-spotted scarf, was clamped in steel curlers and her thin face shone with the cream she had been rubbing on it. She wore rubber boots and a man's topcoat buttoned to the chin, and mittens made from old army socks. She was lugging a large basket of newly sawn logs.

"Do you *mind*?" she said sourly.

He hastened to assist her.

"And don't you go putting none of them on yet. This lot's got to last while tomorrow. We're running short. There'll not be many in with all this skating. You can put the oilstove in the Public, unless you want to go out and do a bit of sawing yourself. Do you no harm, at that. Get your fat down a bit."

"Where's that feller Thompson?" he demanded, aggrieved.

"Where they all are—up at the Tarn. Maggie, too. It's her day off and I couldn't stop her. I says, 'What do you think I'm going to do about the lunches, an' no help?' And she says, 'There's only the First Front, and you can give him the cold lamb and tinned peaches and evaporated, so you've nowt to do but peel a potato or two.' And out my lady walks. You wait until she walks in again, that's all!"

"Cold lamb'll suit me," her spouse offered in a placatory tone.

"It'd better."

"What about a cuppa now, to be gettin' on with, eh?" he wheedled, despising himself.

Her pale eyes flicked over him dispassionately.

"Well, what about it?" she returned, and pushed at the swing baize door, which thumped shut behind her. The draught caused a little gush of smoke, making his eyes water.

He remembered suddenly that she had been a pretty girl. Her hair had been dark and very soft and her eyes so bright that you hadn't noticed their lack of colour. When she'd got all her war paint on she'd looked a real doll and he had been obliged to flatten quite a number of regimental noses before he'd finally got her safely to the altar. Funny, the way life went back on you. . . .

He treated himself to a tot of neat whisky. It would give him hell, he knew, but it would be worth it just to feel the warmth running through him.

He hid the whisky on the shelf below the bar which he began to polish with a concentrated and virtuous expression.

2.

The door leading to the upper rooms burst open and the First Front came in wearing a cerise dressing gown over blue silk pajamas and scratching violently at his chest.

"What goes on?" demanded George loudly. "Is this a pub or is it a family vault? I've been ringing for twenty minutes."

"Ringing?" exclaimed the landlord, pausing in his polishing.

"Ringing. R.I.N.G.I.N.G. Ringing the bell for breakfast. Is it such an unheard-of thing to fancy a bit of breakfast now and again?"

The landlord glanced at the clock. He said repressively: "We don't serve breakfasts after ten. Not without special arrangements we don't. There's a notice to that effect hanging in your bedroom. It's one of the rules of the house."

George gave a prolonged, dramatic and highly profane opinion of the rules of the house which the landlord privately admitted he couldn't have bettered himself. "You mean to tell me I've got to wait until lunch time before I get even a cup of tea in my belly?"

"Ah, now, a cup of tea," replied the landlord. "We might manage that, sir. Cup of tea and a bit of toast, perhaps. I'll just ask the Missus. We're a bit shorthanded today, on account of it's the cook's day off, and her and that feller Thompson's gone up to the Tarn, skating. All the world an' his wife's up there, on account of we don't get real skating weather very often in these parts. When we do, there's no arguing with any of 'em. They just go But a cup of tea, now . . ." He stuck his head round the swing door and yelled, "Min!" in his sergeant-major's voice, and retreated nimbly, but only just in time.

"What now!" Min's face came around the door wearing a belligerent expression.

"It's the First Front," her lord explained in what he hoped were winning cadences. "He'd be very glad of a cup of tea and a slice of toast, if that's convenient to you, love. That's all he wants. Just a cuppa and a bit of toast. He's bin having a lay-in. Not feeling too good, see?"

"Oh, well," said his wife grudgingly, but far more mildly than he had dared hope, "I've just made a pot for myself, so if you want to do the toast you can get on with it. Or he can have his lunch early if that suits him better. Cold lamb and pickles," she added firmly, "and very nice too. Just like we're going to have ourselves."

Every fibre of George's being rejected the cold lamb but, like everybody who came in contact with her, he was frightened out of his wits by the landlord's wife.

"I shan't be wanting any lunch," he mumbled. "Just a cup of tea and some toast, if it's all the same to you." He backed to the door, smirking apologetically. "Much obliged to you, M'am, I'm sure."

The curlers disappeared and the two men exchanged covertly sympathetic glances. George retreated upstairs, shortly to reappear in his customary checks, topped by a yellow tie decorated, for some reason, with mermaids. Cowering over the handful of fire he bolted his tea and toast. The landlord drank a cup of tea with him, sipping at the whisky whenever he thought George wasn't looking.

"Going out, sir?"

"Well," said George, "I believe I'll nip up to the Tarn and have a look at this famous skating."

"It's a goodish walk, or so I'm told; I'm not one for walking much meself."

"Nor me. Any chance of hiring a car?"

"They've got an old Humber down at the garage that they sometimes hire out, I believe. If there's anyone there. Ring double-four."

George rang double-four and obtained the use of the Humber for the day. He drank another cup of tea. He said: "I'll be in to dinner tonight. Unless it's the cold lamb, in which case I'll eat out."

The landlord looked hunted.

"It's on account of us being shorthanded, see?"

"I know, old man, I know! So I'll eat out. All the more cold lamb for you, eh?" He grinned ferociously, smote the landlord painfully between the shoulder blades and went out into the cold brightness of the morning.

3.

The Humber was not just old, it was positively senile. In twenty years George had never seen anything like it.

"They don't make 'em like that no more," said the garage proprietor, wiping his hands on an oily rag and gazing at the Humber like a father upon his first-born.

"No," George agreed. "No, I don't suppose they do."

"Treat her gentle," urged the proprietor. "Take it slow an' steady, an' she'll be okay. Sign here, if you please."

George signed on the dotted line and eased himself into the driving seat. He asked what time the garage shut.

"We-ell, normally around five-thirty, sir. Might be a bit sooner today on account of the skating. I'd like to have a bit of a fling meself, see? But if there's nobody about, just back her into the yard. I don't reckon anybody's going to run off with her."

"I don't reckon so, either," said George reverently.

He pressed the clutch and—you had to hand it to her—she went.

Ignoring a variety of knocks and rattles and coping with a tendency for the nearside door to swing violently open, George drove at a sober pace up the long, winding road to the Tarn.

He was uncertain of his true purpose in making this pilgrimage. It was mainly concerned with the necessity for seeing Alison again, but with what object he was not sure.

Since her absurd—her laughable rejection of his proposal—he had not set eyes on Alison, and now he blamed himself for that. He had flustered her, no doubt of it. He had rushed his fence and put her into a proper tizzy. *Thursday is the Women's Institute*, indeed! It only went to show what a tizzy she'd been in.

It had been another wrong move on his part to go stamping off at that point. He should have known that she wouldn't give in all at once. Not after twenty years. . . . What he should have done, of course, was to seize her in his arms and shout, "Damn the Women's Institute!" Treat 'em rough—they liked it that way. The tiny, sloe-eyed Inez—she had liked it that way. So had Yvonne of those astonishing vital statistics, and Mercedes with her cute little moustache, and Donna, whose bite he still cherished in the region of his left ear. So had Claribel Morgensteiner, of Clonkville, Ohio—and a dozen other charmers. He had treated them rough and they had given him all he had asked. . . .

But Miss Alison Penny, of Greeth, Yorkshire, England—wasn't that something else again?

Soberly he mounted the last rise and brought the ancient Humber carefully to rest on the border of the frozen Tarn.

The skating was in full swing.

Slumped in the driving seat George watched with interest the swoopings and curvings, the figures of eight, the effortless circling and turning, the comical crashes and the clever avoidance of crashes. He heard the peculiar, exciting whine of steel on ice, the shouts of recognition as friends passed each other and the laughing shrieks of the fallen. Hair and scarves streamed out behind flying figures, cheeks were red and mouths gaped in happiness or mock terror. He recognized the meagre, bow-legged form of the man, Thompson, who should have been sawing logs or carting beer crates at The Goat. No doubt the lumpish female he escorted was the cook who had consigned him to cold lamb without pity or regret. He hoped she would fall flat on her back, and at that very moment she did so. But she only shrieked with laughter and started off again.

Incredible. . . .

But at least they were enjoying themselves, and he was not.

Why had he come up here? To see Alison? And if he did see her, what could be said amongst this laughing, whirling, crashing throng of people? He knew very well he should have gone to The Laurels and had the thing out with her in the privacy of the living room.

And so he would have done had not the presence of Miss Plum complicated things. . . .

To do him justice, George really was ashamed of his conduct, for which, he admitted, there was no excuse. Having sulked for several days in his unattractive eyrie at The Goat, he had finally decided to call at The Laurels once again, apologize to Alison and allow her—as was her right—to fix the wedding for whatever date suited her.

Having set out filled with virtuous intentions, it had been a sharp irritation to find, on arrival, no Alison, no cosy fire, no welcome at all: only the scared dark eyes of the little Plum creature peering at him around the door as if she feared rape, murder and arson—in that order, and in quick succession. And Alison, if you please, so far from keeping a solitary vigil regretting her infamous words and bewailing her loss, had been up at the Tarn, fooling around with skates like a two-year-old and enjoying a picnic with a party of friends! It was enough to make anybody mad.

All the same, he'd had no right to force his way into the house and behave as he had behaved. There was no excuse for it.

Or was there?

George lit a cigarette, drawing the smoke deep into his lungs and expelling it with slow satisfaction.

For in the dark eyes of Miss Plum peering around the narrow aperture of the door, there had been something more than apprehension.

Excitement? A hint of pleasure? Hope, perhaps?

He ought not to have demanded a drink: even George was not accustomed to drinking whisky at half-past three in the afternoon. He ought not to have insisted on Miss Plum drinking, too, when she obviously disliked it. He ought not to have kissed her. Even though experience had told him that she was enjoying it, despite her struggles, her small, stifled screams.

Yes, she'd enjoyed it all right. Struggling, protesting, yielding, responding with rapture. . . . It had been Inez, Yvonne and a dozen others whose names he had long forgotten all over again. Even the blow she had finally dealt him with her knuckly little fist had carried memories he had thought decently buried.

The blow had been a challenge. After she had hit him George had been aware that he could either go—or stay. It was up to him, that was as plain as the nose on his face.

Well, he had gone. Let that much be put to his credit.

Fuddled with whisky and bemused by the sharp little toes of Miss Plum hacking at his shins while her arms clung tenaciously around his neck, all that was decent in George had bade him go—and quickly.

He had gone.

A stout old party had been standing on the front step, asking silly questions and inviting silly answers.

George had taken a singular pleasure in telling him to go to hell.

4.

Ronnie had skated past the Humber three times before George recognized him.

That was the kid he had seen in Alison's living room at Christmas; the one who had been flushed out by Ada along with the little Plum. A great hulking fellow with a scowl and an incipient moustache who had turned out to be just a schoolboy: fourteen, was it, or fifteen? No more than that, Alison had assured him. Son of the local parson. Roy? Reg . . . ? Ronnie! That was it, Ronnie.

As the boy passed for the fourth time George sketched a wave and beckoned. After pausing to give him a long, supercilious stare, Ronnie skated to the edge of the ice and said curtly: "Was there something?"

"Good morning," George greeted him, affability itself. "I'm looking for Miss Penny but I can't spot her in this crowd. Do you know if she's gone home already?"

Balanced on the outsides of his skates Ronnie said aloofly: "Alison hasn't been up today."

"Why not?" George asked. "I thought she was mad on skating."

"She's had other things to do," Ronnie replied. And his glance said: "So put that in your beard and comb it, you horrible man!"

After a slight pause George asked: "Such as—?"

"Such as minding her own business I shouldn't wonder," the boy retorted.

George threw out the stub of his cigarette and lit another. He said mildly: "You don't like me, do you?"

"I'm not mad about you. Should I be?"

"I can see no reason why you should either like or dislike me, since we are complete strangers. It's more than twenty years since I lived in these parts, and you weren't even born then. If it's not too personal a question—just why do you dislike me?"

Ronnie glowered. But even he found it difficult to say: "I hate your beard and your clothes and your loud voice and the way you stink of money."

Besides, on this bright and frosty morning, with his blood running warm from exercise and the brief episode of Victoria happily behind him, he was not at all sure that he *did* hate George.

Ronnie was, in fact, feeling lonely and fed-up. Pop was at some ghastly conference in Huffley, Alison and Ada snoring in bed, old Hartley coddling a chill. . . . He knew a great many of the people circling the ice: some of them he had grown up with. But none had shown marked enthusiasm for his company. Moreover it had recently dawned on him that he had forgotten to provide himself with any food, and he felt extremely hollow inside. Consequently, when George suggested with becoming humility that he would be glad of a companion for lunch, Ronnie's defences went down without a struggle. He removed his skates and got into the car with alacrity. He even remarked that it was quite decent of George, in tones that were reasonably civil.

"Not at all," George replied, "you're doing me a favour. I hate eating alone. I think we'll try Huffley. There's nothing but cold lamb at The Goat, and I couldn't face that. I expect you know the best place for a real good blow-out," he added respectfully.

"The Royal's okay," Ronnie said: without the slightest authority, since he had never in his life passed the portals of any Huffley hotel. But the Royal was the largest and most expensive-looking and, since he was doing the man a favour, he might as well cash in on it. Steak, he gloated. A walloping great steak with chips and grilled tomatoes and lashings of gravy. And pêche Melba afterward. And mince pies and Stilton cheese. And coffee that smelled and tasted like coffee.

The car door burst open and he was saved from sudden death only by George's hand grabbing him.

"Blimey!" he muttered, much shaken.

"Sorry about that," said George. "Better hang onto the handle. The old girl's not what she was in Julius Caesar's day. The garage bloke warned me to treat her gently but he forgot to mention how she might treat me. Not hurt, are you?"

"Only shock," Ronnie said, grinning palely.

"We'll soon put that right."

"Haven't you a car of your own?"

"I sold my Cadillac before I came. Reckoned I'd get me a new job over here but somehow I haven't got around to it yet. I hired this valuable antique to save me walking to the Tarn. I loathe walking. I never put one foot before the other, not if I can help it."

"It's not much of a walk from The Goat up to The Laurels if you were so anxious to see Alison."

"That's so. But then Miss Plum's always around, and I kind of figured on getting Alison to myself, see? We've got things to talk about."

I'll bet you have, Ronnie thought, light dawning on him suddenly. Grinning broadly, he favoured George with a man-to-man wink.

"So, *you're* the culprit in this mess! And brother—what a mess! Everybody going around in circles telling each other what to do, and nobody doing it. . . . Boy! I'll say you've got plenty to talk about!"

"Mind that door!" George yelled.

Ronnie grabbed it just in time. Sobered, he went on: "It may interest you to know that I've been out since dawn dealing with your blasted mess. And so have Pop and Alison and Ada. I reckon you owe me a damn good lunch, George."

The Humber screamed and lurched to a stop.

George said: "What are you talking about?" in a queer sort of voice.

"Victoria's hopped it," Ronnie told him with relish.

"Hopped it?"

"Walked out of the house with all her bits and pieces and vanished into thin air, I do assure you. Alison rang Pop at some ghastly hour, and Pop hauled me out, and we all went skedaddling about the place searching for Victoria. Pounding the roads on bicycles, frozen stiff, while you were lazing in bed!"

"Have you told the police?"

"Nope. In this country attempted suicide's an offence against the law."

"Who said anything about suicide?" George said sharply.

"It's just a hunch Alison's got."

"The police must be informed at once."

"But not by you, old man. Not unless you want to gum the works up properly. Take my tip and keep your nose out of this. You've done quite enough damage."

George stared at the boy. Then he said: "Hang onto that door!" His foot came down on the accelerator, the Humber shuddered and leaped forward.

Ronnie shut his eyes.

When next he opened them, they were in the parking area behind the Royal Hotel and George was already out of the car.

"You go in and get a table," he said. "Order whatever you fancy, and the same for me. I'm going to telephone."

"Hello," said Ada's voice. "Who is it?"

"It's George," said George.

"Oh, it is, is it? Well, let me tell you, George, you want your head examined—and then banged agen t'wall!"

"Look, Ada, I want to talk to Alison."

"Then you can want. She's asleep. And she's going to stay asleep. And I don't mind telling you I'd nobbut just dropped oft meself."

"Sorry, Ada. But I've only just heard the news. About Miss Plum, I mean. Ada, Alison's got to inform the police at once."

"Miss Alison will inform the police when she's a mind to," said the voice. And, unconsciously echoing Ronnie, it added: "Keep out of this, George, you've done enough damage already."

"What's all this about damage!" George shouted. "I drank half a bottle of whisky and kissed a girl. Is that a crime? If any damage was done it was to *me*. The whisky got my liver properly and the girl smacked my face. So what?"

Ada's voice said primly: "And serve you right. We don't hold with such goings on, not in Greeth."

"Look, I must talk to Alison, Ada."

"I'm none wakin' her."

"After lunch, then. Surely she'll be awake by then."

"Happen. I don't know if she'll see you. I don't hold out no promises, mind. She's spittin' mad at you, George, an' that's the truth. Best thing you can do in my opinion is keep out of it until she sends for you. Of course, if you should happen to find Miss Plum yourself. . . ."

"Find her? How can I find her? I don't know where to look."

"No more did we. But we *looked*."

"Oh—hell's bells! All right, I'll run around a bit and see what I can do. And tell Alison she ought to get the police on the job right away. Tell her I said so. Be seeing you."

"Ah," Ada's voice said non-committally.

Ronnie was halfway through a plate of steak and chips, grilled tomatoes and a tall glass of iced ginger ale.

"Thought you were never coming," he remarked with his mouth full. "Sorry, the steak's off now. But there's a choice of boiled cod and cold lamb. What you might call poetic justice," he grinned.

George glared at him resentfully.

"Bring me a large whisky and soda," he told the hovering waiter. Presently, poking the pallid cod about his plate he asked: "Where do you want to be dropped off? Up at the Tarn again? Or do you want to go home?"

With the last chipped potato in his mouth Ronnie said: "Home, I think. I don't feel so much like skating any more. And I've got to mend a puncture."

"Right. Have you finished?"

"I ordered pêche Melba and mince pies and coffee," Ronnie mentioned querulously.

"The pêche Melba," George flung over his shoulder. "And another double for me."

He waited until Ronnie could eat no more, which was a very long time. Then he paid the bill and thrust Ronnie into the Humber with the savage recommendation to hang onto the door for all he was worth.

CHAPTER THIRTEEN

1.

HAVING ejected Ronnie at the vicarage gates, George headed north-by-west.

Not that it mattered which way he went. Miss Plum had a good nine hours' start and she could have taken any one of a dozen different directions. By now she was probably miles out of the district; or she was lying behind a stone wall, stiff as a ram-rod and turning a nasty shade of blue.

Of course, it *was* remotely possible that she made a hole in the ice; but it would have been quite a job, and nothing in George's vast experience of women encouraged belief in it. For one of Victoria Plum's peculiar make-up, that gesture would have been too unspectacular and much, much too final.

Sitting down for a breather behind a wall, now—that was a different kettle of fish. It was a thing anyone would feel bound to do after trudging for hours in this ghastly cold, probably on an empty stomach and feeling as dreary as hell, anyway. From sitting down to dropping asleep would be only too easy, the consequences only too predictable. . . .

He drove for a few miles, pondering the subject; shifting his eyes from right to left with neither hope nor reward.

I'm crazy, he thought. This isn't the Antarctic or anything, even if it feels like it. This is Yorkshire, England. In England people don't snuff out just because they've been out in the snow for a few hours. They may go stiff and blue, but it's a safe bet they're not dead. All I've got to do is keep looking behind the walls.

But how did one see behind walls while one was driving a car, with the door crashing open every few yards and the petrol gauge looking decidedly ominous? Let somebody tell George that one! It was not only crazy, it was a sheer impossibility. He stopped the car and got out, climbed the frozen verge and gazed apprehensively across vast, undulating expanses of almost unbroken white. Here and there a few withered trees clung together, their backs hunched against the bitter wind; something that looked like the roof of a shed sloped into the drift; something that might or might not be the legs of a dead sheep stuck up sharply grey against the white. But there were no footprints, no faint cries for help, no smallest sign of human proximity or disaster. On the other side of the road the prospect was almost identical.

He climbed back into the car, drove for another mile and I tried again, with the same result.

He kept on trying; stopping every mile or so to stare helplessly about the deserted countryside. He even tried shouting her name, feeling like a fool yet compelled to do it.

"Victoria! . . . Victoria! . . . Miss Plum!" The name whinnied thinly on the wind and was lost in whiteness.

After the fourth stop the Humber dug in her heels and refused to budge.

George pressed the self-starter. He pressed it again and again—and yet again. The Humber responded with a life-like imitation of an asthmatical old woman about to breathe her last. The needle of the petrol gauge flickered wildly and abruptly ceased to function.

George said all the swear words he had ever learned and made up a few more for good measure.

He got out again and began a protracted search for a starting crank. Time was getting on and the light was beginning to fail. He had no idea where he was or how far he would have to walk to find help. He had eaten nothing all day but a slice of toast and a few mouthfuls of damp cod. His stomach rolled protestingly and his legs felt like cotton wool.

There must be a starting handle somewhere. Nobody rented a car without a starting crank, of course.

Frantically rummaging in the trunk he brought to light a number of oily rags, several sweet boxes, a vacuum thermos minus its screw top, a copy of the Highway Code, (*"Give me strength!"* he snarled), a child's knitted cap, five assorted wrenches, a button-hook and—of all things—a can of baked beans.

There was no starting crank.

He tried the self-starter again.

It was too much for the old woman, and this time she really did breathe her last.

He tried with all his might to shift her closer to the side of the road, but failed to budge her so much as an inch. He tried—and failed—to switch on the headlights.

There was nothing to do except start walking.

When he had been walking for what seemed like hours, George suddenly realized that the hard thing in his hand was the can of baked beans.

He regarded the object with affection, almost with reverence. There had been times in his life when he had kept body and soul together almost exclusively with the aid of baked beans. He'd come a long way since then, but he still liked them. All you needed was a rock, an accurate eye and a bit of luck.

He found a suitable stone and hit the can a mighty whack.

The can leaped into the air and rolled down the bank, disappearing into deep snow.

George followed it. His legs sank deep into the drift and appeared to freeze solid from the knees downwards, but he prodded about doggedly and was presently rewarded by a sharp pain in his hand. He withdrew it gingerly, still clasping a wicked curve of milk bottle. Cursing, he sucked the wound, wrapped it tightly in his handkerchief and went on prodding. He found an old boot, a dead bird and a number of very painful brambles; but the baked beans did finally come to fight.

Staggering up to the road again, he was about to continue his assault upon the can when two facts became only too apparent. Through the jagged hole issued the most appalling smell and a small quantity of greenish liquid.

So they had baked beans as well in Julius Caesar's time, George thought bitterly.

He threw the can down and kicked it violently. It landed twenty yards ahead, slid a few feet and waited for him, bang in the middle of the road.

It was a challenge and George accepted it.

Trudging back along the tracks of the Humber he kicked the can before him, taking a savage satisfaction—almost a pride—in the accuracy of his aim.

No vehicle passed him; no pedestrian. He might indeed have been in the Antarctic, he reflected bleakly.

Yet he did vaguely remember having passed, on the way out, a cottage or a small farm. It seemed a long, long time ago, but he must surely come upon it again, sooner or later.

Doggedly, feeling like death, George trudged on; blowing on frozen fingers, stamping frozen feet, and kicking the can of beans before him.

2.

He brooded upon Victoria Plum; and presently the thought of her obsessed him.

Small and thin and bloodless, without the constitution of a field mouse or the spunk of a rabbit, Victoria had crept from the warm safety of Alison's home and gone out into the darkness, the icy wind, the black, lonely desolation.

If he were feeling like death, what must she have felt? What must she be feeling by now?

Or was she already beyond feeling? Beyond loneliness, hunger, exhaustion, repentance. . . .

Repentance? What had she to repent of?

Was it Victoria's fault if she had been left alone at The Laurels while Alison and Ada went off to enjoy themselves? Was it her fault if he had forced his way in, demanded whisky and made her drink with him? Was she to blame if life had dealt her a raw deal right from the start—right from the font, you might almost say?

Victoria Plum!

Why should anybody think it so funny to be called Victoria Plum? Was it any funnier than Dorothy Perkins, or Dwight D. Eisenhower, or John Smith?

He kicked the can.

He didn't really believe for one moment that she had deliberately set out to do away with herself. Not in the icy blackness of a winter's night. Not carrying all her worldly goods in a suitcase. That didn't make enough sense even for Victoria Plum. No, *sir*. But, uneasily, he had to admit that she might have intended to put a good many miles between herself and Greeth before morning. She might have meant to board an early bus at some point where she wouldn't be recognized. Or perhaps to catch the first train to London. Or to thumb a lift in a truck.

She might have *meant* to.

But suppose she'd missed the bus; had lacked enough money for the tram fare; hadn't seen any truck?

What would Victoria Plum do then, poor thing? What else but sit down in the snow and cry? And freeze? . . .

This is where we came in, George thought wretchedly.

He kicked the can.

The whole setup was crazy. If Victoria had wanted to leave The Laurels, all she had to do was walk out. If Alison wanted to get rid of her, she had only to say, "Scram!" No need to do the whole thing in glorious technicolor on a wide screen.

As soon as he reached civilization—if ever he did reach it— he'd phone Alison right away and tell her straight that if she didn't get on to the police, he would.

Come to think of it, there must have been quite a showdown last night, what with the Plum weeping and trying to explain and Alison being high-and-mighty. . . .

No doubt about it, Alison was no longer the meek and dutiful little daughter he had attempted—and failed—to seduce from parental authority twenty years ago.

Women could be fiends to each other; even the small, soft sheltered ones. Most of all the small, soft, sheltered ones. . . . Look what Alison had done to *him*!

He had returned to the land of his birth, the land of his first and only innocent love, resolved to atone, to reform, to remake both her life and his own.

And what had happened?

Precisely nothing.

He had been dealt with adroitly. He had been relegated to the *very-well,-but-don't-do-it-again* category—and that without any apparent effort on Alison's part or effective protest on his own.

Let's face it, thought George, taking a pot shot at the can and going back for another kick, Alison is tough and Victoria is not.

More and more he sympathized with Victoria.

Victoria was silly: but then, the sort of women George liked *were* silly. They needed a man to stabilize them. They needed a man to tell them what to do and when to do it. They needed a man to tell them when they ought to get married. And when they'd been told, they didn't go jabbering about the Women's Institute.

No, *sir*. . . .

What would have happened had Alison said yes, and flopped into his arms as he had fully expected her to?

With a sudden, appalling clarity George saw the whole thing like a map spread out before him.

He saw Alison's genteel upbringing weaving chains about him; her reserve limiting his lustful appetites; her love of the familiar checking his instincts for wandering. He saw himself bound more and ever more securely into the comfortable life of The Laurels; of church activities; of little bridge parties and little concerts in the village hall, and all the small, stultifying irritations of the Cubs, the Amateur Dramatic Society, the Glee Club, and all the rest of it. He saw himself taking the plate around at Matins, handing cucumber sandwiches at stuffy little tea parties and catching the ten-thirty bus into Huffley for the week end shopping. A Cadillac would be deemed superfluous with the bus being so handy. He would be taken to Bournemouth for two weeks every summer and spend the winter evenings watching television. Even Daddy's port would not last forever. . . .

I must have been mad, George thought, to imagine I could uproot her after all these years and whisk her away into the sun. . . .

He kicked the can.

His feet slipped from beneath him and he sat down heavily in the snow.

Now I've cracked an ankle, he thought drearily. Or slipped a disc, or something.

He sat still awhile, fearful of what injury he might have sustained.

Now I shall know, he thought, what it's like to sit in the snow and die. To go stiff and cold and blue . . . I wonder how long it will take me? I wonder how long it took *her*? . . .

Victoria. Victoria Plum. . . . It was supposed to be a joke.

George had never felt less like laughing in his life.

She was no oil painting; but she'd got something that Alison lacked. Something with which he was familiar, that he knew how to deal with. She had hacked at his shins and smacked his face; but her arms had clung to him and her lips had been hot and surprisingly soft. . . .

Poor little Victoria.

Poor George. . . .

Tentatively waggling each limb in turn, flexing his spine with infinite caution, George found himself able to get to his knees and crawl a few paces.

Where did that blasted can go to? he wondered savagely. He never found out because, at that moment, a blessed sound came to his ears: the sound of a car approaching behind him.

Hooting wildly, the car skidded to a stop and the driver got out. He was a meagre little man in a too large overcoat and a knitted Balaclava helmet. His walrus moustache bristled with concern.

"What's the matter, chum? Had a fall?"

"No," George replied tonelessly, "I'm doing it for a bet. How much farther is it to Brighton?"

"That your car back along the road?"

"I hired it. Just for the one day. That's all I asked of her—just to keep going for one short day. Two pounds I paid for her—and not even a starting handle, if you can believe that. . . . Give me a hand and I'll try to get up."

The man hauled George to his feet, brushed snow from his clothes and assisted him to limp the few steps to the car. He offered to drive back to the abandoned Humber and give a try with his own crank, but this suggestion George rejected with passion. "I never want to set eyes on that bloody car again," he said. "Two pounds I paid for her—just for the one day. She wouldn't fetch more than that for scrap, so I reckon I've bought her. And anyone that likes to bring a starting handle along is welcome to her as far as I'm concerned. Anyway, there's not enough petrol. . . . Where were you heading for?"

"Huffley. Where was you?"

"Greeth. But Huffley will do if there's any chance of getting a taxi."

"That'll be okay. Joe Turnbull will run you there in no time. I'd do it meself, but I'm late as it is and the Missus'll have it in for me. You know what women are."

"I know," George agreed.

"She's doing me a steak-and-kidney pie, and she kind of prides herself on her pastry, my Missus does. If I'm not there on the dot I get it in the neck, see what I mean?"

"Say no more."

The car started with the minimum of fuss.

George slumped in his seat, eyes closed and hands thrust deep into his pockets. His bones ached and his head ached and his stomach rolled interminably. Every now and then he remembered Alison and Victoria Plum, but in the main his thoughts were concerned only with food. Steak-and-kidney pie. With a mountain of mashed potatoes flanking the golden crust on one side and a mountain of Brussels sprouts on the other. And all awash with a sea of thick brown gravy. The very thought of it made George's senses swim. Oh, god, he thought, why do we worry about women when there's steak-and-kidney pie? . . .

The Balaclava helmet chattered away. Dimly George gathered that he was relating the story of his life. He caught a few phrases here and there. "Took me into the business," he heard, and: "Got to go careful, what with three kids and another on the way." There was some trouble, he gathered, about a mortgage, and a good deal of boasting about "The Boy" who had recently, it appeared, been awarded a scholarship for "The Grammar."

George made the noises required of him and thought about steak-and-kidney pie.

3.

When they reached the garage Joe Turnbull was out on a job.

An embittered young mechanic who appeared to be in sole charge could offer no information beyond the fact that Joe might be twenty minutes or he might be a couple of hours. It was all according, said the youth, wiping oily hands on a filthy rag.

"Where's Alf, then?" George's benefactor asked sharply.

"Where do *you* think! Alf's up at the Tarn," replied the youth; and added spitefully: "I hope he breaks the ice. Go down three times an' come up twice, that's what I hope Alf does."

The Balaclava helmet turned this way and that.

"I'd tek you meself if it wasn't for the Missus. I'm late as it is, see?"

"I'll go by bus," George decided wearily. "When's the next bus for Greeth?"

"One just gone," said the young mechanic, not without relish. "Be another along in twenty minutes."

"Just time for a quick one," comforted the Balaclava helmet.

"Not openin' time for another hour," the youth said triumphantly.

"Cuppa tea, then. There's a good café right opposite the bus stop. I'll run you there in a jiffy."

On the pavement outside Mab's Café George's friend shook him warmly by the hand, wishing him Godspeed, coupled with the hope that no internal injuries would subsequently come to light as a result of his fall. "Me Auntie Ellen," he remembered sombrely, "her foot nobbut just slipped off of the edge of the curb, like you might do a hundred times an' think nowt of it. Just slipped off of the curb and—*wham!*—her leg broke like a match stick in two places. Hardly credit it, would you? But there it was. Just slipped off of the curb, an' she were in t'infirmary sixteen weeks! Only goes to show, don't it?"

Hollowly George agreed that it only went to show.

Suddenly the Balaclava helmet doubled up with laughter. He hit George painfully in the region of the solar plexus.

"'Doin' it for a bet'!" he spluttered. "'How far is it to Brighton?' That's a good 'un, that is! I must tell the Missus that one when I get 'ome!"

The tea was thick, dark and sickeningly sweet, but it put a little heart into George. It enabled him to stagger across the pavement just in time to board the bus for Greeth; to find himself a seat; to proffer the correct fare and the demand to be wakened, if necessary, outside The Goat, and there to be set down.

He closed his eyes and tried to relax.

He thought about food.

There would be the cold lamb and the peaches and evaporated. It didn't sound like steak-and-kidney pie, but it sounded pretty good, all the same.

He would take a hot bath, and then he would get straight into bed and they could bring the food up on a tray.

He would order a bottle of Scotch, too.

He would eat and drink and sleep, and forget all about Victoria Plum and Alison Penny; forget about all the women who had ever crossed his path. And tomorrow he would pack his grips and go. Well, not tomorrow, perhaps—in all decency he would have to stay until this mystery of Miss Plum was cleared up one way or the other—but at the earliest possible moment. He'd go to Paris. Or maybe he'd settle for that yacht and go wherever fancy called. Or should he go back to Rio?

Go, anyway. Go was the operative word.

If Alison didn't want him, there were those who did, he thought; and tried to make himself believe it.

The bus bumbled cautiously along the treacherous roads. A conversational hum of flat, north-country voices rose all around him, punctuated by the sharp *ping* of the ticket machine. His head nodded. He started up aggressively when his shoulder was shaken, wincing with the pain the sudden movement gave him.

"What the hell!" he snarled.

"Come on, chum, wake up," shouted the conductor, imperturbably cheerful. "You asked for it, didn't you? Show a leg, now, if you want The Goat."

Painfully George descended from the bus and went into the pub through the private entrance. Home at last: it did actually feel like home.

The landlord sat with his feet up beside the fire, dozing over yesterday's newspaper. To him George related, with suitable omissions, the saga of the day's doings, and issued instructions for the proprietor of the garage to be informed of the approximate whereabouts of the Humber, in the unlikely event of his wanting it back. "I," George added, "am now going to give myself a great hot bath and go to bed. Bring me a bottle of Scotch when I ring. And food. Lots of food. Even if it *is* the cold lamb and the peaches and evaporated."

"And that," said the landlord, with something approaching animation, "is just where you're wrong. We got some hikers in for lunch and she worked the cold lamb off on them. Then she had to set to and make a pie for your supper. No kidneys, I regret to say, but as nice a piece of steak as you'd come across in a day's march. And though I says it as maybe shouldn't, I've yet to find the woman that bakes a better pie than my old trouble-and-strife. Provided she's in the mood. Smell that!" he added, throwing open the baize door with a dramatic gesture.

George sniffed the lambent air. His very bones seemed to dissolve in a lush anticipation. Oh, boy! Oh, boy, boy, boy! . . .

"A bath," he muttered, "and bed. And steak pie. And a bottle of Scotch. And sleep. . . . It's too good to be true."

"And that," said the landlord, dropping into depression again, "is where you happen to be *right*. About the sleep, I mean. Because I don't reckon you're going to get much of that, not yet awhile." He scratched his armpits in some embarrassment. "You got a visitor," he explained. "Turned up just after lunch, she did, asking for you. I told 'er I'd no idea when you'd be back, an' she said she'd wait. Said she'd wait in your room, see? Said she'd bin on the go for hours an' had got to lie down . . . I didn't rightly know what to do. The wife had popped up to the butch-er's, and there was I, alone with a strange female who looked ready to pass out any minute. Well, I mean to say, what *could* I do? . . . I made her a cuppa and showed her up to your room . . . I haven't told the wife yet. I reckoned that was something you'd do better than me, see what I mean?"

The two men stared at each other, united in male appre-hension.

"Get me a double Scotch," George said hoarsely.

The landlord gave him a double Scotch, and one for himself too.

"Cheers," they told each other timidly.

After the Scotch George recovered a little.

"I expect it's my sister," he offered, and the landlord nodded. "That's what I thought."

"Supposing my sister wants to stay the night—can you fix it?"

"No problem there. The single room next to yours is empty. Only wants the bed aired."

"Okay. Let's have another."

They had another.

"Go easy with the wife," begged the landlord. "Think up a good story and stick to it, see? That's all I ask. She's in a good mood at the moment, see what I mean?"

George set his glass down with a thump and grasped the landlord's hand. He said with emotion: "What a world this could be, if there were no women in it."

"There wouldn't be no world," the landlord reminded him.

Slowly and painfully George ascended the stairs.

Outside the door of his room he hesitated, pressing chilled hands against throbbing temples.

It *could* be Alison—but he knew very well it was not.

Alison would never stoop to such tactics. Alison's life was ordered and controlled; bounded by the church, the Cubs, the Glee Club, the Women's Institute on the one hand and two weeks at Bournemouth on the other. Alison was strong, serene, self-sufficient.

Alison had no need of him, or of any man.

It could only be Victoria Plum.

Weak, clinging, aggravating, silly little Victoria, who had never known security, never profited by experience; who possessed, nonetheless, some quality that Alison lacked; that George could understand; that George needed. . . .

There, upon the threshold of that dingy bedroom at The Goat, Greeth, Yorkshire, England, George bade farewell to his mis-spent youth, to romance and all nostalgic dreams; opened his heart to reality, to the known and familiar; and opened his bedroom door with a sudden surge of relief, a pleasure that was surprisingly warm.

"Hello, honey," he said softly, "were you wanting me?"

CHAPTER FOURTEEN

1.

"IF YOU ask me," Mrs. Platt said, looking Stanley straight in the eye, "I think you're looking for trouble."

Stanley buttoned his overcoat, returning Mrs. Platt's gaze as severely—or nearly as severely—as he had received it. He said with a nice mixture of dignity and humour: "As I recall it, Mrs. Platt, I did *not* ask you." He pulled on his sheepskin gloves. "Whether I like it or not, Mrs. Platt, I am obliged to go out whatever my personal feelings on the subject may be. Nothing, I assure you, but the strongest feelings of duty prompt me to what may well be considered a foolhardy project. When I return I shall go straight to bed and there remain until I am fully recovered. That much I can promise you."

Mrs. Platt sniffed. Stanley ignored the sniff and went out into the cold, steel-grey twilight. He marched with a purposeful stride in the direction of The Laurels.

He brooded over Mrs. Platt with some misgivings. This morning she had flounced, this afternoon she had sniffed. Could it possibly be that Mrs. Platt was getting out of hand? Would it become necessary in the not-too-distant future to take a firm line with Mrs. Platt—even to the extent of giving her notice to leave?

Should Mrs. Platt continue to flounce and to sniff and air her opinions on the way he conducted his life, then he and Mrs. Platt would have to part.

Profoundly Stanley hoped it would not come to this. It was ridiculous to think of any woman as being irreplaceable; yet in the light of previous experience he feared that such was the truth. It was a most depressing thought.

Yet what were the alternatives?

Marry Alison Penny?

That would mean leaving the intricate web of comfort he had woven around himself with such care, and going to live at The Laurels: he had no illusions about that.

The Laurels was well enough, but it did not embody his specialized notions of comfort. It would need a lot of reorganization before it came up to his own standards; and it was certain that Alison would take a poor view of being reorganized.

Then, too, there was Ada.

If Mrs. Platt flounced and sniffed, Ada would go a lot further. Ada would put her hands on her hips and tell him, in vulgar parlance, where he got off. Ada was a very frightening woman.

There was this mysterious George to be reckoned with, also. George who, if Mrs. Platt's information were true, had come back from foreign parts after twenty years with the intention of marrying Alison and whisking her away to the other side of the world. If that was what Alison wanted, Stanley thought distastefully, then let her get on with it. After his one brief encounter with George he had no intention of repeating the experience.

The only other alternative, as far as Stanley could see, was to marry Mrs. Platt.

The very thought of this was anathema!

In any case it wouldn't work. Housekeepers could be dismissed and wives could not. Housekeepers might flounce and sniff but wives could employ far more subtle and sinister methods. Wives could ignore your likes and dislikes, impose their own conceptions of your needs over your expressed commands, and get away with it. If the worst came to the worst wives could—and frequently did—take you to court upon such flimsy pretexts as mental cruelty, et cetera. . . .

Stanley turned up the collar of his overcoat. The wind was keener than he had anticipated and he wondered if it might not be more prudent to turn back at once, retire to bed again and, for once in a way, admit that Mrs. Platt was right.

He was now, however, much nearer to The Laurels than to his own home, so he pressed on, hoping against hope that Alison and not Ada would open the door to him.

He thought suddenly: I could marry Miss Plum. . . .

The thought took him in the midriff, temporarily winding him.

Miss Plum would marry him like a shot. He had no illusions about it: he knew very well that Miss Plum would marry practically any man who asked her to do so. Miss Plum, he believed, was looking for security rather than romance.

But neither was Stanley looking for romance.

Miss Plum was silly but she was teachable. She would be grateful for the smallest kindness and only too anxious to repay. She had, apparently, no relations to complicate matters. She was quiet. She was not bad-looking and would no doubt blossom in the security and dignity of wifehood.

Hitherto marriage had played no great part in Stanley's design for living. Now it began to assume an enormous significance increasing with each step that brought him nearer to The Laurels.

It did, of course, largely depend on whether or not Miss Plum were still alive. This fact struck him sharply as he clicked the gate behind him and began to climb the steep path to the front door.

Alison admitted him.

She was paler, he thought, than usual, but appeared composed as she led the way into the living room where tea was laid on a small table beside the fire.

"I will ring for another cup."

"Not for me, dear lady. I had tea before venturing out into this wind, which is small but treacherously keen."

"Would it not have been wiser to remain indoors, seeing that you have a chill?" Alison suggested rather coolly. She took a neat bite from a fragment of thin bread and butter, avoiding Stanley's eyes. "If only you were not so stubborn about having the telephone installed you could have saved yourself a journey."

"Now, Alison, you know perfectly well how I detest the telephone," he said pettishly. "I have been a slave to the thing all my life and am only too thankful to be rid of it. I did not come here to talk of telephones. Or—yes, in a way, I did, because I came to urge you to lose no more time in calling the police, if you have not already done so."

"I have not done so," Alison stated, taking another piece of bread and butter.

"Why in the world not? I told Hubert most emphatically that it was the only possible course to take. I am surprised he did not pass on my message to you."

"Oh, but he did. What is more, he tried to persuade me himself. They all tried."

"And you refused?"

"Until all other methods had failed—yes."

"But *why*?"

Alison set down her cup and turned her clear blue eyes upon him.

"Victoria Plum has lived in my house for more than two months," she said slowly. "I cannot and will not put up with her any longer."

Stanley's first impulse was to say: "And why should you, indeed!?" But then he recalled that he had almost decided to marry Miss Plum, which put him in a quandary. Inclining his handsome head and drumming manicured fingernails upon the arms of his chair, he waited for Alison to continue which, presently she did.

"If the police search for and find Victoria, they will go very thoroughly into her history. After which she will either be put into an institution of some sort which, in my opinion, would be the end of her, or some person will be made responsible for her future. And that person, Stanley, will be me! *Now* do you understand?"

Stanley understood only too well. Alison's solemn statement, with all its implications, absolutely petrified him.

He ventured feebly: "Do you not think you take too gloomy a view of this poor girl's condition?"

"I have lived with Miss Plum, Stanley, and you have not."

There was a pause while Stanley thought about this.

"And if you should find her yourself?"

"If I find her myself, I shall immediately do what I should have done long ago: find her lodgings in Huffley, put her in touch with the Labour Exchange, and wash my hands of her."

They gazed at each other across the blazing hearth. Absent-mindedly Stanley reached for a buttered scone, nibbling it pensively.

"You realize, of course, that this poor creature may already be beyond any human jurisdiction?"

"In which case," Alison said briskly, "there is no problem."

Stanley put down the half-eaten scone. He was shocked. Shocked to the very core. That Alison—*Alison*, of all people— should say such a thing! It struck at the very foundations of one's belief in human nature. It undermined the whole social structure. It was monstrous. Unthinkable . . .

He said: "It is your affair. You must do as you think best." In deep displeasure he got to his feet and went out into the hall; put on cardigan, overcoat, scarves, galoshes, hat and sheepskin gloves as if he clad himself in armour.

As indeed he did. Armour against women. Against any woman. Against all women who aired their opinions and pursued their paths in the face of authority and experience; women who ran away and had to be found in a killing east wind; women who flounced and sniffed; women who openly despised him.

Women. . . Stanley disliked them all. However, he reminded himself with bitter triumph, he could do without women. He had done without them all his life and was none the worse for it. He could continue to do without them. If the worst came to the worst, he could cook and clean for himself as he had done for many years, with admirable results.

Plunging homeward, head down to the bitter wind, which had risen alarmingly in the last hour, Stanley thought vindictively: One more flounce out of Mrs. Platt! One more sniff—that's all! . . .

Hubert's crazy little car passed him and stopped with a shriek of brakes. The left-hand door opened and an untidy head appeared.

"Hop in!" cried Hubert; too exuberantly, as usual.

After the briefest hesitation Stanley accepted the invitation, ensconcing himself with great caution and testing the door handle several times while Hubert revved the engine without mercy, and with no worthwhile result.

"Any news of Miss Plum?"

"No!"

"What?"

"NO!" Stanley bellowed, shaking his negative gestures with his hands.

The roaring ceased. Hubert shouted: "Has she told the police?"

"No."

They stared at each other. They knew, both of them, that the police should be informed; but each knew that neither of them would do it.

"I thought you were supposed to be ill," Hubert said reproachfully as the car finally responded to persuasion.

"I am ill," Stanley replied hollowly. "Nonetheless, I felt it my duty to visit Alison and try to persuade her . . ."

"And you failed?"

"I failed."

Hubert took a corner perilously.

"You ought to have a telephone," he said.

Stanley let that one go. He was almost sure his chest felt tighter, and when he swallowed there was a small sting at the back of his throat which terrified him.

Home, he thought, panic-stricken. Home, with aspirins and hot milk and whisky, and two hot-water bottles. Home to Mrs. Platt. . . .

2.

As soon as Hubert had decanted Stanley at the gate of his house he drove back to the vicarage and parked the car in the leaky little outbuilding that served for garage, tool shed and repository for outworn furniture and unwanted articles of all description. He turned the key in the flimsy padlock and stood for a moment in the windy darkness looking toward his home.

The vicarage stared back at him with sightless eyes. Its bulk loomed black against the blackness, shut in by moving shapes of trees that creaked menacingly.

There was no light anywhere but in the kitchen, and that, Hubert rightly guessed, had nothing to do with any activity on the part of his housekeeper, who was still too poorly to do anything but skate. No savoury smell would greet him as he entered. No cosy fire awaited him. No gentle, womanly hand and voice were there for his comfort and delight. Edna, he thought sadly. . . . But even that secret and special sorrow was merged and lost in the all-pervading weariness that beset him.

He was tired to death. He had been up at crack of dawn, cycling about the countryside in the abortive search for Miss Plum. He had attended his conference in Huffley, which had dragged out drearily far beyond the expected hour. In a café he had picked at a meal whose sole merit had been that of cheapness. He had driven several miles out of his way in order to visit a supposed invalid, and had received no answer to his knocking. He had returned home to find a scribbled message from Ronnie that another parishioner, now located ten miles in the opposite direction, was lying on a bed of sickness and asking for him. *"Old Marsdon's popping off,"* Ronnie had written. *"He wants to see you pronto."*

A faint smile touched Hubert's lips. Poor Ronnie: so young and full of life; so much in need of care and attention and companionship. Yet his needs must give way to the needs of an ancient, dying man who, by the time Hubert reached him, had been too far gone into the shadows to know or care whose hand he held, whose voice prayed, whose tears were shed. . . .

Well, old Marsdon had popped off at last and Hubert had been free to return home.

And then there had been Stanley with the news that Miss Plum had not yet been found; and the even more disturbing news that Alison was still refusing to inform the police.

He gave a great jaw-cracking yawn and began to stumble toward the house. *Bed*, he thought. Never mind about fires and food. Just let me get into bed and sleep—that's all.

*

The kitchen door opened and Ronnie burst out, whistling shrilly and nearly knocking his parent flat.

"Cripes!" he yelped. "This you, Pop? What on earth are you mooning out here for? I'm afraid the kitchen's in a bit of a mess, but at least it's warm. I've got a good fire going, and I've opened half-a-dozen cans and bunged the lot in a saucepan together, and it smells terrific. Have you locked up? I was just going to get another wrench. I'm mending Ada's bike, so watch your step. As a matter of fact, you can give me a hand . . ."

Hubert surrendered the garage key and went into the kitchen, watching his step as he had been well advised to do.

The place was a shambles. Surely no one bicycle could contain so many parts! Straddling the debris Hubert shut his eyes tightly and concentrated on keeping awake. He had kept awake for the dying, who had neither heeded nor needed him. Now he must keep awake for the living.

The warmth of the fire revived him a little. The smell of Ronnie's stew revived him even more. It certainly smelled good. He had not realized how hungry he was until he smelled Ronnie's stew. It was good of the boy, he thought gratefully, divesting himself of his outer garments and picking his way delicately among the bits and pieces that had once been—and must again be—Ada's borrowed bicycle. It certainly looked as if he were needed to lend a hand.

Ronnie returned, shutting the door upon the night. Shutting out the black cold, the loneliness, the bitter, bitter loneliness. . . .

"Just hold this," he ordered. "Hold it steady. I shan't be a jiffy."

"I thought it was only a puncture?"

"That's what I thought until I started investigating. Between you and me, I don't know why Ada didn't break her blooming neck on this contraption. Anybody but Ada would have. Hold it steady, for God's sake! . . . Sorry, Pop. But hold it steady, will you? I might as well make a proper job of it, now I've started. I've got nothing else to do."

"Did you go up to the Tarn?"

"I did. And what do you know—that fellow of Alison's took me out to lunch. At the Royal, of all places! I ate so much I would have broken the ice afterward, so I got him to run me home instead. . . . There, that's done it, I think. Now I've only got to shove this in—so. And this—so . . ." He worked away manfully while Hubert held things and handed things, secretly marvelling at his son's dexterity.

In no time at all, it seemed, the bicycle was reassembled and Ronnie was standing up, brushing off his hands with pardonable pride. "This," he solemnly asserted, "is my good deed for the entire holiday. From now on I shall probably be a bastard of the first water. Sorry, Pop, but you know what I mean."

Hubert knew what he meant.

It's what he means, he thought, not what he says. What he says doesn't really matter at all. Even what he *does* isn't all that important. It's what he means that matters. . . .

The stew smelled delicious. He got two plates out of the cupboard and put them on the side of the stove to heat. He cut thick slices of bread. He found a reasonably clean cloth and set the table while Ronnie cleaned up the floor and washed grease from his hands. He thought gratefully, humbly: he's a good boy, really.

With the clear, uncanny prescience that is given at times to all parents, he knew that everything was going to be all right, if only he held on long enough.

"Do the cleaning-up tomorrow, eh?" Ronnie said, yawning.

"Yes. Anyway, tomorrow Mrs. Hart may feel well enough to stop skating," Hubert said hopefully. "You get to bed, you've had a long day." He stood hesitantly before the fire, rubbing up the back of his hair. He would have liked to kiss Ronnie good night, but he knew he must not do this. "I shan't be long after you," he mumbled.

He struggled into his overcoat and went out. Ronnie heard the *crunch-crunch* of his feet going around the side of the house and then the gate slamming to and fro in the wind. Hubert always forgot to shut gates.

He knew where Pop was going. Nearly every night Pop went into the dark, empty, echoing church and stayed there for a time, all alone. Praying, he supposed. What does he get out of it? he wondered gloomily. What is there in it for him. Or for me? It doesn't bring Mother back. It doesn't make anything easier, more comfortable. It doesn't get us any money. It doesn't make us understand each other. . . . Does anybody ever understand anybody else?

He kicked at the shabby hearthrug and smoked half a cigarette. He went upstairs and brushed his teeth. He put a hot-water bottle in his bed and another one in Pop's. He pulled his tie undone, staring at himself in the mirror. God, what a sight! he thought. All these pimples. And fuzz in between the pimples. How do you avoid pimples when you shave? How long is Pop going to be? He was practically asleep on his feet when he got home. Why couldn't he go straight to bed? It'll be cold as death in the church. Cold as death. And he might fall asleep. He might be asleep already. . . .

After a while he went downstairs again, pulled on an overcoat and a scarf and followed his father out into the night.

Hubert was kneeling on the chancel steps in the flickering light of a single candle. He did not stir when the church door creaked open, clicked shut. He did not stir when the footsteps approached. A clumsy elbow knocked a hymn-book to the floor but still he knelt there, motionless.

Ronnie slumped in the pew and watched the back of his father's head which was lifted to the rose window above the altar. He thought: where is he? Who is he with? What does he hear and see? He felt lonely and rather frightened. "Pop," he whispered. But the small, tense, humble figure did not move. He covered his eyes and tried to pray too; but praying had never been Ronnie's strong suit; praying always made him feel a bit of a fool. "Stop me from being such a beast to him," he tried; but he still felt like a fool. So he just went on kneeling there, waiting for Pop to come back from wherever he was before his hot-water bottle got cold.

Come on, Pop, he fretted. His knees were getting sore and the cold was eating into his bones.

Could ye not watch with Me one hour?

The words dropped into Ronnie's mind from somewhere; words he had been familiar with all his life and never understood; words he had heard a thousand times and never heeded.

In the silence of the dark church they dropped into his mind as a stone drops into still water. At first there was only the small shock of stone cleaving water. But then the ripples began. Small ripples, barely ruffling the surface, but moving outward and ever outward into the uncharted regions of eternity.

Presently he got to his feet and went to kneel beside the small, lonely figure on the chancel steps.

He slipped his hand into Pop's hand. It closed around his chilled fingers in a grasp of astonishing warmth, of most reassuring strength.

3.

"I'm going out, Ada," Alison said, poking her face around the kitchen door. "I don't suppose I shall be long. Will the shepherd's pie be all right for supper?"

"It looks all right an' smells all right. More than that, I won't commit meself."

"Good," Alison said brightly. "What a good thing we're both so fond of shepherd's pie, isn't it?" She shut the door and opened it again to ask (in her little-girl's voice): "Will you make me some apple fritters, too, Ada dear? My first thought when I woke was: *apple fritters. Nobody makes them like you!*"

"Happen," Ada said; adding pointedly: "Sooner you get off, sooner you'll be back."

Her hand reached for the apples even before the front door slammed.

Now what's she up to? she wondered. It can't be t'police or she'd have used the telephone. Her knife whipped around the huge apple with a vicious competence. She's going to George, that's what it'll be. She's going to George. . . . An' what's going to come of *that*, for goodness sake!

As the gate clicked behind her the wind met Alison in full force. It had risen considerably, she noticed, since morning. Probably this meant the end of skating.

And the end of what else?

Plunging head-down into the wind Alison had a vision of Miss Plum's body floating beneath a thinning scum of ice; saw a room crowded with a white blur of faces, curious, condemning, inimical; heard the coroner's dry voice asking: *"And what was your reason, Miss Penny, for withholding information from the police?"*

"I didn't wish to be responsible for Miss Plum," she heard herself stammering. *"Not any more?"*

"Why not?"

"I felt I had done enough for her."

"You felt you had done enough for her. And exactly what had you done, Miss Penny, for this poor creature?"

"I gave her a home. I nursed her when she was ill."

"And when you and your servant were ill, Miss Plum looked after your home and nursed both of you. Am I correct in saying this?"

"Oh, yes, of course. We—we were grateful to her."

"You were grateful. . . . It is the opinion of this court, Miss Penny, that you showed your gratitude in a most peculiar way."

"Rubbish!" Alison said vigorously. She said it aloud. And the assistant postmistress, who had just wished her a civil good evening as she passed, took grievous umbrage and was never quite the same to her again. Alison was often to wonder why.

George will help me, she comforted herself. He must help me. He *must*. Even if I have to marry him next week. Even if I have to leave my home, my friends, my dear Ada, and go to some frightful foreign country and eat nothing but spaghetti with chopsticks, she thought wildly. It's no good asking help from either Hubert or Stanley. Hubert is too humble and Stanley too conceited, and both would be wax in the hands of Miss Plum. If she is still alive, of course. . . . The police will either prosecute her for attempted suicide or put her in an institution. In either case I shall have to visit her. And when she comes out I shall be expected to meet her at the gates with a car and a bunch of flowers or something. . . . No. No, I cannot! I will not.

Quite definitely, and rightly or wrongly, I have *done* with Miss Plum.

4.

The windows of The Goat sent welcoming splashes of yellow light across the road. A comfortable hum of voices punctuated by laughter issued from the closed doors. The sign swung creaking in the wind.

In all her life Alison had never yet entered a public house, either accompanied or alone, and for a moment she hesitated. But only for a moment. She had never lacked courage when it came to making a vital decision. In the circumstances, she reasoned, it was only right and fair that she should come to George rather than demand that he come to her.

The door marked *Saloon Bar* was much quieter than that marked *Public Bar*, so, taking a grip on herself, she pushed and entered. Warmth and light came at her in a welcome but rather overpowering blast, and she stood for a moment, peering through the smoke-laden atmosphere, trying to get her bearings. She had a confused impression of red carpet, the leap and glow of a log fire, the wink of brass on beamed walls.

All the occupants of the bar were men. Four of them were acquaintances who greeted her arrival with subdued astonishment and rather embarrassed bonhomie. Two strangers shot cursory glances in her direction and continued their conversation, heads close together.

Behind the bar the landlord's wife was polishing glasses. A long string of amber beads slid to and fro over a tight dress of black satin, clashing against the bar from time to time. A crest of rigid waves topped a ready, metallic smile.

"*Good* evening," said the landlord's wife.

"Good evening," Alison returned, timidly approaching the bar.

"And what can I get for you, dear?"

"Oh, I don't . . . I mean—yes, well, perhaps I might have a small port, thank you very much."

"A small port, dear? Certainly. . . . There you are, dear. Two and six, if you please. Thank you very much."

"Thank you very much."

The till *pinged* sharply. The amber beads clashed. The landlord's wife gave a small, genteel cough and continued to polish glasses. "Terrible weather we're having," she remarked.

"Terrible," Alison agreed. She sipped at the port and wondered frantically how to get at George without first being turned inside out by this repellent-looking female. "Though, actually, I quite like cold weather."

"Oh, so do I, dear," said the landlord's wife without turning a hair. "Healthy, that's what I always say."

"Yes, indeed."

"Keeps the circulation going."

"Oh, yes, it does."

"Not like the hot weather. Enervating, hot weather is."

"Yes . . ."

Somebody butted in with: "Same again, Miss," and Alison sipped discreetly at her port until the landlord's wife was free again. Then she said: "You have a gentleman staying here, I believe . . ."

The landlord's wife shot her a curious glance.

"When you say *gentleman*," she said through a tight mouth, "that, if I may say so, is a matter of opinion." She pushed at the furrows of her coiffure with a sparkling hand. "And it's *was*— not *is*—if you see what I mean."

"Was . . . ?" Alison echoed, bewildered.

"What I mean to say, this is a respectable 'ouse, and so I aim to keep it, meaning no offence, dear, if he was a friend of yours. I put up with a good deal. A *good deal*," she emphasized, "I put up with. But what I mean to say, there's a limit, as I'm sure a lady like yourself will agree."

"Same again, Bright-eyes," said another voice. "Large ones."

Beer frothed. Bell pinged. Amber beads clashed.

"So, naturally, when I found out what was going on, I put a stopper on it right away. Well, I mean to say, dear, you can't 'ave *that* sort of thing going on, not in a respectable 'ouse, can you?"

"What sort of thing?" Alison faltered, feeling rather ill.

The landlord's wife sniffed.

"Well, of course, he *said* she was his sister. My hubby come out in the kitchen and he says: 'The First Front's got his sister staying the night,' he says. 'So there'll be two for dinner.' 'Is that so? I says. Well, I'll just have a look at this sister,' I says, 'before I do another thing!' So up I goes. And they hadn't locked the door, so in I barges—as I had every right to do. And there they were, dear, as bold as brass, and if she was his sister, then I'm a duchess! And what he could see in her, dear, beats me. Peaky little thing she was. Nothing *to* her, if you see what I mean, and crying like she hadn't got a hope left. Well, that's neither here nor there, and I'm not one to poke my nose into other folks' business. My business is to keep this 'ouse respectable, and so I told him. I gave him an hour to pack his bags and go. Of course, my hubby took his part. 'Give the fellow a chance,' he says. 'Let 'em wait until tomorrow. It's a cold night,' he says, 'to go turning folks out, an' yon girl's right done up.' Well, you know what men are, dear, they always hang together. And that's what I say they *should* do, the whole boiling of 'em—hang together! The world," said the landlord's wife, pouring herself a Guinness with a tot of rum in it, "would be a sweeter place."

"I think," Alison said faintly, "I had better be going."

But she was no match for the landlord's wife who, wiping beige froth from her upper lip, ploughed inexorably on: "I told him straight. 'This is a respectable 'ouse,' I says, 'and we've got our licence to think of, so the sooner you pack your bags and get the hell out,' I says, 'the better for all parties concerned.'" She served a gin-and-It, a large whisky and soda and a pint of mild. "So that's what they did, dear. They packed their bags and went. He paid up, I'll say that for 'im, there wasn't any hanky-panky there. He paid up to the last penny and he rang for a taxi and they went. Don't ask me where—that's no business of mine. They went, and that's all I asked of him. Well, he wasn't a bad sort of feller in some ways, but no class, if you see what I mean. Are you feeling all right, dear? Have another port."

"No, thank you," Alison managed.

"Go on, dear. Have it on the house!"

"No, really. It s very kind of you, but I must get home."

"Well, I'm sure!" said the landlord's wife huffily. She had recognized Alison immediately and was bitterly disappointed at not getting to the bottom of the mystery while she had the chance. "If I was you, dear, I should sit still for a bit and have another port. Quite white you look, I must say. I hope I haven't said anything to upset you. Of course, if he was a friend of yours . . ."

"Same again, please," a voice interrupted.

"I must go." Alison slipped off the high stool and turned toward the door.

"What about my hubby running you back, then?"

"No, thank you. The air will do me good. Good night, Mrs.— er . . ."

"Same again, darling, *when* you've got the time."

Alison slipped out thankfully into the clean, cold darkness.

What a horrible woman! What a horrible situation to be caught in! Now she knew what a fly felt like entangled in the sticky strands of a spider's web.

She thought helplessly: I wish I knew what it was all about. Well, I suppose I do know, really . . . I wish I could *understand*.

She leaned against the wall of the inn under the creaking sign. Her limbs trembled uncontrollably. I must get home, she thought urgently. Home to Ada. To order and safety and decency. . . .

A touch on her arm made her jump violently and she slewed around to confront the solid bulk of the landlord.

"Sorry if I startled you, Miss. It's just that he asked me to give you this letter. I meant to bring it up in the morning but seeing as you're here . . . I could run you home in a matter of minutes, Miss, if you'd like?"

"Oh, thank you, Mr.—er. Thank you very much, but I'd rather walk, truly I would. I am perfectly well. It was just the contrast, you understand, between the heat in there and the cold out here."

"That's right," said the landlord stolidly. "It gets a bit stuffy in there and well I know it. Very stuffy it gets. Well, Miss, if you're quite sure?"

"Quite sure, thank you. I shall enjoy the walk."

"Very good, Miss. Well, good night, then."

"Good night, landlord."

He turned to go; turned back and stood there gazing at her under the swinging sign, as he might have gazed at some rare creature in a cage at the Zoological Gardens. He said abruptly: "He wasn't a bad sort of chap. Not takin' him by and large, see what I mean?"

5.

When the landlord had gone Alison opened George's letter and read:

> Dear Alison,
>
> I found Victoria Plum. Or she found me, if you like it better that way. We're off to London tonight, bound for God-knows-where at the earliest possible moment. If it's any comfort to you, we're going to get hitched, all legal and proper. May work out or may not, but that's a risk everybody's got to take, so try not to worry. Expect I shall drop you a line as per usual next November. No promises, mind, but no harm in looking out for my horrible scrawl.
>
> Yours as ever,
> George.
>
> P.S. Vicky sends her love.

Alison read the letter through twice. Then she tore it into tiny pieces and threw it to the wind. But she picked up as many of the pieces as she could recover and pushed them deep into the pockets of her coat.

She began to walk slowly homeward. The wind was now at her back: it felt like strong hands urging her on her way to Ada and safety; to shepherd's pie and apple fritters and dreamless sleep in a warm, soft bed.

Strength gradually returned to her limbs. She began to step out more quickly, more confidently.

Well, she thought, so all is over and done with. Now I can forget Victoria Plum and remember only George. I can go on remembering George as I remembered him for over twenty years. I can forget that beard, those awful clothes, the horrible reek of whisky, and remember a boy on a bike, with his hair blowing and his white shirt ballooning out in the wind. I can remember the way he used to kiss me under the larches in the spring dusk; the way he pleaded with me to go away with him. He cried once, she recalled suddenly, and felt a constriction in her throat. He laid his face in my open hands, and I felt the tears trickle warmly between my fingers. Poor George. Poor little boy. . . . But Mummy and Daddy knew best. Truly they did. Everything has proved that up to the hilt. Everything. . . .

A voice from a passing bicycle called a greeting and she responded eagerly; neither knowing nor caring who called, but content with the small, familiar incident. Everybody in the village was known to her and she to everybody. Wherever she went there was a voice calling, the nod of a head, a grumble, a cup of tea, an item of gossip.

She looked at the lighted cottages with love. Behind each blossoming curtain was an old person she had helped to nurse, a woman who had served with her on a committee or a child she had taught in Sunday School. In the living rooms of the larger houses she had played bridge, watched television, rehearsed plays and drawn up innumerable lists relating to the annual Flower Show.

All these small, dear, familiar things she could now continue to do—now that she could forget Victoria Plum and remember George. . . .

She thought inconsequently: I shall never know what actually happened to the three travelling salesmen. . . .

She passed the road leading up to Stanley's house and, for a moment, her pace slackened. Should she call on Stanley and tell him her news?

On the whole, Stanley would be pleased, though he had certainly made a mild pass at Victoria himself. But Alison had no illusions about Stanley. Instinctively she was aware that Stanley did not wish to become involved with any woman, least of all a woman like Victoria. Stanley liked to play with the idea of marrying a woman like herself. Just as she herself liked to play with the thought of marrying Stanley. Nothing, she knew, would ever come of it. It's a sort of game we play with ourselves, she thought in a sudden burst of honesty. A sort of game we play with each other.

In any case, Stanley would by now be tucked up in bed, doped with aspirins and simmering gently between hot-water bottles, with Mrs. Platt on guard between him and the outside world.

Stanley could wait.

And now here was the church, and the vicarage, dark behind the pointing trees, its gate banging in the wind. Hubert, she remembered with tolerance, was quite incapable of shutting gates.

Light flowed from the kitchen window. There was light also, feebler but far more significant, in the church.

There was no service tonight, no choir practice. It might possibly be Mr. Sharples about to run over the hymns for next Sunday—but Mr. Sharples would surely need more light than that?

If it were Hubert, it might be well to look in and set his mind at rest about Miss Plum. He had been very good, poor Hubert, dashing about in the dawn as if not only the girl's life but his own depended on it. Poor Hubert. He meant so well and accomplished so little. Look how he had failed with Ronnie. Of course, he had never really got over Edna.

Yet even Hubert had not been indifferent to Miss Plum. . . .

She thought: I can do it just as well by telephone. I will call as soon as I get home. Tonight I am not in the mood for Hubert.

Leaving the church behind her, Alison continued on her way.

She was filled with a sober happiness, with a sense of well-being. The immediate past was a nightmare from which she had awakened, an illness from which she had made sudden and complete recovery. The past of long ago was once more established in the golden mists of a comfortable nostalgia. The future was assured.

Now she could stay in her comfortable home, in her dear village, and Ada would look after her forever and ever. There would be the Cubs, the Dramatic Society, the Glee Club, the Flower Show, the carol singing to fill her days. There would be the two weeks at Bournemouth and the occasional week-end visit to friends. She would continue to give little tea parties; to exchange cookery recipes with Stanley and help him with his Father Christmas effort; to advise Hubert about his neglected garden.

And I will read *Under Milk Wood,* she thought determinedly. I really will—all the way through! I'll take it up to bed with me tonight.

And when her birthday came around again, there would be the letter from George. . . .

Life, thought Alison Penny, as the gate of The Laurels clicked to behind her, was a strange affair but, on the whole, it was good. Very good indeed.

Opening her front door she called out (in her little-girl's voice):

"Here I am, Ada, all in one piece. And oh—*what* a delicious smell!"

THE END

FURROWED MIDDLEBROW